D0422416

From his dwelling place he watches
all who live on earth—
he who forms the hearts of all,
who considers everything they do.

—Psalm 33:14-15 (NIV)

MIRACLES &
MYSTERIES
of **MERCY**
HOSPITAL

Where Mercy Begins
Prescription for Mystery
Angels Watching Over Me
A Change of Art

MIRACLES & MYSTERIES
of MERCY HOSPITAL

A Change
of ART

LESLIE GOULD

Miracles & Mysteries of Mercy Hospital is a trademark of Guideposts.

Published by Guideposts Books & Inspirational Media
100 Reserve Road, Suite E200
Danbury, CT 06810
Guideposts.org

Copyright © 2021 by Guideposts. All rights reserved.

This book, or parts thereof, may not be reproduced, stored in a retrieval system, or transmitted in any form or by any means, electronic, mechanical, photocopying, recording, or otherwise, without the written permission of the publisher.

This is a work of fiction. While the setting of Mercy Hospital as presented in this series is fictional, the location of Charleston, South Carolina, actually exists, and some places and characters may be based on actual places and people whose identities have been used with permission or fictionalized to protect their privacy. Apart from the actual people, events, and locales that figure into the fiction narrative, all other names, characters, businesses, and events are the creation of the author's imagination and any resemblance to actual persons or events is coincidental.

Every attempt has been made to credit the sources of copyrighted material used in this book. If any such acknowledgment has been inadvertently omitted or miscredited, receipt of such information would be appreciated.

Scripture references are from the following sources: *The Holy Bible, King James Version* (KJV). *The Holy Bible, New International Version* (NIV). Copyright ©1973, 1978, 1984, 2011 by Biblica, Inc. Used by permission of Zondervan. All rights reserved worldwide. www.zondervan.com

Cover and interior design by Müllerhaus
Cover illustration by Anton Petrov, represented by Deborah Wolfe, LTD.
Typeset by Aptara, Inc.

Printed and bound in the United States of America
10 9 8 7 6 5 4 3 2 1

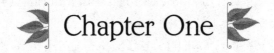

Chapter One

Joy Atkins stopped in the middle of the Grove, on the grounds of Mercy Hospital. Ahead was the Angel of Mercy statue. Overhead was the lush canopy of an eastern redbud tree, thick with heart-shaped leaves.

All around in the peaceful setting were more trees, pots of flowers, and tables and chairs arranged for staff, patients, and visitors.

On three sides of the Grove were the hospital buildings. As she walked to the entrance door, her bag in one hand and a bundle of zinnias from her garden in the other, she breathed out a prayer of gratitude.

God had provided a new home for her in Charleston, South Carolina, and a new job and community at the hospital.

As she stepped into the lobby and started toward the gift shop, a new painting in the hallway leading to the emergency department caught Joy's attention. Had another month gone by already?

Abrielle Fleury, the proprietor of Belina House Gallery, changed the artwork every month. She had gotten off to an early start today. It was only a quarter to seven.

The paintings of summer flowers by local artists were gone, and it looked as if the theme for September was Charleston architecture. The first painting was of the Colonial-style Old Exchange building.

The second was of the Gothic Revival Huguenot Church, which Joy knew Abrielle attended. The third was of an Italianate-style, three-story building with flower boxes filled with white angel's-trumpet. Joy stepped closer. It was the Belina House. She smiled. That was Abrielle's art gallery, which Joy had been meaning to visit.

The fourth painting was titled *The Fleury Estate*. It was of a Georgian-style home behind a gate, probably built in the late 1700s or early 1800s, surrounded by a lovely garden.

"Joy!"

She turned toward the voice. It was Abrielle, her blond hair piled high in a bun and her brown eyes, framed by dark eyebrows and lashes, bright and lively. She wore a turquoise blouse, a black flowing skirt, and heels. She stood with the posture of royalty.

"Hello," Joy responded. "I was just admiring the artwork."

"These are some of my favorite pieces." Abrielle, who was at least a half foot taller, smiled down at Joy. "From my family collection. All of the properties are dear to us."

Joy pointed to the fourth painting. "Is that where you grew up?"

"It is." Abrielle smiled.

Joy asked, "And where Claire lives now?"

"That's right," Abrielle answered. "The property has been in the family for centuries. Daddy moved into the guest cottage a year ago, so Claire and Lloyd live in the big house by themselves now. Doc Fleury, one of the founders of the hospital, lived there for most of the 1800s."

"Is that Dr. Arthur Fleury? The one in the portrait that's been restored?"

Abrielle nodded. "Everyone calls him Doc Fleury, to this day. Even his descendants. The plan is to unveil the portrait at the art auction and then hang it in Garrison's office." She smiled again. "It's going to be delivered in a few days. We've been doing some other work with the same consultant, although I haven't given Claire all of the details yet."

Claire, who'd been away part of the summer, was one of Joy's volunteers in the hospital gift shop. She had invited Joy to join the art auction planning meeting and attend a brunch for the group the next day—at that gorgeous home in the painting.

"What a lovely property, and how wonderful that it's been in the family for so long."

Abrielle pointed toward the painting of her gallery. "The Belina House Gallery has only been in the family for a century. We're celebrating one hundred years this month."

"Wow." Joy stared at the painting.

"I live on the top floor," Abrielle added.

"How interesting," Joy said. She couldn't imagine having deep roots in an old city like Charleston. Yes, she'd grown up in Houston and lived there as an adult, but her parents weren't from there. They'd moved to the city as newlyweds.

And how nice that Abrielle and Claire had each other too. Joy had a sister—Hope—but they weren't exactly close. Joy felt a twinge of jealousy. "Well," she said to Abrielle, realizing she'd become lost in her own unhealthy thoughts, "I'd better get things ready in the gift shop."

Abrielle adjusted the shoulder strap of her purse. "I have to get going too. I'm expecting a call about three paintings we're having authenticated. It's rather exciting."

"That sounds fascinating."

"It is. I'll tell you all about it tomorrow. I'll be at the brunch too." Abrielle took a step toward the front door and then stopped and turned to Joy again. "Oh, and Claire plans to stop by and talk with you about the art auction this morning."

Joy waved and said, "I can't wait to see her." Claire had spent August on Lake Champlain, in Vermont, at her husband's family home. Something they did every year.

Claire had volunteered in the gift shop a handful of times before she left, just enough for Joy to know she considered the woman a friend.

Moving to Charleston to be close to her daughter, Sabrina, and grandchildren had definitely been the right decision for Joy. And getting to know women such as Claire and Abrielle was an added blessing, along with her hospital coworkers. Evelyn Perry, who worked in the records department, had already become a close friend. And Anne Mabry, the volunteer extraordinaire, whose husband was a hospital chaplain, was also part of her new group. Shirley Bashore, an African-American nurse who worked everywhere from the emergency department to surgery floor, rounded out the group. Well, almost. Shirley's spitfire of a mother, Regina, had become one of Joy's favorites too.

Approaching the gift shop, Joy gazed through the wall of windows at the shelves of colored glassware—red, green, indigo, and azure. She unlocked the door and stepped out from under the painted-sky ceiling of the lobby into her own spectacular domain of beauty.

She had worked hard to order just the right pieces, anticipating what visitors, guests, and employees needed, and then displayed them to draw customers into the shop. The collection of candles filled the air with the scent of lemongrass, and the items hanging from the ceiling—Japanese lanterns and origami cranes—added texture to the shop. And all the glassware bounced color and light around the room. Her planning had paid off. The place was bright and vibrant.

After she secured her bag in the bottom drawer of her desk and put the zinnias in a vase full of water by the cash register, Joy put on her smock, inhaled the scent of the coffee that was brewing, and saw to the details of opening the shop for the day.

A few moments later Joy pulled her phone from the pocket of her smock. She'd texted Sabrina the evening before to see if she and her family could come for Sunday dinner after church. There was still no response.

At eight, as Joy flipped the sign to OPEN, Claire came waltzing through the door in a navy blue dress with a wide skirt and heels. She wasn't as tall as Abrielle, but she still towered over Joy by a few inches. Claire had the same shade of blond hair as her sister, the same dark eyes, and the same book-on-top-of-her-head posture. But instead of wearing whimsical blouses and skirts like Abrielle, Claire wore tailored fifties-style dresses, skirts, and sweater sets. She also wore bright red lipstick.

She gave Joy a hug and then kissed her on the cheek. "It's so good to be back!"

Joy hugged Claire and said, "It's great to have you back. How was Lake Champlain?"

"Wonderful!" Claire said. "Of course, it nearly broke my heart to be away from our grandgirl that long." Her first grandchild had been born in June. "So I've been spoiling Talia every single minute since we got home."

Claire held up her phone and showed a photo of herself with the baby. The little one had a pink bow on her bald head and a serious expression on her face.

"She's darling," Joy said.

"She's getting baptized on Sunday." Claire slipped her phone back into her bag. "You should come. Have you attended our church yet?"

Joy shook her head. The historic Huguenot Church had been on her list of churches she wanted to visit.

Claire clapped her hands together. "Come on Sunday."

"You might be tired of me, after the brunch tomorrow," Joy teased.

"Never." Claire beamed.

"I'm not sure if I have plans yet or not," Joy said. "If I don't, I'll keep it in mind."

"Wonderful," Claire said.

"Just one question." Joy clasped her hands together. "Is the service in French? Because *je ne parle pas français.*"

Claire laughed. "You're in luck. Only one service a year is in French, and it's not this Sunday. Now as far as tomorrow…" She went on to discuss the brunch. She'd called Joy the day before, asking Joy to be on the committee because one of the members had bowed out at the last minute to be in Ashville with her pregnant daughter who was on bed rest. "Anne and Evelyn will be there," Claire said. "And so will Roger."

Joy raised her eyebrows. She'd heard about Roger Gaylord—a new benefactor to the hospital—but hadn't met him yet.

Claire grabbed Joy's forearm and gave it a squeeze. "We're going to have so much fun!"

Joy didn't hear back from Sabrina until the next morning as she approached the gate across the walkway to Claire's home for the eleven o'clock brunch. SORRY, Sabrina texted. SUNDAY DINNER WON'T WORK. WE ALREADY HAVE PLANS WITH ROB'S FAMILY. MAYBE NEXT WEEK?

As she slipped her phone back into her bag, Joy decided she'd take Claire up on attending church for her granddaughter's baptism. If she couldn't spend time with her own family, she might as well spend time with Claire's.

She squared her shoulders and straightened her jacket, ready to press the button on the box by the gate.

"Joy!"

She turned around. Evelyn and Anne, along with Anne's granddaughter, Addie, hurried toward her. Lili, Addie's mom and Anne and Ralph's daughter, was serving with the Air Force in Afghanistan, so the little girl was living with her grandparents.

Anne's blond hair shone in the morning light, and Evelyn had her silver hair pulled back in a barrette that matched the dragonfly pin on her lapel. Both women wore blouses and skirts, and seven-year-old Addie wore a yellow sundress.

Joy hoped her pantsuit wasn't too casual. She did have a gauzy scarf around her neck that added an element of elegance. "Hello, y'all!" she called out.

"Hi!" Anne and Evelyn responded.

Addie yelled, "Howdy!"

Joy smiled and waved. Addie ran ahead of the others, her dress twirling around her knees and her sandals flapping on the sidewalk.

"Have you buzzed the gate yet?" Anne asked.

Joy shook her head.

"Hold on. I know the code."

As Anne punched in the number, Evelyn said, "I've always loved this house. It was built for the Fleury family, who had a shipping business with ties to Europe. They were—still are—Huguenots, otherwise known as French Calvinists. When Louis XIV forced many of them from French society, some of the Fleury family went into hiding in France for a time. But one branch of the family arrived in Charleston in the late 1600s."

Intrigue filled Joy. "Now that's fascinating."

The gate clicked open and Anne, followed by Addie, led the way onto the property. Joy knew a little bit about the Huguenots. Many found freedom of religion in the New World, along with so many other faith groups that arose out of the Reformation.

"Oh, look at Claire's Japanese maple tree," Evelyn said. "Isn't it gorgeous?"

It was to the right of the path in a well-shaded garden and about three feet high. The leaves, all bright red, shimmered in the morning light, casting shadows over hostas, coleus, and coral bells.

"Claire definitely has a green thumb." Evelyn held up her hand. "Unlike me."

Joy laughed. Evelyn had many skills, including organizing and historical sleuthing, but gardening wasn't on the list.

"We should go around to the patio," Anne said, pointing toward the left as she reached for Addie's hand. Ralph, Anne's husband, was working his once-a-month Saturday shift at the hospital. Joy was delighted to have Addie tag along on this outing.

Joy's gaze shifted from the perfectly kept grounds to the house as she walked. It was three stories and made of bricks with cream-painted columns framing the front door.

They followed the pathway to another, smaller gate. As Anne opened it, she called out, "Hello!"

"Come on in, y'all!"

The three women and Addie stepped through the gate onto a large patio, adorned with potted palmetto trees and lush plants. Claire, who wore a black polka-dot dress, stood with a stack of cloth napkins in her hands. She wore her hair in a flip, right at her shoulders. She greeted the women with a sweet, "Welcome."

A large table was set with cutlery and plates. Platters of scrambled eggs, bacon, fruit, and pastries covered another table.

Two men chatted by a fountain near the back door. Abrielle placed a bouquet of cosmos on the food table, and Claire put the napkins around at each place setting on the table.

As the women chatted, one of the men approached. His dark eyes shone, and he gave Joy a warm smile.

"Roger Gaylord," he said, extending his hand.

Joy took it and said, "Pleased to meet you. I'm Joy Atkins."

"Pleased to meet you also." He smiled again. "You work at the hospital, right?"

"Yes," she said. "In the gift shop."

Claire then introduced her husband, Lloyd Walter, to Joy.

Claire added, "Lloyd can only join us to eat. He has to rush off to Savannah to look in on his aunt Mae."

Abrielle's head shot up. "What about Talia's baptism tomorrow?"

"I'll spend the night there and leave early in the morning," Lloyd said.

Joy knew it was only a two-hour drive. He could easily be back for the baptism.

Claire turned to Lloyd. "Honey, would you please say a blessing for us?"

After the prayer, everyone filled their plates and then sat around the table. From her place, Joy could see a guest cottage, most likely where Claire and Abrielle's father lived, on the edge of the back garden, and to the left of it a garage that looked as if it had been a stable at one time.

"Isn't Daddy joining us?" Abrielle asked.

Claire shook her head. "He had some errands to run this morning."

"He's out walking?"

Claire nodded. "He's fine." She glanced at Joy. "Our father is eighty-four but in good shape. He had an irregular heartbeat, but his new medication has corrected it."

Joy smiled. "What a relief." Claire and Abrielle were fortunate to still have their father with them.

Addie arranged strawberries on her plate while the discussion around the table turned to the art auction. Everyone else at the table had been involved in the auction in the past. Joy listened intently, trying to catch up. The auction would be held at Belina House Gallery in one week. Abrielle and her staff would hang the exhibit next Friday. A local caterer was donating the food—a collection of canapés—and drinks at cost for the event. Claire, with Anne's help, had seen to the details of that. The tickets had already been sold. It sounded as if all the details had been seen to.

"What can I do to help?" Joy asked.

"Well, besides attending the infamous art auction dinner for the planning committee on Thursday here"—Claire gestured toward the house—"we need you to stand by the back door of the gallery and direct people into the workroom, where one of the food tables will be. Mostly we don't want anyone going in or out the back door, for security reasons. And would you like to help arrange the flowers the morning before the event? Our usual florist just went out of business." She made a sad face, which quickly transformed into a happier one. "We could visit the gallery today, and I can show you exactly what we'll need."

"I'd love to," Joy answered.

"Perfect." Claire beamed. "Roger will be on duty in the hallway during the event too."

Joy glanced at Roger, who was taking a small notebook and pen from his shirt pocket. He jotted down a couple of notes.

Abrielle's cell phone rang. "Excuse me," she said. "I've been waiting for this call and need to take it."

She stepped away from the table toward the guest cottage. When she returned, Claire gave her a questioning look. Abrielle gave her a quick nod and then said softly, "I'll fill you in later."

But then Abrielle had another phone call, a short one, and when she returned she said, "I need to get to the gallery." She turned to Joy and then to Claire. "I'll see you two soon." She told the others goodbye and slipped through the patio gate.

Anne, Addie, Evelyn, and Roger all needed to leave right after the brunch, but Joy helped Claire clean up. Then the two walked the eight blocks to the gallery, past the Dock Street Theatre and onto the cobblestones of Queen Street. A right turn took them straight to Belina House Gallery.

Just like in the painting, the Italianate building was painted white with black trim, and the window boxes overflowed with white angel's-trumpet.

Claire bounded up the steps, the skirt of her dress swaying back and forth. Joy imagined the Fleury sisters as girls, running the blocks between their house and the gallery. Claire opened the door and called out, "Hello! We're here!"

A young man with a shock of dark hair and bright eyes smiled. "Claire! How was your trip?" He stepped out from behind the counter.

Claire gave him a hug and a kiss. "It was wonderful," she answered. "But I'm happy to be home!"

She turned to Joy. "This is our friend, Joy Atkins. She manages the gift shop at the hospital." She gestured toward the young man. "And this is Grey Monte. Abrielle's assistant extraordinaire."

"Nice to meet you." Joy extended her hand.

Grey had a firm grip. He appeared to be in his late twenties and had a sweet smile.

"Abrielle's in the office, on the phone with the authenticator again."

Claire's eyebrows shot up. "Again?"

He nodded. "It's the third call since she arrived."

"So, bad news?" Claire asked.

"It seems to be mixed," Grey answered.

Claire grimaced. "We'll head back that way."

As they walked down the hall, Claire said, "We have three French paintings from the early 1870s. An art dealer we've worked with saw the paintings and is convinced they're very early Theodore Joubert paintings."

Joy tried to pull the name *Joubert* out of the files of her brain, but she came up empty. "Sorry, I don't know who that is."

"Don't worry—lots of people who aren't in the art world don't," Claire said. "He was a French painter, 1870s through 1880s. On the outer edges of Impressionism—he studied with some of the greats. That sort of thing. He has some nice Paris scenes and landscapes with figures. A few portraits. He died in the early 1880s at the age of forty-two, so fairly young."

"What are the paintings of?" Joy asked.

"Three young women—*Abrielle Overlooking the Village*, *Belina in the Garden*, and *Claire at the Church Steps*."

Joy stopped. "What?"

"Right?" Claire smiled. "We're named after the paintings."

"You and Abrielle and the gallery?"

Claire turned her head. "Something like that... Anyway, it turns out Joubert had three sisters. An art authenticator who also does restoration work told us that. Can you guess their names?"

Joy smiled wryly. "Abrielle, Belina, and Claire."

"Exactly. When the art dealer said he thought the paintings were early Jouberts, our research showed Joubert had sisters with names that had been in our family since the 1800s." Claire smiled again. "That was the first clue that he might be the painter."

"Goodness," Joy said. "What a mystery."

"Hopefully the authenticator has been able to sort it all out," Claire said.

She suddenly stopped walking. "If all three were done by Theodore, it would mean they're worth a lot of money. But then it becomes a bit of a quandary. How our family came by the paintings is somewhat of a mystery. The family story is that the paintings were a gift from friends in France. But others maintain that our great-great-great-grandfather, Doc Fleury, stole them."

Joy froze. "The same Doc Fleury who was one of the founders of the hospital? Whose portrait is being restored and will be unveiled the night of the auction? The portrait that will be hung in Garrison's office?"

Claire nodded. "There's a theory that's been floating around the internet by an anonymous blogger about an unaccounted-for early Joubert that went missing sometime in the early 1870s."

"That's a big deal, if Doc Fleury stole the paintings, or if it's even assumed he did."

Claire shrugged. "I'm sure he didn't. He's always been described as a man of character. And besides, even if he did, it happened a hundred and fifty years ago."

Joy had done enough nonprofit work to know it could be a big deal, if the information reached the wrong hands—or the right hands, if in fact he had stolen the paintings. "What do you know about him?"

"He was one of the founders of the hospital, as you know. A pillar of the Huguenot Church." She lowered her voice. "Just between you and me, I've never been that interested in family history, so I actually don't know much about him."

"Claire!" someone yelled from the next room. "Claire! I hear you out there. Get in here!"

Claire grabbed Joy by the arm and dragged her into the office. Abrielle sat on the desk, her long legs crossed and her phone in her hand. "So," she said, "I just got off the phone with Pamela DePass. She said she can only authenticate *Belina in the Garden* as a Joubert."

"Then who painted the other two?" Claire asked.

"She doesn't know. Most likely someone who knew Theodore, perhaps someone who painted with him and spent time with him. Maybe one of his classmates even, who visited the family. It turns out he had four brothers and five sisters all together."

"Wow," Claire said. "Were any of them painters?"

"Pamela hasn't found that information yet. The sisters could have been, but back then women usually painted only landscapes and that sort of thing. But perhaps one of his brothers copied him."

"Are the other two very different from the authentic one?" Claire asked.

"As much as I was hoping all three were Theodore's," Abrielle said, "I can see it. I mean, we grew up thinking the same artist did all three, but now I can see the differences."

"So," Claire said, "does that mean Pamela thinks Arthur Fleury stole *Belina in the Garden*?"

Abrielle slid off the desk. "She said if he did, hopefully no one will make a big deal out of it."

Joy bristled. "Oh, someone will. And from a PR standpoint for the hospital, it could be bad. The unveiling of Doc Fleury's portrait is taking place the night of the auction. If it comes out in the news that he's suspected of stealing a Joubert, that won't be good for the hospital."

Abrielle grimaced. "Or for the gallery."

Claire wrinkled her nose. "Or for our family." She sighed.

Abrielle crossed her arms, opened her mouth, and then closed it. Finally, she said, "You're right, Joy. Absolutely. This won't be good. And Daddy will be crushed. Doc Fleury has always been his biggest hero."

Claire mimicked her sister's stance and said, "I suppose we should get to the bottom of whether Doc Fleury stole the Joubert or not."

Abrielle sighed. "As if we don't have enough to deal with right now."

"Right." Claire agreed. "Maybe there's information stored away somewhere that would clear him."

"Maybe at the college." Abrielle turned to Joy. "Someone in our family a long time ago donated Doc Fleury's papers to the South

Carolina Historical Society archives, but they're stored in the college library."

"Oh." The college was close. Just a few blocks away.

"Well." Claire looked at Abrielle. "Where are you keeping the three sisters these days?"

"In the safe, of course." Abrielle stood. "Want me to show you the differences between *Belina in the Garden* and the other two? Then we can talk about the auction—and how to figure out if Doc Fleury was a thief or not."

Claire nodded in agreement.

Joy was relieved the two were taking the accusation against Doc Fleury seriously.

Abrielle headed for the door with Claire behind her. Joy followed along. She looked ahead to the end of the hall and the back door, to where she'd be stationed the night of the auction.

Claire increased her pace to keep up with her sister. "How much did she say the painting is worth?"

"That depends on quite a few factors that she hasn't determined yet," Abrielle answered, stepping through a doorway to the left.

Abrielle flipped a switch and soft lights came on. Joy noted there were no windows. There were two large worktables, supplies, and a large safe at the front of the room. Abrielle entered the combination, leaning down as she did, and then pulled open the door. There were a few small paintings. Joy had imagined the paintings of the three sisters to be much larger.

Claire peered over her sister's shoulder. "Where are they?"

"Gone." Abrielle turned to her sister, her face ashen. "They were here last night."

Claire's voice wavered as she took a step backward. "Was the alarm set when you opened up this morning?"

"Yes. We didn't open until noon. I disarmed the alarm. I unlocked the door. Everything was in order."

"Well something wasn't in order." Claire pointed at the safe. "We've been robbed."

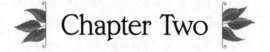

Chapter Two

Fifteen minutes later, Detective Rebekah Osborne arrived at the gallery. She wore her hair pulled back in a low ponytail, showing off the gray at her temples that matched the blouse she wore under her blue blazer. Joy had become acquainted with Rebekah when the Angel of Mercy statue was stolen from the hospital a few months before.

"Ladies," she said. "Hello. Tell me what happened."

Joy waved to her and stepped backward against the lobby wall, making room for Abrielle and Claire to speak with the detective. Rebekah opened her notebook. As Abrielle relayed the timeline of her arriving at the gallery and deactivating the security code, Rebekah took notes.

She asked, "Was anything out of order when you arrived?"

Abrielle shook her head. "Nothing."

Rebekah made a note. "Who all knows the code besides you?"

"I do," Claire said.

"And Grey does," Abrielle added.

"Anyone else?" Rebekah asked.

"No," Abrielle answered. "We installed a new system about a month ago and keyed in a new code. I haven't touched the security footage or any of that."

"Good." Rebekah closed the notebook. "Let's start with the safe. We'll have it dusted for fingerprints and then take a look at the video footage after I finish getting the initial information from you. The entire gallery is now a crime scene, as are the entries and the exterior of the building. We'll tape the whole property off."

"How long will the gallery need to be closed for?" Abrielle asked.

Rebekah put her notebook and pen in her pocket. "At this point, I don't know…"

"We have an auction scheduled for a week from tonight."

"Do you have an alternative location?"

This time Abrielle looked at Joy, who hesitated and then said, "The mezzanine at the hospital, perhaps? We can ask Garrison."

Abrielle nodded. Then she turned back to Rebekah. "I live upstairs."

"Is there somewhere else you can stay?"

Abrielle glanced at Claire and raised her eyebrows.

"Of course," Claire said. "Your room is always available."

The front door opened, and Officer Jason Williams stepped into the gallery with a clipboard under his arm. He'd also investigated the stolen statue. Joy waved.

"Hello, ladies," he said and then looked at Grey, who remained behind the counter—but now appeared frozen. "And Grey."

"Good afternoon," Grey answered back.

"How are y'all doing?" Williams asked. "Considering?"

Claire answered with a soft murmur, and Abrielle said, "As well as can be expected."

Rebekah was all business. "Tape off the property, front and back, check for footprints in the back alley and around the exterior door, and then let the crime unit in the back door so they can dust everything. The safe is in the workroom."

"Down the hall," Abrielle said. "Last door on the left."

"I'll tape everything off first." As Officer Williams headed back outside, Rebekah addressed the rest of them. "We might as well get the basic questions out of the way. Where were each of you last night? And who were you with?" She focused on Grey.

He cleared his throat. "I was at my parents' cabin about thirty minutes south of here, with my sister and a couple of her friends. I came into town this morning, around ten. Got a shower at my apartment and was here at noon."

"I was already here and had the place opened up," Abrielle said. "Last evening, I got takeout for dinner and went to bed early."

"You live on the top floor, right?" Rebekah asked.

Abrielle nodded.

"And you didn't hear anything?"

"Not a thing. There's an outside entrance with three flights of stairs up to my apartment. So I don't come through the gallery to go up there."

"Is there an interior door that connects the apartment and the gallery?"

Abrielle nodded again. "But it's bolted from the gallery side—and my side. I don't use it."

"Why is that?"

"When we put in a new security system, that was the recommendation."

Rebekah dug out her notebook again. "What about this morning?"

"I left my apartment around nine thirty and went to Claire's for a brunch."

"Did you come down to the gallery before you went to Claire's?"

Abrielle shook her head. "We don't open until noon on Saturdays. There was no reason for me to come down."

Rebekah turned to Claire. "How about you? Where were you last night?"

"Home. Daddy had dinner with me, and then I helped him get settled in his cottage. After that I watched the news and headed to bed."

Rebekah wrote in her notebook and then asked her, "What about this morning?"

"I was home getting ready for the brunch that Abrielle came to." She motioned to Joy. "Joy was there too, along with Evelyn Perry and Anne Mabry, who also work at Mercy. We're planning the art auction for the hospital. Like I said earlier, it's a week from today, hopefully here."

They waited as Rebekah wrote a few more things in her notebook.

Then she said, "We'll go through the entire gallery to check for prints and any clues. We can't have you contaminating the crime scene. If you need to get any personal belongings from the premises do that now, but show me what you plan to take. We're setting up a canopy outside with a table and chairs under it. You can wait there or retreat somewhere else. We'll have officers watching the building until we're done."

"I have a few personal belongings in my office," Abrielle said, "and, of course, also upstairs that I'll need."

"All right." Rebekah put her notebook in her pocket again. "Let's take a look at the security video first. Then you can collect your things in your office, and after that I'll escort you upstairs."

"The security system is on the computer in my office." Abrielle pointed toward the hall.

Joy cleared her throat and said, "Should I leave? Am I in the way?"

Rebekah smiled at her. "Do you mind staying?"

"Not at all," Joy said. "But how about if I go get coffees for everyone?"

"That would be much appreciated," Rebekah said. "I'll take mine iced."

Joy remembered from the previous case that Rebekah was a fan of coffee and quickly took everyone's order, including Grey's.

"Grey and Claire, you should wait outside," Rebekah said. "The crime unit will be working in here."

"Can I go home?" Grey asked.

Rebekah shook her head. "You need to stick around."

Claire and Grey followed Joy out the front door. There was a canopy set up on the sidewalk. Grey stopped there, but Claire said to Joy, "I'll help you get the coffee."

As they crossed the street to the coffee shop kitty-corner from the gallery, Claire asked, "Who would take the paintings of the three sisters?"

Joy had the same question. She didn't say it out loud, but she wondered what it would mean for Doc Fleury's legacy. Now that

Belina in the Garden, a genuine Joubert, had been stolen—perhaps for the second time—it would likely draw even more negative attention to Doc Fleury—and the hospital too.

As Joy and Claire started back across the street to the gallery, balancing the coffees in two holders, a young woman with a book bag strapped over her shoulder started up the steps of the gallery even though the CLOSED sign hung on the door.

Joy quickened her step and called out, "You can't go in there. It's closed."

The woman, who wore her sandy hair long, turned toward her with a surprised look on her face. "I have some questions for the police. I'm with the *Dispatch*. Daniella Hattel. I heard on the police scanner that there was a burglary here."

Joy raised her eyebrows. "I'm only the coffee service. I can't comment on that."

She handed Grey his coffee and then placed hers and Rebekah's on the table under the canopy. Claire placed the two she carried on the table too.

Daniella addressed Grey. "How about you? Do you work here?"

"I do." Grey took a sip of his coffee. "But I can't comment either."

"Who can?" Daniella asked.

Joy pulled out her phone. "I'll let the owner know you're here."

Daniella shrugged and sat down in the chair next to Grey. "All right."

Joy sent Abrielle a text and then waited. When she didn't answer after a few minutes, Claire said, "I'll call her."

When Abrielle didn't pick up, Joy said, "I'll take her coffee to her and tell her you're here."

Daniella stood.

"No," Joy said. "You stay here. Go get a coffee or something and come back."

She sat down.

Joy grabbed two coffees and headed up the stairs to the gallery. She knocked on the door and listened but heard nothing.

She opened the door and called out, "Knock, knock. Coffee delivery."

Rebekah called out, "Come on down. Just don't touch anything."

As Joy walked down the hall, she peered into the first gallery room and caught sight of large abstract paintings with blocks of color—reds, purples, blues, and oranges. In the next room was a collection of Charleston scenes. The paintings on display at the hospital were probably from this collection. A Classical Revival house with a horse and buggy in front of it. A wrought iron fence with pink vine roses wound around it. A Queen Anne Cottage set back in a stand of trees.

When the gallery was open again, she'd return and take time to look at each painting.

As Joy entered the office, the two women looked up from where they were huddled around a computer screen.

Joy handed out the coffees.

"Thank you," Rebekah said.

"You're welcome. Have you found anything?"

Abrielle shook her head. "Not yet."

"There's a reporter outside, wanting to talk with someone about the burglary."

Abrielle sat up. "So soon?"

Joy nodded. "She seems content to wait."

"Could you take her card?" Abrielle asked. "Tell her I'll call when I have a chance."

"She might camp out," Rebekah said.

Abrielle took a sip of her coffee. "That's all right." She leaned forward and clicked the mouse again.

"I'll tell her," Joy said.

As she started toward the door, Rebekah said, "Wait a minute. The video just jumped forward twenty-seven minutes."

"What?" Abrielle peered at the screen.

"It jumps from 2:03 a.m. to 2:30 a.m."

"How can that be?" Abrielle asked.

"Maybe the thief is familiar with your security system," Rebekah said. "Look. There's a shadow that passes by the back door at 2:33."

Grey's voice, out in the lobby, called out, "Hey! What are you doing?"

Joy swung open the office door. Daniella stood in the hall.

"Were you eavesdropping?" Joy asked her.

Daniella's face reddened, and she shook her head.

"I'll walk you back outside," Joy said.

When they'd exited the building, she asked Daniella, "Do you have a business card I can give to the owner? Someone will call you."

She shook her head.

"You don't have a card?"

"No," she answered. "Because I know how this will work. No one will call me back."

"Someone will," Grey said.

Daniella shook her head. "I'll wait."

Grey led the way down the stairs back to the canopy. Claire sat on one of the chairs, the skirt of her black polka-dot dress tucked around her legs.

When Joy reached the table she pointed to her coffee and asked Daniella, "Would you like this? I'll go buy myself another one. It's black, no sugar." And clearly iced.

A confused expression settled on Daniella's face.

"Or I can go get you a special order. What would you like?"

She shook her head. "Why would you do that?"

Joy smiled. "Why wouldn't I?"

Daniella hesitated. "I like black iced coffee," she said finally. "I'll take yours."

Joy grabbed it off the table and handed it to the reporter.

When she returned a few minutes later with her own iced coffee, Grey was asking Daniella where she went to college.

"University of Richmond," she said. "I grew up in an old mining town in Pennsylvania but always liked Richmond."

"And what brought you here?" Grey asked.

"Well, the job. But I vacationed here with my parents. My dad's a history teacher. We visited Savannah. St. Augustine. Chattanooga. New Orleans. San Antonio."

"Sounds like a great childhood."

Daniella smiled and then took a long sip of her coffee. "I minored in history in college, hoping to combine it with journalism.

Getting a job here was a dream." She shrugged. "But I'm seen as an outsider and sometimes it's hard to get people to talk to me." Daniella leaned forward and asked Grey, "How about you? Are you from around here?"

Grey smiled. "Seven generations back."

"Lucky you."

Joy studied the facade of the building. The Belina House Gallery wasn't on the Broad Street Gallery Row, but Joy guessed its reputation drew plenty of tourists and locals alike. A century was a long time for a gallery to be in business, even in Charleston.

Claire stepped to Joy's side.

"How are you doing?" Joy asked.

Claire took a drink of her iced coffee and then said, "I'm in shock, I think. I don't know how this could have happened."

A commotion on the front porch of the gallery caught Joy's attention. Abrielle and Rebekah, along with Officer Williams, were coming out the front door.

"The crime unit didn't find any prints in the workroom," Officer Williams said to Rebekah. "The perp either wore gloves or everything was wiped. There were a few footprints out back." He looked at Abrielle. "Women's shoes. Size nine."

"That would be me," she said.

Officer Williams nodded. "I thought so. The unit is ready to dust the rest of the gallery for prints now."

"All right," Rebekah said.

Abrielle headed down the stairs and toward the canopy with her coffee in her hand and addressed Grey. "Hopefully we can open within a couple of days, but it depends on the investigation. I'll let you know."

"Am I a suspect?" he asked.

Abrielle shrugged and then lowered her voice and spoke with Grey quietly.

Claire said, "It seems as if we know less now than we did an hour ago."

Abrielle turned toward her sister. "It's a mess. There are missing sections of the security code log and of the video footage. I left a message with the security company. Hopefully they'll call me back soon."

"Did you call the insurance company too?"

Abrielle's face reddened. "I'll do that next."

Daniella stood and approached Abrielle, extending her hand. "Daniella Hattel from the *Dispatch*. I heard you had a break-in."

"Yes, we did," Abrielle said.

"Could I ask you a few questions?"

Rebekah stepped forward and said, "It's an ongoing investigation, so no one has a comment at this time."

"Is it true that you have a Theodore Joubert painting?"

"No comment at this time," Abrielle answered.

"Is it true it was stolen?"

"Who told you about the painting?" Abrielle asked.

Daniella shrugged.

Rebekah stepped forward. "I'd like to know too. The answer could help the investigation."

"An anonymous source." Daniella smiled wryly. "So, no comment at this time."

"That's all the reporter said? That she had no comment?" Shirley's black hair, which was braided and piled high on her head, shook a little as she spoke.

Joy was having dinner at the Hassell Street Café with Shirley, her mother, Regina, and Evelyn, whose husband, James, was at a humanities department event for the evening.

Joy nodded in response to Shirley's question. "Yes, because she'd gotten the information from an anonymous source."

"How did she know only one painting was a Theodore Joubert?" Evelyn asked. "Before today, Abrielle and Claire thought all three might be Jouberts, right?"

"Exactly." Joy cut a slice of fried green tomato. "And they were only told this morning that it was confirmed the one was a Joubert. Abrielle called the authenticator, but she said she hadn't breathed a word to anyone."

"Y'all, who else would have known about the painting?" Regina's brown eyes were wide with concern.

"Claire couldn't think of anyone else," Joy said.

Regina raised her eyebrows. "Well, somebody told somebody."

Joy couldn't help but smile. "That's for sure."

"Claire and Abrielle are all right with you telling us about this though?" Evelyn asked.

Joy nodded. "In fact, they asked me to. Well, Claire did. She knows your research abilities and"—she turned to Shirley—"how interested all of us are in a good mystery, including Anne. She's hoping we can find some answers to who stole the painting now and answers to another mystery too."

Shirley's eyebrows shot up. "What else is going on?"

"The authenticator suspects Doc Fleury stole the Joubert painting all those years ago in France and brought it to the US. Even if he didn't steal it, if he's only falsely accused, it will shed a bad light on the hospital considering his portrait is supposed to be unveiled at the art auction. And it would bring all sorts of bad publicity to the gallery. We need to also prove Doc Fleury is innocent."

Evelyn narrowed her eyes. "But why in the world would the authenticator—what's her name?"

"Pamela DePass," Joy answered. "She's from Savannah."

"Why would she think Doc Fleury stole the painting?" Evelyn asked.

"Because there's a theory on a blog about a Joubert that went missing sometime in the early 1870s," Joy said.

"Interesting," Evelyn said, "What are Claire's and Abrielle's thoughts on the theory?"

"They've both grown up thinking Doc Fleury was a good man, but neither of them seems that interested in the history of their family. Which surprised me. If I had an ancestor like Doc Fleury, I'd want to know everything I could find out about him."

"Wait," Shirley said. "Who exactly is Doc Fleury, besides an ancestor of Abrielle and Claire's?"

Regina's eyes lit up. "One of the founders of Mercy Hospital."

Shirley laughed. "Mama—"

"Regina is absolutely right," Evelyn said. "Doc Fleury was a young doctor when the hospital was founded in 1829, and then he served on the board for the next fifty-five years. Through the War, through the destruction of most of the hospital, and then through the rebuilding of it too."

"The family came to Charleston early," Regina said. "I think in the 1700s."

Evelyn nodded in agreement. "Yes, ma'am, that's right."

"They've been part of the Huguenot Church from the beginning," Regina said. "Their box is on the left-hand side, in the middle."

"Mama." Shirley titled her head. "How do you know so much about the Fleury family?"

Regina smiled and raised her eyebrows again. "Oh, I have my sources."

The waitress arrived with their entrees—shrimp and grits for Regina and Joy, pan-roasted halibut for Shirley, and barbecue shrimp for Evelyn.

The conversation shifted to the upcoming art auction. "The Fleury sisters do such a good job with the fundraiser," Regina said. "It's always been one of my favorites."

"Mama," Shirley said. "You've been keeping secrets from me. Not once in all these years have you mentioned going to an art auction for the hospital."

Regina laughed. "Well, Shirley, I never have—and still don't—tell you everything."

Shirley shook her head and laughed too.

There were some days that Regina thought Shirley was her sister. But this wasn't one of them. Thankfully Regina was having a good day. She was a delight—no matter if it was a good day or a bad day.

As they finished their meal, Joy said, "I have decaf and a lemon meringue pie back at my house. How about dessert there?"

"Did you make the pie?" Regina asked.

Joy put her finger to her lips. "Shh." She leaned forward. "And you wouldn't have wanted me to. I got it at the bakery."

"Yum, yum." Regina pushed her plate back an inch. "I'm in."

Fifteen minutes later, Joy unlocked her front door and swung it wide open for her guests. Her charming, newly remodeled two-story home with its piazzas and small garden was a haven for her, and she hoped others felt welcome here too.

"Go ahead and make yourselves comfortable," Joy told her friends. "I'll start the coffee."

"I'll help," Shirley said.

Evelyn took out her phone. "And now that I have better service, I'll see what I can find out about Dr. Fleury online."

Joy led the way to the kitchen and took the pie out of the fridge. "You can go ahead and cut this," she said to Shirley, nodding toward the knife rack.

Shirley took the pie from her and Joy turned her attention to the coffee. Keeping her voice low, she said, "So what do you think your mom knows about the Fleury family?"

Shirley shook her head. "She might have just been teasing me. It's hard to tell. But I'll take it. She's alert and having fun."

"The location of the Fleurys' church box sounded pretty convincing…"

Shirley laughed. "Mama can think on her feet and could have easily made that detail up. Honestly, it could be part of her confusion."

Joy started the coffee maker. "Well, it's been a lovely evening."

Shirley plucked a knife from the rack. "And it's not over yet. We still have this delicious pie to devour."

A few minutes later, Joy carried out cups of coffee on a tray while Shirley delivered pie to each of the women.

"Listen to this, y'all," Evelyn said. "I found something on a Theodore Joubert appreciation website about the Fleury paintings that was posted just today. About two hours ago. Word is out about the current theft, and Claire is right about the speculation that it was stolen back in the 1870s too. This post claims, without a doubt, that Dr. Arthur Fleury stole the painting."

"Oh dear." Joy placed Regina's coffee on the end table beside her wingback chair. "Who posted that?"

Evelyn grimaced. "An anonymous blogger."

"Of course," Joy said. "Should I let Claire know?"

"Wait and tell her tomorrow. There's nothing that can be done tonight."

"You know," Regina said, "that family isn't as perfect as everyone thinks. They have their problems too."

"Mama." Shirley sat down on the end of the couch, balancing her piece of pie. "What have you been dancing around all evening? What do you know about the Fleury family?"

Regina smiled, this time slyly. "Oh, I'm not sure. You know I'm old. My memory—it comes and goes."

Shirley shook her head. "So basically you're thinking that one of the founders of Mercy Hospital was a thief? The ancestor of the family who continues to raise big bucks for the hospital every year?"

Regina shrugged.

"I hope not." Joy wrapped her hands around her mug, wondering how they could possibly discover if Dr. Arthur Fleury was innocent—or not.

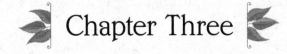

Chapter Three

THE NEXT MORNING, AS JOY sat on her patio dressed in a skirt and blouse and drinking her French roast coffee, her phone buzzed.

Sabrina. DINNER TODAY WORKS AFTER ALL. SEE YOU AT CHURCH!

"Oh dear," Joy said out loud. Should she change her plans with Claire? Theoretically she could go to church with Claire and then host Sabrina and her family for dinner, but she didn't go to the grocery store yesterday and didn't have anything on hand to fix for dinner. She'd have to skip church to make it work.

No. She needed to be honest with Sabrina and keep her commitment to Claire.

She sent Sabrina a quick text, explaining that she'd already made plans to go the baptism of a volunteer's granddaughter.

Sabrina sent back a sad face, followed by OK. SEE YOU SOON!

But then her phone rang. Joy answered it with a cheery, "Hi, sweetie."

Sabrina's voice had a hint of teasing to it. "So you're going to the baptism of someone else's granddaughter instead of seeing your own granddaughters?"

Joy laughed. "Something like that. This is the Fleury family—they own the Belina House Gallery. A great-great-great grandfather helped found the hospital. And the family is still a big donor."

"Ooh la la," Sabrina said. "So you're standing us up for Charleston's elite?"

"No."

Joy's voice must have sounded hurt because Sabrina said, "I'm just teasing."

Relieved, Joy said, "You won't believe what happened at the gallery yesterday. They have these three paintings—"

The sound of a crash startled Joy. "What happened?"

"Gotta go!" Sabrina said. "I'll catch up later."

"Is everything all right?"

"It's fine. Mallory just knocked the bowl of pancake batter off the counter. Bye!"

"Bye—" The call ended. Once Joy got past the image of sticky pancake batter splattered all over Sabrina's kitchen, she moved on to hoping Sabrina really was just teasing her. She'd moved to Charleston to be close to her daughter, son-in-law, and granddaughters, but it was a juggle to balance everything, both for Joy and Sabrina. Joy wanted to be as available as possible, but that didn't mean she needed to drop everything at a moment's notice.

Preplanning really was key.

Joy took the last drink of coffee. She knew Sabrina understood that. She was a wife, mother of a nine-year-old and five-year-old, and now a college student too. Basically, she was a supermom.

Joy imagined her daughter on her hands and knees mopping up pancake mix, probably not feeling super about anything at the moment. That sort of thing always seemed to happen on Sunday mornings before church.

Back in the house, as Joy rinsed her coffee cup, her phone dinged again. She picked it up, expecting a reply from Sabrina with an update about the pancake batter.

But it was from Joy's sister Hope instead. She read the text once and then a second time. And then a third. I'M MOVING TO CHARLESTON! I WAS GOING TO SURPRISE YOU AND SABRINA, BUT I CAN'T MOVE INTO MY APARTMENT FOR A COUPLE OF DAYS AND NEED TO STAY WITH YOU! SEE YOU TOMORROW! CAN'T WAIT.

Hope was moving to Charleston and arriving tomorrow? Without even mentioning it to Joy first?

Joy leaned against the counter and took a deep breath. Hope was already on her way and would arrive tomorrow.

She and Hope got along. They weren't close like Claire and Abrielle, but they weren't distant either. Not exactly. But Joy, as much as she hated admitting it, wasn't sure she wanted Hope to move to Charleston.

Hope loved surprising people. Joy hated to be surprised. Hope was spontaneous. Joy was a planner. Hope had long, flowing hair. Joy wore hers short and styled. Hope was both accident- and drama-prone. Joy avoided both whenever possible.

Joy and Hope were four years apart and as different as could be. Joy had married, had a baby, and lived a settled life as a wife and mom. Hope moved around the country from place to place, never marrying, working one job after another, coming home to Houston every few years, sometimes living with their folks for short bursts of time.

There were a few times when Hope seemed down and out, but she had an eternal optimism and always managed to bounce back. Joy just hadn't ever expected her to bounce to Charleston.

She stood up straight and said a little prayer, asking the Lord to help her be gracious to Hope—and for help being excited that she was moving to Charleston.

She sent her a quick text. SEE YOU TOMORROW! THE SPARE BEDROOM WILL BE READY.

Hope had been one of Sabrina's favorite people when she was a girl. And no wonder. Every time Hope waltzed into town she had a gift for her niece. A vase. A book. A bracelet. All small but sweet gifts. And Hope always had time to spend with Sabrina. She'd play dress-up when Sabrina was little. Take her shopping when she was older. Hope had made Sabrina's wedding veil, beading it with a thousand faux pearls, something Joy never would have had the patience to do.

But Hope wasn't always as careful as she should have been with Sabrina. One time, when Sabrina was five, Hope took her to the park. Sabrina wanted to climb up the ladder of the big-kid slide, and Hope, who said she hadn't understood when Joy explained that Sabrina needed to stay on the small slide, let her. Then Sabrina got scared and wouldn't come down, so Hope climbed the ladder and started carrying her back down. But halfway, Hope stumbled and fell, with Sabrina still in her arms. Sabrina was fine, but Hope broke her ankle and ended up losing her job at a garden center because she was immobile for two months.

Joy needed to let Sabrina know right away about Hope's plans. She texted: IS EVERYTHING OKAY WITH THE PANCAKE BATTER? WHAT A MESS. Then she texted, I JUST HAD A MESSAGE FROM HOPE. SHE'S MOVING TO CHARLESTON. IN FACT, SHE'S ARRIVING TOMORROW AND WILL BE STAYING WITH ME FOR A FEW DAYS. ISN'T THAT CRAZY!? ☺

She waited a minute, but Sabrina didn't text back, so Joy tucked her phone into her purse, stepped out her front door, locked it, and started walking through the French Quarter toward Church Street.

She passed shops and restaurants, mixed in with houses, and a few minutes later reached the grounds of St. Philip's Church, the oldest church in the city. On her right was the cemetery and to the left the stucco brick church. She greeted parishioners as she walked by—single women, young families, couples, and older men. All wearing dresses and suits.

Just past Queen Street was the Huguenot Church. Joy had admired it many times on her walks through the French Quarter. It was also constructed of stucco, although in a Gothic style. It was painted with a light tinge of pink that contrasted strikingly with the wrought iron fence around it.

Joy stepped through the open gate and read the sign to the left of the door.

THE FRENCH PROTESTANT CHURCH

ORGANIZED ABOUT 1681

FIRST CHURCH BUILT 1687

THIS BUILDING

THE THIRD ON THE SITE

WAS ERECTED IN 1845

The wooden door was open and a young man greeted her with a hearty, "Welcome!" as he handed her a bulletin.

"Thank you." Joy took the bulletin from him. "I'm visiting today, for the baptism. I'm a friend of Claire Walter's."

"Well, a double welcome then," the man said. "Claire's already here, in one of the Fleury boxes. Middle of the left side."

Joy thanked him and then smiled as she stepped into the lobby. Regina was right.

The church was nothing like the sprawling megachurch she'd attended in Texas, of course, where everything was bigger. She smiled, keeping herself from thinking *and better*. She loved Charleston. Things were different here, was all.

Everything in the church was compact. The lobby. The restroom tucked under the staircase that led to the balcony. She headed toward the far end of the lobby and then entered the sanctuary.

She stopped a moment. The pipe organ at the front of the church caught her attention first. Then the rows of wooden boxed pews. And lastly, the chandelier hanging from the ceiling.

"Joy!" Claire stood in the side aisle, waving and smiling. "We have a place for you here."

Joy waved and started down the aisle toward her friend. "Where's the baby?" she asked as she reached Claire.

"Running late. You go in first. We'll let the family sit on the outside."

Claire held the door to the box open and Joy stepped up into it, sidestepping along the wooden floor to the far end of the box. Then she sat down on the cushion as Claire hugged a woman in the aisle.

In the box in front of her was Abrielle, who turned around, a smile on her face. "Joy. Hello." She took Joy's hand, squeezing it. "I'm so glad you could make it." She put her other hand on the arm of the man next to her. "Daddy, I'd like you to meet someone."

Mr. Fleury, who had thick, snow-white hair and wore a black suit and red tie, turned around also. He smelled of soap and expensive cologne.

"This is Joy Atkins," Abrielle said. "She manages the gift shop at Mercy."

Mr. Fleury stood and reached out to Joy. She took his hand.

"This is our father," Abrielle said. "Marshall Fleury."

"I'm so pleased to meet you," Joy said.

"Likewise," Mr. Fleury said. "Welcome to our church."

"Thank you," Joy said. As she let go of his hand, he gave her a kind nod and then turned and sat back down.

"How are you?" Joy asked Abrielle. "How's everything going at the gallery?"

Abrielle wrinkled her nose. "All right. No new news."

"You seem so calm," Joy said.

Abrielle sighed. "I'm not."

Mr. Fleury patted his daughter's arm. "I'm struggling too, but we all need to try not to worry…"

Joy wondered if he was worried about the reputation of his ancestor along with the loss of money. Although the gallery's insurance would surely cover the losses if the paintings weren't recovered.

As Claire sat down beside her, Joy asked, "Where's Lloyd?"

"He had to stay in Savannah," Claire said. "Aunt Mae ended up in the ER last night."

"Oh no. Is she all right?"

"I think so," Claire said. "They're back at her place with some new meds. She has congestive heart failure."

"I'm sorry," Joy said. "And sorry that Lloyd has to miss the baptism."

Claire folded her bulletin. "We didn't want to postpone it. Evan—that's our son-in-law—has his family in town from Raleigh. It didn't seem right to postpone when it was all planned."

The organist started playing "Jesus Come with Clouds Descending," and people began taking their seats. A young couple with an infant slipped into the box and settled on the pew next to Claire, passing her the baby. The little one was dressed in a white dress with an embroidered bodice. Claire held the little one close then shifted her so Joy could see her too. "This is Talia," Claire whispered.

"She's beautiful," Joy whispered back.

"I know." Claire beamed. She nodded to her left. "Brooke and Evan." She smiled. "I'll introduce them later."

The service began with a hymn and then a reading, followed by a prayer, led by the song leader. "'Oh, Lord God! We render thanks unto Thee, that Thou hast called us to the knowledge and profession of the Christian faith…'"

The congregation followed along, reading from the bulletin. And then all concluded by reciting the Lord's Prayer.

Reverend Martin—according to the bulletin—stepped to the pulpit on the right side of the stage and read from Matthew 19:14. "'But Jesus said, Suffer little children, and forbid them not, to come unto me: for of such is the kingdom of heaven.'"

Then he began his sermon by saying, "Children aren't impressed by their own greatness. They're impressed by the wonder of the world, by a drop of rain, a dragonfly, a wilting flower. Jesus wanted His followers to emulate the humility of children."

The reverend smiled over the congregation. "Just a chapter before, when the disciples came to Jesus, saying, 'Who is the greatest in the kingdom of heaven?' He answered them by calling a little child unto him and saying, 'Except ye be converted, and become as little children, ye shall not enter into the kingdom of heaven.

Whosoever therefore shall humble himself as this little child, the same is greatest in the kingdom of heaven.'"

This time the Reverend Martin's smile landed on Talia, snuggled in Claire's arms. "In a while, a little one will be baptized today. Her parents will be tasked with bringing her up to know the Lord. Her mother was brought up in this church and her mother's mother and the grandmother's mother, and the father, who is here today, and more generations before him. There is great value in generation upon generation of a family following the Lord, living humbly, and serving others. Remember that." The reverend continued with the sermon.

Joy's eyes wandered to the right and then to the left as she listened. On each of the interior walls were plaques commemorating Huguenot families through the years with dates starting in the late 1600s. Some had settled in South Carolina, and others had settled in Virginia, Pennsylvania, and New York.

But for some reason, only the Huguenot Church here in Charleston had survived through all the years. The Fleury family seemed to have played a role in preserving it.

At the end of the sermon, Reverend Martin invited Brooke and Evan to join him. Claire placed Talia into her daughter's arms.

The little family made their way to the front of the sanctuary. When Brooke, Evan, and Talia reached Reverend Martin, he led them to the baptismal.

Brooke slid Talia, who was still asleep, into his arms.

Reverend Martin, with his eyes on the congregation, said, "May our trust be in the name of the Lord, who made Heaven and Earth."

The congregation responded, "Amen."

He turned to Brooke and Evan. "Do you offer this child to God and to His Holy Church, requiring that she should be baptized?"

They answered, "Yes."

Reverend Martin continued, speaking of the parents' responsibility in raising the child in the Lord. "You then promise to instruct this child in the doctrine of the Christian faith…" Finally he said, "May the Lord give you grace to faithfully perform this promise."

Just as he reached into the baptismal for the water, Talia opened her eyes and startled. Then she began to cry. Reverend Martin held the baby close and rocked back and forth.

The congregation seemed to sigh in unison when Talia stopped crying.

Then Reverend Martin said, as he sprinkled water on Talia's head, "I baptize thee in the name of the Father, and of the Son, and of the Holy Ghost."

Talia didn't stir, not even as the congregation said, "Amen."

Tears filled Joy's eyes at the beauty of the ceremony. They all needed grace to perform their promises to God, to raise the next generation, to encourage each other.

She herself needed grace in her relationship with her sister. She needed God's grace.

After the service ended, Reverend Martin invited the congregation to meet in the fellowship hall for refreshments and to meet Talia.

Joy was surprised there was a fellowship hall. The church didn't seem big enough for one, and she hadn't noticed an attached building.

After introducing her to more people than Joy could remember, Claire pointed at Brooke and Evan. They were accompanied by a couple who appeared to be in their fifties and a gaggle of young people. "That's Evan's parents and his siblings. They must have sat in the balcony. Let's follow them to the fellowship hall."

"Where is that?" Joy asked.

"On Queen Street."

Joy followed Claire out the front door, onto Church Street, and then they turned left onto Queen Street. A few buildings in, Claire turned to the right and headed up a walkway toward what looked like a two-story home. But the plaque on the outside read HERITAGE HALL. The front door was open and a man wearing a suit greeted Claire, saying, "You, my dear, must be delighted."

She beamed. "I am, of course. I'd like you to meet my friend, Joy Atkins."

The next couple of minutes were another blur of introductions. Joy felt nearly overwhelmed with the care and goodness of the congregants, all in the cozy environment of Heritage Hall that felt much more like a home than a church fellowship venue, as she was used to. Yes, Charleston, South Carolina, was as different from Houston, Texas, as could be.

Finally they reached Brooke, Evan, and Talia, who were near the back of the first room, with Marshall Fleury at their side.

Beyond them, around the refreshment table in the second room, stood Evan's parents and siblings.

"Brooke and Evan," Claire said, "I'd like you to meet Joy."

"Finally!" Brooke stepped forward and gave Joy a half hug. "Mom's told me all about you."

Joy smiled. "Thank you so much for including me. The service was lovely, and Talia is absolutely precious."

Brooke beamed with the same wide smile as her mother. What a legacy the Fleury family had, going back over three hundred years, all in the same location.

As Joy tried to find the words to express what she felt, there was a commotion at the front door.

"What's going on?" Claire took a step away from the group.

"Fire!" a man's voice shouted.

Claire, followed by Mr. Fleury, who was surprisingly quick on his feet, hurried toward the door.

A woman shouted, "The church is on fire!"

Chapter Four

CLAIRE DARTED OUT THE DOOR first, but Mr. Fleury seemed determined to catch up.

Joy hurried to his side and took his arm. "I'll help," she said.

Out the door they went as people surged forward on either side of them, up the walkway and onto Queen Street.

Joy and Mr. Fleury followed, turning onto the sidewalk.

Claire had reached the front of the church and yelled, "Has someone called 911?"

Abrielle waved from the front steps. "I did." The scarf around her neck was askew, and her face was red. Behind her stood Reverend Martin.

The faint sound of a siren could be heard as Mr. Fleury called out, "Abrielle, come down from there."

"It's all right, Daddy. The fire was only in the custodian's closet. Raymond found it and put it out. We just need the fire department to make sure everything is all right."

"What a relief," Claire called out. She turned toward the crowd. "The fire's out—it was in the custodian's closet. A truck is on its way so the crew can make sure everything is all right, but the church is safe."

Joy turned to Mr. Fleury. "Do you want to go back to Heritage Hall?"

He shook his head. "I'll stay right here until I know the church is fine. I've worked too hard to keep her going all these years to turn my back on her now."

Joy smiled.

"Our home. The Belina House Gallery. And Mercy Hospital are all dear to me." His brown eyes grew misty. "But the church…" He exhaled. "I can't imagine losing it."

Joy couldn't either. It seemed Claire and Abrielle had been raised by a man of integrity, something Joy wanted to think was passed down from Doc Fleury and probably from the generations before him. But, all of these years later, who could really know?

The siren grew louder and then blared as the truck rounded the corner onto Church Street a block away. It stopped in the middle of the street, in front of the church. Three firefighters, dressed in full gear, jumped down and headed toward the church.

Reverend Martin held the door open for the firefighters while Abrielle said, "The custodian put the fire out—it's at the far end of the lobby."

Once the firefighters were inside, Reverend Martin followed them, but Abrielle stayed on the front steps.

Claire came to Joy and Mr. Fleury's side and took her father's arm.

A minute later, Brooke approached. "Everything all right?"

"I think so," Claire said.

"What about Sunday dinner?"

Claire pulled out her wallet, opened it, and took out a credit card. "You should go with Evan and his family. Make sure to pay. Granddaddy and Abrielle and I will come if we can." She handed the card to Brooke.

"Mom…"

"I know. This isn't what we planned. But we can't leave until we know the church is all right."

Brooke sighed. "Okay."

Claire gave Brooke a hug. "I'm sorry. First Dad had to go to Savannah and now this. We'll make it up to you."

Brooke shook her head. "Don't worry about that. I understand. Evan's family has to get on the road right after dinner, so we'd better go ahead and keep the reservation."

"All right," Claire said. "Apologize for me."

"They'll understand." Brooke turned toward Joy. "It was nice to meet you."

"You too," Joy said.

Brooke kissed her grandfather on the cheek. "See you soon, Granddaddy."

He kissed her back, on one cheek and then the other. "One of those kisses is for your baby girl."

"Sure thing," she said. "We'll stop by tomorrow after her morning nap."

Joy watched Brooke head back to Heritage Hall. The Fleury family all seemed so idyllic. Mr. Fleury was in good health and an active part of the family. Claire and Abrielle were close. Brooke was a loving daughter and granddaughter.

Joy fought a wave of grief at the passing of her own parents and that her relationship with Hope wasn't closer, but then it passed. Every single family was different, and none was perfect. She was blessed to live in Charleston and be so close to Sabrina and her family. That was what she needed to concentrate on.

Someone speaking loudly at the front door of the church caught Joy's attention. A firefighter held two flat objects, wrapped in brown canvas, that came up to his hip. "The custodian said to ask Abrielle and Claire if these look familiar. He heard some paintings were missing from the gallery."

Abrielle hurried up the steps, her heels clicking against the concrete. Claire followed her. They pulled back the canvas on both items.

Mr. Fleury gasped. "The paintings."

"Well, two of the paintings," Joy said. Maybe the other one was still in the church.

Detective Rebekah Osborne arrived fifteen minutes later in her unmarked car, which she parked behind the firetruck. Joy still stood with Mr. Fleury on the sidewalk. She guessed he was tiring, but he insisted he wasn't.

Rebekah climbed out of her car and looked up at the church, shaded her eyes, and called out, "Abrielle. Claire. Which paintings were found?"

Abrielle called back, "Two of the three, but not *Belina in the Garden*."

"Oh." Rebekah started toward them. "I see."

Abrielle motioned to the two paintings still wrapped in the brown canvas. "Here are the two."

"Where was the fire?"

"In the custodian's closet. That's where the paintings were."

"How many people were in the church at the time of the fire?"

"Just a handful," Abrielle answered. "Most of the congregation had gone to the fellowship hall. The ones I know of who were in the church are still around."

Rebekah nodded. "I'll need to speak with anyone who was in the building at the time of the fire. Is there possibly a list of the congregants who attended the service?"

"I think so," Abrielle said. "At least members. A record of the names of guests won't be available unless they filled out a registration card."

"All right." Rebekah took a step toward the front door. "I'll speak with Reverend Martin about that." She pointed at the paintings. "I'll need to take those as evidence of the theft."

"We'll need to have them looked at as soon as possible, to evaluate any damage," Abrielle said.

"Of course," Rebekah said. "But we'll need to brush them for prints first."

Abrielle nodded. "All right."

A couple of minutes later a young man wearing black slacks and a navy blue polo shirt stepped out of the church. He was followed by Rebekah, who stopped him with, "Mind if I ask you a few questions while the firefighters check out the rest of the building?"

"Of course not," he said.

"That's Raymond Cooper," Mr. Fleury said softly. "He's our new custodian."

Joy leaned toward him. "How new?"

"A couple of months or so. He's a nice young man. He comes in around seven on Sunday mornings and makes sure everything is ready. Then he cleans up after the service and takes care of Heritage

Hall after the fellowship time ends. During the week he sees to all of the maintenance, plus he sets up for weddings and other events."

Rebekah and Raymond sat down on the steps. Joy could see that they were talking and every once in a while caught a word, but she couldn't tell what they were saying specifically.

Both Abrielle and Claire stood at the bottom of the steps, off to the right.

"What a relief that Raymond found the fire before the church burned down." Mr. Fleury shivered, even in the heat. "The thought is unimaginable. As much as I value the paintings, I value the church far more. It's the heart of our community, of our family too."

Joy sympathized with him but her concern fell, again, to his well-being. "Are you sure you aren't tiring? Do you want to go back to Heritage Hall?"

He shook his head. "I'm fine. But you don't need to stay."

"Oh, I want to," Joy said. "I'm finding this all quite intriguing, especially the possible connection to Doc Fleury and the hospital."

Mr. Fleury sighed. "Claire told me about the authenticator's speculation that he stole the paintings all those years ago. And that there's some sort of post online about that too. Doc Fleury is one of the sturdy trunks in our family tree. He was a selfless doctor, husband, father, and grandfather."

"Are there any family documents about him?"

"Of course. They were all donated to the South Carolina Historical Society archives years ago, before I was born."

Joy remembered what Abrielle had said the day before, about the documents being stored at the college. Perhaps she should make a trip to the college library. "Tell me about the paintings that were in the closet."

"I have photos of them on my phone," Mr. Fleury said. "Would you like me to text them to you?"

"I'd love that," Joy said.

He took his phone from his pocket and asked for her number. Then he texted her the two pictures.

Joy took out her phone as it dinged and opened the text.

"The first one is *Abrielle Overlooking the Village*," Marshall said.

The painting was of a young woman wearing a yellow cotton dress. Her dark hair was piled on her head, her eyes met the painter's straight on, and her feet were bare. She sat on a stone wall, and off to the left, in the distance, was a village with a church steeple in the middle. Joy loved art but she knew nothing about it, not like the Fleury family did.

But she was truly drawn to the painting. The girl appeared confident, as if she was completely in charge of her life.

"It's beautiful," she said.

"Isn't it? All three paintings are."

Joy swiped to the next photo.

Mr. Fleury said, "That's *Claire on the Church Steps*."

Joy glanced up at Claire and Abrielle on the church steps in front of her and then back at the painting.

The figure in the painting was younger than the figure in the previous painting, and her lighter brown hair was down around her shoulders. She wore a light green dress and sat on the steps in front of a wooden door. Without the title of the painting, Joy wouldn't have known it was a church. The girl appeared innocent and hopeful.

"Do you know where the painting was done? Have you been able to match the village and the church?"

Mr. Fleury shook his head. "Perhaps the authenticator has an idea."

"Do you have a picture of *Belina in the Garden* too?"

"Of course." Marshall took out his phone again and sent another text.

Joy tapped on the picture as soon as the text came through. The girl in the painting seemed to be older than the one in *Claire on the Church Steps* and younger than *Abrielle Overlooking the Village*. She wore a pale pink dress, and her hair was dark. She was barefoot and stood in the middle of a garden, her hand holding on to a trellis covered by a climbing pink rose.

"I don't understand," Joy said.

"Understand what?"

"Your family knew all these years what the names of the paintings were but you didn't know who the artist was?"

"That's right," Mr. Fleury said. "I was always told the paintings were given to Doc Fleury. Each one had the title written on the back in English, and none of them were signed."

"So you named the gallery and your two daughters after the paintings?"

"Three daughters."

"Three daughters?"

Mr. Fleury nodded. "Sadly, we haven't seen Belina in years."

Joy rolled the name "Belina" over and over in her mind as Rebekah approached and asked, "May I ask you a few questions, Mr. Fleury?"

"Of course," he answered.

"Has anyone contacted you about the paintings in the last few years?"

He shook his head. "But I never ran the gallery. My wife operated it until she passed away. Then I hired someone to do it until Abrielle took over."

"Who technically owns the paintings?"

"Our family corporation. The gallery and my law firm are all part of the corporation."

"Who runs the law firm, since you're retired?"

"Claire's husband, Lloyd."

Rebekah glanced around. "Is he here?"

Mr. Fleury shook his head. "No, he's in Savannah. His aunt is ill."

"When did the paintings come into your family's possession?"

"I don't know the exact date," he said. "My grandfather, Michael, and great-grandfather, Alexander, opened Belina House Gallery in 1901 and owned the paintings then, but that's all I know. The family had various businesses—the gallery, for example. And the law firm, which was established in 1869. And another one before that."

"Which was?"

"A shipping business. From the late 1600s until the 1870s. Doc Fleury was the first in the family to pursue work other than the shipping business. Then his son, Alexander, became a lawyer and later started the law firm, Fleury & Sons, which has survived all these years. Sadly, the shipping business did not."

"I see," said Rebekah. "Anything else as far as the paintings? Who might want them? And who might want *Belina in the Garden* in particular?"

He shook his head. "Although it seems likely that if it is an authentic Theodore Joubert, whoever knew that might be a viable suspect. Don't you think?"

Rebekah smiled. She handed him her card. "Would you call me if you think of anything else? Or if anyone contacts you?"

"Are you thinking someone might want to ransom the painting?"

"I'm not thinking anything in particular, just trying to cover all the bases," said Rebekah.

Mr. Fleury slipped the card into the breast pocket of his jacket. "Of course. Thank you."

The firefighters came out of the church. One said, "So far there's no other sign of fire or any other kind of damage in the building, but we're going to do a more thorough inspection." He motioned to Rebekah. "You can come back inside."

Rebekah turned to Abrielle and Claire. "I need to talk to the two of you as well."

"All right," Abrielle said.

"We need to go get some dinner for Daddy," Claire said. "He has low blood sugar."

"Can I meet you somewhere?"

"Sure," Claire said. "Let's get a sandwich and a cup of soup at the little shop around the corner."

"I'll be there in about a half hour or so," Rebekah said. "The crime unit is on the way to dust the closet door and other surfaces for prints."

"What will you do with the paintings?" Abrielle asked as a police car pulled up behind Rebekah's car.

"Officer Williams will take them back to the station. We'll dust those and the tarps, and trace the tarps and see if we can figure out where they came from. Then we'll put the paintings in the safe. I'll get you a receipt for them at the station and get it to you later today."

"How long will you keep them?" Abrielle asked.

"That depends on how the investigation goes," Rebekah said.

Abrielle nodded. Officer Williams wore gloves and had two large plastic bags in his hands. One at a time, he placed the paintings, still wrapped in the canvas tarps, into the bags.

Claire started down the steps and said to her father, "Let's go get something to eat."

Joy let go of his arm. "It was so good to meet you, Mr. Fleury."

"Come with us," Claire said to Joy. "You need something to eat too."

"I don't want to impose."

"Nonsense. You'd be doing us a favor."

Marshall linked his arm back through Joy's. "Please, do come with us."

"All right." She patted his arm. "If you're sure."

"I'm sure," he said. "And please, call me Marshall."

Abrielle joined them, and they walked past the church to Broad Street.

Marshall exhaled loudly.

"What's the matter, Daddy?" Claire asked.

"Oh, I was just thinking about how thankful I am to have three daughters. I was thrilled when you were little—and I'm even more so now. It was meant to be."

"Oh, Daddy," Claire said, but Abrielle didn't seem to hear what their father had said.

Joy couldn't help but wonder where Belina was and why neither Abrielle nor Claire had mentioned her, but she didn't ask. The fact they hadn't mentioned her seemed to indicate Belina was a touchy topic.

They turned off Broadway and stepped into the sandwich shop. Only a few of the tables were filled, unlike most of the eateries in town after church.

After they ordered, they sat down at the large table in the back of the shop and waited for their cups of soup and half sandwiches.

Abrielle pulled out her phone and said, "I'm going to call Pamela to let her know two of the paintings have been found and ask if she can evaluate them as soon they're released."

Claire nodded in agreement.

A moment later it was obvious Abrielle had reached the authenticator's voice mail. "It's Abrielle Fleury with an update for you. Please give me a call ASAP."

After Abrielle ended the call, Claire asked, "Did you give Rebekah Pamela's contact information?"

Abrielle nodded. "She was going to have a detective in Savannah speak with her, but I don't know if that's happened yet."

As Abrielle slipped her phone back into her purse, Daniella Hattel walked into the shop.

"Oh no," Abrielle whispered.

Daniella waved and headed toward them. "I heard two of the paintings have been found."

Claire flashed a cordial smile. "That's right."

"Any suspects yet?" she asked.

"You'll have to speak with Detective Osborne about that."

Daniella turned to Marshall. "Mr. Fleury. I'm Daniella Hattel from the *Dispatch*."

Marshall extended his hand. "Pleased to meet you. We appreciate your work as a journalist, but, as you know, we aren't at liberty to answer any questions at this time about the investigation."

"Of course," Daniella said. "I have a personal question though." She turned to Abrielle. "Can you tell me why you were with the Belgian art collector Jacque De Villiers on Friday night, the same night the paintings went missing?"

Joy looked at Abrielle. By the expression on her face she seemed to know exactly what Daniella was referring to.

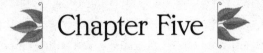

Chapter Five

AFTER ABRIELLE HAD REFUSED TO answer the question and Daniella left to go find Rebekah at the church, Claire said, "Abrielle, what was Daniella talking about?"

"Nothing," Abrielle said.

Claire leaned toward her sister. "Don't lie. I can read you like a book. You knew exactly what Daniella was talking about."

Abrielle shrugged as the number for their order was called.

Marshall started to stand. "I'll get it."

"I've got it." Joy quickly stood and headed toward the counter with Abrielle right behind her.

"I'll help," she said, which was one way not to have to answer her sister's questions.

When they returned to the table with the sandwiches and soup, Marshall led the group in a simple prayer of gratitude.

After he said, "Amen," the conversation shifted to Lloyd.

"Did you tell him two of the paintings have been found?" Marshall asked Claire.

"Yes," Claire said. "We've been texting."

Just as they finished up their food, Rebekah arrived with Daniella right behind her. Rebekah marched right to their table and said, "Abrielle, we need to talk. If you'd prefer, we can go down to the station where we can have some privacy."

"I'll answer you here," she said. "Claire and Daddy should hear what I have to say. I don't care if Daniella overhears, although what I'm saying is off the record." Abrielle gave Daniella a pointed look and then nodded toward a chair at the nearby table. "Pull up a chair," she said to Rebekah.

"All right." Once Rebekah sat down she asked, "Who is Jacque De Villiers?"

"He's a Belgian art collector," Abrielle answered. "He has a large collection, including seven Jouberts."

"How do you know him?"

"He works with an art dealer named Patrick Ray." Abrielle leaned backward in her chair. "Patrick lives in New York but comes to Charleston frequently. I've worked with him before."

Rebekah pursed her lips and then asked, "Was De Villiers interested in the three paintings?"

Abrielle nodded. "He's interested in anything that might be a Joubert, so he was interested in all three. Of course, now he'd only be interested in *Belina in the Garden*. I doubt he knows it was the only one authenticated though."

"If he does know, who would have told him?"

"It would have had to come from Pamela DePass, the art authenticator from Savannah," Abrielle said. "She's the one who made the decision. But it would be highly unprofessional of her to tell anyone else."

"How did De Villiers know the paintings might be Jouberts?" Rebekah asked.

"Patrick saw them in the gallery last winter when he was in town. I display them every few years. I'd seen Joubert's work, of course, but these would have been early in his career and quite different than the impressionistic work he's famous for, so I hadn't even thought it was a possibility." Abrielle exhaled. "Anyway, Patrick connected me with Pamela, but it took a couple of months until she could start the evaluation and then another couple of months until she completed it."

"Tell me about your contact with De Villiers."

"Patrick shared my contact information with him on Friday, and we went out to an early dinner at the Broad Street Grill after I left the gallery at five."

"Did he meet you at the gallery?"

Abrielle nodded.

"Interesting," Rebekah said as she jotted in her notebook. She glanced back up at Abrielle. "Why didn't you tell me all of this on Saturday?"

"I didn't think it was significant…" Abrielle's voice trailed off.

"Of course it is." Rebekah shook her head. "Where is De Villiers now?"

"He left for New York Friday evening, which is why we had an early dinner," Abrielle said. "I assumed he flew, but now that I think of it, perhaps he drove. He mentioned how much he loves to drive and see the countryside. Then again, he could be back in Belgium already. I don't have any idea."

Rebekah twirled her pen along her fingers. "What is your relationship with De Villiers?"

Abrielle frowned. "I only met him Friday."

"Did you show him the paintings?"

Abrielle nodded. "Friday afternoon, before we went to dinner."

"What was his response to the paintings?"

"He believed that *Belina in the Garden* seemed to have more promise as far as being a Joubert, so I wasn't that surprised when Pamela called with that verdict on Saturday morning."

"Were you hesitant to show him the paintings? Or eager?"

"Definitely eager," Abrielle said. "He was our best contact. If we decided not to sell, he would have been a good connection to the European art world, to museums who might have included the painting or paintings in exhibits and paid us a fee. If we needed to sell, he wanted to buy."

Marshall cleared his throat and said, "We're not selling."

"Daddy, we might have to sell," Abrielle said. "You know I'd never sell any of the three paintings without your approval—I couldn't do that—but if it comes to keeping the gallery or keeping the painting, well—"

"We're not selling any of those paintings," Marshall said adamantly.

Rebekah stopped writing, and her head shot up. "The gallery is having financial problems?"

Abrielle sighed. "You could say that."

"Let me guess," Rebekah said. "You didn't think that was important information for me to have either?"

Abrielle shook her head. "I'd like to preserve as much dignity for myself and our business as possible."

"Believe me," Rebekah said. "Dignity doesn't solve crimes. Honesty does. And full disclosure." She stared at Abrielle for a long moment. "Anything else you need to tell me?"

Abrielle shook her head, but Joy wasn't sure if she was telling the truth. By the expression on Claire's face, she wasn't sure either.

As Joy stood outside the sandwich shop with Claire, Abrielle, and Marshall, a storm brewed. The humidity was on the rise and a hot stickiness made it hard to take a deep breath.

Marshall turned to Joy. "Will you help us find the missing painting?"

Joy pursed her lips, not sure she had the resources to find the missing painting. But Marshall's request seemed heartfelt. "I'll do anything I can," she said.

He turned to Claire and then Abrielle. "Will you two commit to doing everything you can to find the painting?"

"Of course, Daddy," Claire answered immediately.

Marshall narrowed his eyes. "Abrielle?"

"Yes, sir. I already am."

Joy took her notebook from her purse. "I'll work on a list of what we have so far."

"Good," Marshall said, glancing from Joy to Claire to Abrielle. "You three keep in touch, keep talking. We have to get the painting back. Not because it's worth a lot of money and it could save the gallery. We need to get it back because it belongs to our family."

Claire nodded, and Abrielle wrinkled her nose.

"The truth," Marshall said, "always comes out sooner or later. Make sure it's sooner."

This time Abrielle nodded along with Claire.

Marshall took Claire's arm. "Let's go home."

"I'll see you tomorrow," Claire said to Joy.

"Oh, you don't need to come in," Joy said. "You have other things to deal with."

"No." Claire shot a look at Abrielle. "I'll be there. I'll need the distraction. And we can work on your list."

"Decide in the morning," Joy said.

Claire nodded but didn't say anything more.

Joy turned to Marshall. "It's been a delight to meet you. I promise I'll do as you requested."

Marshall smiled, just a little.

Joy added, "And I hope I'll see you again soon."

"You will," Abrielle said. "Daddy practically holds court during the auction."

Joy smiled, unsure of what to say. She assumed the auction might be canceled unless the investigation wrapped up quickly and the Belina House Gallery wasn't still a crime scene. Or if Garrison said they could use the mezzanine at the hospital.

"Well," Joy said, "I'll keep y'all in my prayers, and the current situation you find yourselves in. We'll figure this out—we'll find the painting and the thief."

"Indeed," Marshall said.

"Thank you for all your help today," Claire said. "And yesterday too. We appreciate it."

Abrielle and Marshall nodded in agreement, and then Abrielle sank down into one of the chairs in front of the sandwich shop and pulled out her phone.

Joy waved and started back to the church as Claire and Marshall started walking the opposite direction.

As Joy rounded the corner, she saw the fire truck still in front of the church. Two of the firefighters sat on the steps. Perhaps the third one was back inside, triple-checking everything. They certainly had a responsibility to ensure there were no other fires.

As she retraced her morning steps to St. Phillip's, her phone dinged.

THAT'S GREAT HOPE IS MOVING HERE. I CAN'T WAIT TO SEE HER!

That was Sabrina. All good cheer and optimism. Joy tucked her phone back into her bag as she walked through the property surrounding St. Phillip's. Several people still milled around, visiting on the grounds, but when thunder rumbled most waved to each other and started toward the parking lot.

Joy hurried her pace as she thought about Abrielle and Claire. Sibling relationships could be so complicated. Abrielle was the oldest and Claire the youngest. And now it turned out there was a third sister—Belina. What impact did she have on Claire and Abrielle's relationship?

Joy thought of Hope. What if they had another sister? Would that have made their relationship better or worse?

Another crash of thunder, this time closer, startled Joy as she left the grounds of St. Phillip's. When it started raining she increased her speed, as if she could perhaps outrun the drops. Of course she couldn't. She laughed as rain drenched her—flattening her hair and running down her face. Her dress was quickly drenched and by the time she crossed Market Street, she was dodging mud puddles too.

When she neared her house, someone called out her name. She lifted her head.

Evelyn, with a practical umbrella over her, stood on Joy's stoop.

Joy waved and hurried toward her. When she reached the stoop she took out her key as thunder crashed again.

After she unlocked the door, she swung it open and said, "Come on in" to Evelyn, who closed her umbrella and then quickly stepped inside.

Once they were both in the entryway, Joy closed the door. "What are you doing here?"

"I was out for a Sunday stroll and had some thoughts about what we talked about last night. I was hoping you'd be home." Evelyn leaned her umbrella against the wall. "I was afraid I had missed you and then, voilà, here you are."

"I went to Claire's granddaughter's baptism this morning and then some stuff happened I need to tell you about." Joy grimaced. "And then we all got sandwiches."

"Oh dear," Evelyn said. "It sounds as if there's more to the story."

"There is." Joy glanced up at her wet hair plastered above her eyebrows and then down at her dress. "I need to change first."

"Of course. How about if I put the water on for tea?"

"Perfect." Joy slipped out of her shoes, picked them up, and headed straight for the stairs.

Ten minutes later, Joy and Evelyn sat in the living room sipping Mandarin orange tea while the rain splattered against the patio door, making the home seem even cozier than usual.

Joy filled Evelyn in about the fire in the custodian's closet and two out of the three paintings showing up. Then she explained that

Abrielle had dinner with a prospective buyer Friday evening but hadn't told Officer Osborne when the paintings went missing.

"Because?" Evelyn asked.

"She claims she didn't think it was important information."

Evelyn frowned. "I took Abrielle Fleury to be smarter than that."

Joy exhaled. So had she. "What new information did you find?"

Evelyn opened her bag and took out a folder. "You know I've been slowly going through the archives at the hospital, trying to file everything in the appropriate place. It's a long process."

Joy nodded. She knew. Everyone at Mercy knew Evelyn was working to organize the archives. She, with her meticulous personality, was the perfect person to do it. Nearly two centuries of documents, some important and some rather odd, had been stuffed into boxes and files and cabinets in the windowless room.

Opening the plastic folder, Evelyn said, "I'd already started a file on Dr. Arthur Fleury. I found a few certificates of his. A couple of bills—one paid in bricks." She grinned. "I wonder if the bricks were used in any of the walkways around the estate?"

Joy smiled. That was a thought.

"Anyway," Evelyn said. "There are also a couple of newspaper articles that are quite fragile. I've been putting them in these archival sleeves." She opened the file and pulled one out. There was a one-column, four-inch, yellowed article in it.

"What is it about?"

Evelyn handed the sleeve to Joy. "It's a society column piece about Dr. Fleury going to France in April of 1871 on a business trip."

Joy took the sleeve. "A business trip? That had to do with medicine? Or the shipping business?"

"The shipping business," Evelyn said. "They had partners in France. However, the South Carolina branch of the business closed by 1872."

"I see." Joy read the article.

> *Our very own Doc Fleury is taking a leave of absence from Mercy Hospital to travel to Europe on a business trip for Fleury Shipping. He'll be gone no longer than six months and will spend the majority of his time in France. We wish him a good trip and a speedy return. Bon voyage.*

Joy lifted her head and met Evelyn's eyes. "So he was in France around the time the early Joubert went missing?"

"It appears so."

"How would the blogger have known that?"

Evelyn shrugged. "I emailed the blogger and asked. Hopefully he or she will get back to me."

"Don't you think it's quite a leap to think that because Doc Fleury went to France in 1871 he stole the painting?" Joy asked.

"Oh, I'm not saying it proves he stole the painting. Just that it places him in France around the time it may have disappeared."

Joy nodded in agreement and then took a sip of her tea, her head spinning with possibilities. She'd try not to speculate about Dr. Arthur Fleury—or Abrielle Fleury—until actual evidence was uncovered.

Monday morning, Joy rose earlier than usual. After she was ready for work, she grabbed her shears and went out onto her patio to cut a bouquet for the spare room. She cut lavender and heliotrope, red roses, and coleus as an accent. Then she arranged the flowers in a vase, filled it with water, and walked upstairs with it. Morning light filled the room.

Sabrina's bedroom set from her teen years occupied the room. A double bed with a wrought iron bedstead and an old, distressed bureau and bedside tables. Three throw rugs complemented the hardwood floor.

Joy placed the vase on the top of the bureau. The reflection of the flowers in the mirror added extra warmth to the room. She said a prayer for Hope as she traveled and for her new life in Charleston.

Then she headed back downstairs, grabbed her bag and her umbrella in case the predicted thunderstorm materialized in the afternoon as it had yesterday, and headed out the door to Mercy. She felt unsettled.

She hoped Claire would come in to volunteer after all. Someone in the family needed to see the article Evelyn had found—and Joy figured Claire would take it seriously while Abrielle would only try to ignore it, or at least minimize it.

The rain from the day before had completely dried. A clear blue sky shone overhead, and the morning was a little cooler. A faint scent of fall hung in the air as Joy cut through the French District.

Joy had been told that Charleston, with its winding cobblestone streets that were dotted with cafés and boutiques, was the closest urban area the United States had to a European city. When it was established in 1670, on the west bank of the Ashley River, its founders patterned it after what they had left behind.

Joy turned south toward the hospital and when she reached it, after a detour to the Grove to say good morning to the angel statue, she slipped in through the front door and headed straight to the gift shop. She'd barely unlocked the door and stepped inside when Shirley, wearing a pair of scrubs, appeared at the open door.

"Got any coffee?" Shirley called out.

"Of course." Joy motioned for her to step into the shop and then closed the door, happy that the coffee was set to start brewing every weekday morning at six forty-five. As she started toward the back, she asked, "Did you work last night?"

"Uh-huh," Shirley said. "I picked up a night shift in the ER. I only had a nap yesterday afternoon." She yawned. "I'm getting too old for this."

Joy didn't know how people worked the night shift. She'd be a mess. "How's your mom doing?" she asked as she poured a mug of coffee.

"Good," Shirley said. "I called her at the end of my shift, and she was already up, drinking her coffee and reading her Bible."

Joy smiled. What a sweet image of Regina.

"Seriously," Shirley said. "I know it's only ten minutes home, but I'm so tired I figured I shouldn't drive without a little caffeine first. Once I get home, I'll make Mama and myself some breakfast and then sleep for a few hours."

Joy handed Shirley the mug. "You don't work tonight?"

Shirley shook her head.

Joy poured coffee for herself. "Did you get any more information from your mom about the Fleury family?"

Shirley hesitated. "I'm not sure. I thought maybe she worked for them at some point, but that doesn't seem to be the case. She said she knew Marshall Fleury 'way back when.'"

"Really?"

"But who knows." Shirley took a drink of her coffee. "Sometimes she has these odd memories that are based on a nugget of truth, but then it becomes a fantasy."

"She can't help it," Joy said.

Shirley replied, "Oh, I know. And usually her stories are strictly entertaining. But every once in a while they involve a real person." She shrugged.

"Well, she was right about where the Fleury family box is at the Huguenot Church. Middle, left side."

Shirley shook her head. "Maybe she just got lucky." She took a long drink. "You're a lifesaver."

Joy laughed. "Actually, *you* are the lifesaver, literally." Joy had always appreciated the services of medical workers, and working at Mercy had enhanced that appreciation exponentially.

Shirley took another long drink, draining the cup. When she finished, Joy extended her hand.

"Oh, I'll wash it," Shirley said.

"Oh, no you won't." Joy grabbed the mug from her. "You need to get on home to your sweet mother."

Shirley smiled. "Thank you."

"Tell her hello."

"I will." Shirley spoke over her shoulder as she headed toward the door. "She'll be thrilled to hear from you—you're one of her favorite people. Bye!"

Joy waved and then headed to the back room to wash the mug.

At eight o'clock sharp, just after Joy turned the sign to OPEN, Claire came through the door.

"Hello, Joy!" she called out, as cheery as ever. She wore a tailored white blouse, a red full skirt, and red pumps. "How are you today?"

"Good." Joy's voice dropped in concern. "How are you?"

"Just fine."

"Any new developments as far as the missing painting? Or the found paintings?"

"Not a thing," Claire said. "Except that Rebekah texted Abrielle last night to say they hadn't finished the investigation yet and the gallery can't open today or tomorrow. We'll see if it can open later in the week."

"Oh, that's too bad," Joy said.

"She wondered if you could talk to Garrison about the mezzanine."

"Of course," Joy answered.

Evelyn came through the door, a pencil stuck through the bun on her head and her mug in hand. "I smell coffee," she said.

"I have some!" Joy pointed to the counter.

Evelyn headed toward the coffeepot. "Claire, did Joy tell you about what I found?"

Claire shook her head.

Joy said, "I haven't had a chance yet."

As Evelyn poured coffee into her mug she said, "An article about your great-great-great-grandfather taking a trip to Europe."

"Oh, that wouldn't be news. The Fleurys have always traveled a lot, even back in the seventeen and eighteen hundreds. It was part of their shipping business."

"Well, the date of the trip may be significant."

"What do you mean?"

"He traveled during the spring and summer of 1871, at the time the blogger claimed the painting was stolen."

Claire's expression clouded for a moment, but then she said, "That doesn't prove anything."

"Of course not," Evelyn said. "But it does raise suspicion. Do you have any idea why Dr. Fleury would have closed the shipping business down the next year?"

Claire shook her head. "Maybe this historical mystery will all fade. We need to focus on the present, on the stolen—"

"Have you seen this?" Anne held up a newspaper as she came through the door.

Evelyn, Claire, and Joy all shook their heads in unison.

Anne unfolded the paper and held up the front page. The title of the lead story read: *Has history repeated itself? Painting connected to the Fleury family goes missing. For the second time in the last one hundred fifty years.*

No surprise, the article was written by Daniella Hattel. Anne spread it out on the counter, and Joy and Claire began reading it.

"I didn't think she'd do it," Claire moaned. "I didn't think she had enough information."

"The anonymous source gave her quite a bit of information," Evelyn said.

"Do you think it's the blogger?" Joy asked.

Evelyn shrugged. "Perhaps... Or maybe there's more than one person who believes Doc Fleury stole the painting—or paintings—from France."

Daniella Hattel wrote that the paintings had all been stolen from Theodore Joubert's village, from a place called Itteville in the early 1870s, and that it seemed Dr. Arthur Fleury, a prominent physician in Charleston at the time and one of the founders of Mercy Hospital, was the prime suspect.

She went on to write that from an early age, it was apparent Theodore was an artistic protégé. By the time he was twenty, he was studying art in Paris.

Daniella claimed *Belina in the Garden* was one of Theodore Joubert's early paintings. The origins of the other two paintings were unknown, but because the themes were so similar experts believed the paintings were connected in some way.

"Experts?" Claire asked. "What expert is involved besides Pamela?"

Evelyn read out loud, "'Patrick Ray, an art dealer in Manhattan, says he was struck with how the other two paintings resembled Joubert's style and yet were more primitive in their composition.'"

Joy kept reading. "Any mention of Jacque De Villiers?"

"No one by that name is mentioned," Anne said.

Claire crossed her arms. "I don't know what to believe."

"Have you finished reading?" Anne asked.

"No," Claire answered.

Anne urged, "Keep going."

Joy kept reading too, apparently at the same pace as Claire because just as she gasped, Joy read, *The Belina House Gallery insurance policy is in question.*

Claire reached for Joy, as if she might fall. Evelyn pulled Joy's office chair out into the shop for Claire. After Claire sat down, Joy poured her a cup of coffee and carefully handed it to her.

The article wrapped up quickly after that with the line *The Fleury family owes the people of Charleston answers—about both the past and the present. Especially when a portrait of Doc Fleury is scheduled to be unveiled Saturday at the Mercy Hospital Art Auction. Does the city want to celebrate a possible thief?*

Evelyn read the last lines out loud and then rolled her eyes. "What does the city of Charleston have to do with all of this? If the paintings were stolen in the past, they were stolen in France, not Charleston. It sounds as if the reporter is being sensational and trying to draw attention to herself."

"You have a point," Anne said. "However, it's bad publicity for the hospital no matter what."

Joy agreed.

Anne folded up the paper, and said, "I'm sorry, Claire."

"No, don't be sorry. I usually read the paper in the morning, because Lloyd gets it off the porch and puts it on the breakfast table. But he's still gone, and I totally forgot about it."

Claire took another sip of coffee and then said, "Abrielle is the one who always renews the gallery's insurance policy." She tightened her grip on the mug. "I can't believe she would let it lapse."

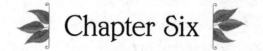

Chapter Six

A HALF HOUR LATER, EVELYN and Anne had left the gift shop, and Claire had seemed to regain her composure in time for a rush of customers.

A new father bought a bouquet of glass-blown roses for his wife. A mother bought a teddy bear for her little girl on the pediatric floor. An older man bought a box of chocolates for his wife who had been admitted for tests.

When they all left, Joy stood at the counter and asked Claire how she was doing.

"Better," she answered, standing by the display of candles. "Although I haven't heard back from Lloyd. I shot him a text about the insurance policy."

"What about Abrielle? Did you text her?"

Claire shook her head. "Not yet. I will—later."

"In the meantime, do you want to talk about the case more? Do some brainstorming?"

Claire shrugged.

Joy spoke quickly. "Someone took the paintings. Someone put two of them in the church and set the fire. Someone still has the Joubert painting. We need to identify who that is." Joy had a notebook tucked in beside the cash register that she used from time to time for notes to herself. She picked it up. "Let's start that list we talked about yesterday."

"All right," Claire said.

Joy opened her notebook. "Let's do a historical one too. We want to clear the good name of the Fleury family before the auction Saturday night. Otherwise, I'm afraid no one will show up."

"Let's start with the historical then." Claire pursed her lips and said, "How in the world could we have any idea who might have taken the pictures besides Doc Fleury?"

"Perhaps someone traveled with him," Joy said.

Claire shrugged again. "Face it, we're not going to figure out the historical mystery."

Joy kept her voice calm. "Maybe Evelyn will find more information in the archives."

When Claire didn't answer, Joy said, "We'll revisit the historical mystery later." She tapped her pen against the notebook. "How about what's going on now?"

"I hope Abrielle didn't stage all of this," Claire said, "but put her name on the list. She's been acting secretive lately. The fact that she had dinner with De Villiers and didn't tell Rebekah—that's just weird. Why would she do that? I don't think she staged the theft or started the fire, but I do wonder what she's up to."

Joy wrote down Abrielle's name. "What about the art consultant, Pamela DePass?"

"Yes, ma'am, definitely put her on the list. She seems to be a hub of information—or disinformation."

Joy added Pamela DePass to the list.

"You'd better add Grey," Claire said. "Even though he has an alibi. Grey could have driven into town that night. And I could have left my house in the middle of the night. I'm sure we're both on Rebekah's list."

Joy jotted down Grey's name and then added Claire too. She knew the security code. She could have sneaked out of her house in the middle of the night.

Claire spoke softly. "I wonder where Belina is."

Joy held the pen in midair.

When Claire didn't say any more, Joy asked, "You don't know where she is?"

Claire shook her head.

"Does she live in South Carolina? Or somewhere else?"

"It's hard to tell," Claire said.

"Does your father know?"

"I don't think so," Claire said, "although he hasn't always been up front with me when he's had contact with her."

"Why is that?"

Claire sighed. "It's a long story."

Joy hesitated and then said, "Would Belina know the painting was a Joubert?"

"That's hard to know too." Claire sighed again. "Belina studied art. At one time, it was her whole life."

"Really?" Joy mused over that. "Would Belina have motivation to steal the painting?"

Sweeping her hair away from her face, Claire stared past Joy, a defeated look on her face.

"Claire? Would Belina have motivation?"

She nodded and then made eye contact. "Absolutely."

Two hours later, Lacy, a regular volunteer of the gift shop, arrived. Claire was just finishing her shift as Joy readied to take her lunch break.

"I'm going to walk over to the church to check in with Reverend Martin," Claire said. "Want to keep me company?"

"I'd love to." Joy could eat the sandwich she'd packed when she returned. "I'll just grab my bag."

They stepped out of the hospital and onto Franklin Street, into the bright sunshine and sticky warmth. The hint of autumn in the morning air was long gone. It felt like summer again. And as if another thunderstorm might be a couple of hours away.

Joy's phone dinged, and she took a quick look. It was from Hope. I'm in Columbia. See you in a couple of hours!

She was making better time than Joy expected. "It's my sister," Joy said to Claire. "She's moving to Charleston and is on her way."

"Wow," Claire said. "I had no idea."

"I only found out yesterday. Her apartment won't be ready for a few days so she's going to stay with me. I just need to text her back."

"Of course."

Joy stopped for a moment and texted, Great! Come by the hospital and I'll give you the key. I don't get off until 3.

They continued down Queen Street.

"What's your sister's name?" Claire asked.

"Hope."

She smiled and made quotation marks with her fingers. "'Matching' names, just like my sisters and me."

Joy laughed. "To go with the matching outfits."

"You too?" Claire clapped her hands together. "We had some doozies. Plaid jumpers. Magenta turtlenecks. Even bell-bottoms."

Joy smiled. "Ditto, along with velvet Christmas dresses and fluffy Easter outfits."

"With white gloves and bonnets?"

Joy laughed again. "Exactly."

"Do you and Hope get along?" Claire asked.

"Pretty much," Joy said, "although I wouldn't say we're as close as you and Abrielle."

"Well, today's not the day for me to comment on how close I am with Abrielle, not after that article. But…" She paused a moment and then said, "Perhaps now that you and Hope will live in the same city, you'll grow closer."

"Perhaps," Joy answered.

They took a left on Queen Street. Claire's pumps clicked along the sidewalk while Joy's more practical shoes made a soft thud.

"I plan to talk with Abrielle after I check in at the church about the insurance," Claire said. "I'm keeping my chin up, as Mama used to instruct us to do."

"How long ago did your mother pass away?"

Claire's voice grew soft again. "I was fifteen. Belina was seventeen and Abrielle was nineteen."

"I'm so sorry," Joy said. "You were all so young. And your father was too. He never remarried?"

"No. He was absolutely devoted to our mother." Claire's voice was barely audible. "She was the sweetest person you could ever meet. None of us ever totally recovered from her death, although I believe it was hardest on Belina. Abrielle had already gone off to college, I still had a couple of years of high school, but it was a week before Belina's high school graduation, and the funeral was the day before. Belina refused to attend her graduation. She went from being prom queen to hardly leaving the house all summer. She went off to Savannah for art school and then on to Paris to study for a few years, but she dropped out right before she graduated." Claire shook her head. "Then she moved around a lot. She'd land these really cool jobs—and then quit after a short time."

That sounded like Hope, although Joy's mother hadn't died. And Hope's jobs weren't all that cool.

They stopped at Meeting Street, waited for the break in the traffic, and then kept walking.

"When I reached the age Daddy was when Mama died—forty-five—I realized how young he was. He should have remarried. But he's always said he never found anyone to replace Mama." She smiled. "Not that he looked." She grew serious again. "Now that I've been married for thirty years, I realize what a good marriage they had." She hesitated for a moment and then said, "I assumed I'd have one just like theirs."

"What do you mean?" Joy asked.

Claire lifted her head. "Oh, nothing. Just that it's a lot more work than I thought it would be, even after all of these years."

"I think all marriages are more work than one expects. Your parents' marriage might have been too—they just kept that from you."

"Perhaps…"

They'd reached the church steps. "I'll leave you here," Joy said.

"Oh, come in with me," Claire said. "The church is such a peaceful place." She smiled again. "Especially when it's empty."

Claire pulled out her phone and sent a text. "Reverend Martin will let us in," she said.

A couple of minutes later the door swung open.

"Reverend Martin," Claire said. "I'd like you to meet my friend Joy Atkins."

"Welcome," he said, holding the door wide. "I recognize you from yesterday."

Joy smiled. "I enjoyed the service," she said. "I moved to Charleston eight months ago and have admired your church ever since. I was so happy to finally have a chance to visit."

He smiled in return. "I'm so glad you did," he said. "Come on in."

Joy followed Claire into the lobby, expecting the acrid smell of smoke. Instead, the scent of cleansers filled the air. Disinfectant and wood cleaner, mostly.

"How is everything today?" Claire asked.

"Besides a burned floor in the custodian's closet and smoke-damaged walls, everything seems fine. I'm getting a bid on the floor repair and the cleaning tomorrow." He stopped in the middle of the lobby. "Thank goodness Raymond smelled the smoke. I was heading out the door to the fellowship hour and hadn't even noticed it."

"Any idea how it started?" Claire asked.

"There were only a handful of us still in the church, but a back door was unlocked."

Claire's eyebrows shot up.

Reverend Martin nodded. "That door is never used. But someone must have a key, although I have no idea who. The lock was intact, and nothing was broken."

"The plot thickens," Joy said.

Claire crossed her arms. "Apparently so."

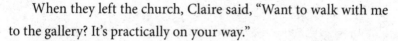

When they left the church, Claire said, "Want to walk with me to the gallery? It's practically on your way."

"Sure," she said. They hadn't been at the church long. Joy still had plenty of time to get back to the gift shop.

As they approached the gallery, which had a CLOSED sign hanging in the window, the door opened and Abrielle stepped through and then locked the door behind her.

"Hi, Sis," Claire called out.

"Oh, hello." Abrielle started down the steps, shading her eyes with her hand. "What are you doing here?"

"I came to talk with you. Did you see the article in the *Dispatch* today?"

Abrielle stopped on the next-to-the-bottom stair. "I heard about it but haven't had a chance to read it yet."

"Is it true you let the insurance on the paintings lapse?"

Abrielle's face reddened. "Who told you that?"

"It was in the article."

"But who would have known that?"

Claire crossed her arms. "You."

Joy took a step backward, feeling uncomfortable listening to the conversation.

"I haven't heard back from the insurance company," Abrielle said. "Lloyd put in a call today, but he hasn't heard back from our agent either."

"I need better answers than that," Claire said. "Let's go talk in the gallery."

Abrielle shook her head. "I can't let you inside."

"But you just came out of there."

"I just grabbed some papers is all, with Rebekah's permission. I was headed around the back and up to my apartment—she said I can stay there tonight."

Joy took another step backward. "I need to get back to the gift shop," she said.

"Thanks for walking with me," Claire said. "See you soon."

Abrielle took the last step. "See you soon, Joy." But she didn't sound very enthusiastic about it.

"Goodbye." Joy waved and turned north toward the hospital. Abrielle did seem secretive. Joy never would have taken her to be a deceptive person—not even a secretive one—but it appeared she might be.

The Fleury family had trusted Abrielle with the gallery only to have her keep secrets, it seemed, and possibly not see to basic business practices.

Joy would soon have her own sister to interact with. In an hour or so, Hope would arrive.

As Joy neared the hospital, she said a prayer that she would be gracious and loving toward Hope. It was incredible how patterns from childhood could intrude on a relationship.

She stepped out of the muggy air and into the cool lobby of the hospital. As she headed for the gift shop, Evelyn came from the hallway that led to the records department. "Joy!" she called out. "There you are. Do you have a minute?"

Joy nodded. "Want to sit with me in my office while I eat my sandwich?"

"Sure," Evelyn said.

A few minutes later, Joy said hello to Lacy, and Evelyn followed her into the office. Joy unwrapped her turkey sandwich as Evelyn said, "I found another folder in the archives of clippings and documents on Dr. Arthur Fleury."

Joy swallowed her first bite. "Ooh. Anything important?"

"Not yet," Evelyn said. "All of it is fascinating—articles about his medical practice, parties at the family home, and civic events he attended. Also some bills, inventory lists, and notes he took at meetings. But I've only gone through the first third of the file, so hopefully something related to the paintings will show up. I'll let you know."

"That'd be great," Joy said and then took another bite.

"I also spoke more with James about the Huguenots. He did some research on them for an article for the South Carolina Historical Society a few years ago. He said the diaspora—"

"What diaspora?"

"The Huguenot diaspora," Evelyn said. "It started in sixteenth-century France and continued through the eighteenth century. Huguenots ended up in England, Belgium, South Africa, and throughout the New World, from New York to Florida."

"I find it fascinating that so many left and yet the Huguenot Church here is the only one left in the United States."

Evelyn nodded. "It's because most groups assimilated into their new communities within a couple of generations. Although some kept their culture and ties to their relatives in other parts of the world. The Charleston church stayed Huguenot because there were no laws in the Carolinas that they couldn't, and they retained a stronger sense of identity."

"Interesting," Joy said.

Evelyn added, "The other important response James had when I told him the names that have come up so far concerning the missing paintings, is that De Villiers is a Huguenot surname."

"Really?"

Evelyn nodded again. "Of course, that's not saying the art collector Jacque De Villiers is Huguenot or that his family was. But it's a connection worth pursuing."

It certainly was. "Speaking of names connected to the paintings, do you know anything about Belina Fleury, who was named after the missing painting?"

"I know she's the middle Fleury sister," Evelyn responded. "The girls are a decade and more younger than I am, but I was aware of them. Especially at the time their mother passed away. That was a real tragedy."

"How did she die?"

"A car accident," Evelyn said. "I don't remember all of the details. I do remember that Belina eventually went to Paris to study art. I think she worked as a model at one time and then worked in the fashion world, out in California." She shrugged. "I have no idea what she's doing or where she's at now. Every once in a while I'll ask Abrielle or Claire how Belina is doing and they'll say she's fine. About five years ago Abrielle said Belina was living in Santa Monica and working with a designer there. Mostly I get the idea that Abrielle and Claire don't want to talk about her much."

Joy found that sad. But maybe they had a good reason.

As she took the last bite of her sandwich, her phone rang. *Hope.*

Joy swallowed and then said, "It's my sister." Joy hit accept.

Using her cheeriest voice, she said, "Hello, Hope!"

"Joy." Hope was crying as she spoke. "I just caused an accident. Behind the hospital. On Magazine Street."

Joy's heart clenched as she heard sirens in the background. "I'll be right there."

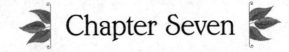

Chapter Seven

JOY RAN THROUGH THE LOBBY of the hospital, past the coffee shop and the windows looking out over the Grove. As she approached patient discharge, Anne called out from the counter, "Joy! What's wrong?"

"My sister's been in an accident." She slowed and pointed toward the back exit.

Evelyn, who was a little out of breath, caught up with Joy, but Joy kept going, with Evelyn at her heels. Anne followed.

The automatic doors slid open and all three hurried through, into a splattering of rain and thunder off in the distance. To the right, a police car with its lights flashing was parked in the middle of the intersection.

A white car pulling a U-Haul trailer had been broadsided by a pickup truck.

A woman with shoulder-length blond hair and a man stood beside the pickup, which had a damaged bumper and hood. Steam was shooting out from the engine. The woman was tall and seemed familiar. Joy walked quickly along the sidewalk, dodging pedestrians. As she neared the intersection, the wail of another siren grew louder and a fire truck arrived.

Joy stepped into the intersection, nearing the white car. "Hope?" she called out.

The woman standing beside the truck pointed to the car. In a husky voice she said, "She's in there. The door won't open."

The driver's door of the car was completely smashed and the window was broken. It was worse than Joy had assumed from the quick conversation with Hope.

Joy's heart raced faster. "Hope?"

Her voice was so soft, Joy could hardly hear it. "I'm here."

Joy leaned down, brushing raindrops from her face. "Are you all right?"

"I think so."

The airbags had deployed and were now deflated all around Hope. She had a gash in her head that was bleeding, matting her dark hair.

Another crash of thunder startled Joy. But then the rain stopped. She quickly took the scarf from around her neck and reached through the window with it. "Your head is bleeding," she said to Hope. "Can you press this against it?"

Hope took the scarf and held it to her head.

"Does anything else hurt?"

"My left foot. Somehow it got wedged under the brake pedal."

"Can you move it?"

Hope pulled on her leg. "No." She looked up at Joy. "I ran the red light."

"Shhh," Joy said. "Don't think about that right now. The insurance companies will sort that out. I'll get the other driver's information and speak with the police officer. Right now, your health is what's most important."

Three firefighters approached, and Joy stepped back. Evelyn and Anne both moved to her side.

"What can I do to help?" Anne asked.

"Could you go back to the gift shop and stay until I get back? Lacy is scheduled to go home soon."

"Sure," Anne said.

"What can I do?" Evelyn asked.

"Stick around for a few minutes. Make sure I don't forget anything as far as getting the information Hope will need from the officer and the other driver."

Evelyn nodded. She was always so levelheaded and thorough and just the right kind of person to have on hand during an emergency.

Joy approached the officer, explaining that she was the driver's sister.

The officer said, "I'll need to speak with the driver, if she's able."

"Of course," Joy said.

One of the firefighters announced, "We're going to have to cut into the car to get the driver out, so I need everyone to step back onto the sidewalk."

Joy's heart raced as she followed Evelyn to the sidewalk. Poor Hope.

Two firefighters placed blocks behind the wheels of Hope's car while another firefighter spoke with her through the window. Then a fifth firefighter appeared with a neck collar, which she put around Hope's neck.

The first firefighter approached the car with a tool, while the others all stepped back, and he started cutting the front hinge of the door. The hum of the cutter and the smell of metal filled the air.

Another siren wailed and an ambulance arrived. Paramedics climbed from the back and pulled a gurney out.

Joy shivered, even in the heat.

The cutting continued until the door began to wobble. Then two firefighters stepped forward and held on to it as the last cut was made. As they carried the door away, Hope was exposed to the crowd that had gathered. She looked so small and vulnerable. Joy's bloody scarf was wadded in her left hand, and the neck collar was already covered with blood.

Joy fought back tears.

The paramedics approached, leaving the gurney at the back of the car. A tow truck arrived, and the two people who were in the pickup stepped over to talk with the driver.

Joy kept an eye on them, not wanting to miss her chance to get their information and to give them Hope's phone number. The paramedics blocked Joy's view of her sister but soon they had her moved onto the gurney.

Joy approached, with Evelyn at her side. "I'm assuming you'll take her to Mercy," Joy said to the closest paramedic.

The man nodded.

Joy turned to Hope. "Do you want me to take your purse and meet you in the ER?"

"I'll take it," Hope said. "Could you stay and talk with the tow truck driver? And find out where they'll take my car and trailer?"

"I'll do that," Evelyn said.

Joy knew the car was totaled, but there was no need to talk about that right now. The trailer definitely needed to be kept in a secure location.

A firefighter stepped forward with Hope's purse and an overnight bag from the back seat. He placed the purse on the gurney, and Joy took the bag.

"Where's your phone?" Joy asked.

"In my purse." Hope clutched it. "Could you give my number and insurance information to the driver of the pickup and get his number?"

Joy nodded. "And then I'll see you in the ER."

Hope's eyes filled with tears. "I'm sorry, Joy."

"Whatever for?"

"Making life more complicated for you."

Joy reached out and touched Hope's arm. "Don't say that. Just be all right."

"I am," Hope said. "Don't worry about me."

Joy had been worrying about Hope her entire life. Why would she stop now?

As the paramedics wheeled the gurney toward the ambulance, Joy opened the passenger door of Hope's car and opened the glove box. She half expected not to be able to find the insurance information—Hope wasn't always very organized—but it was in a folder with the car registration. As a second tow truck arrived for Hope's car and trailer, Joy took the folder and approached the couple standing to the side while the tow truck driver loaded their vehicle.

"I'm Joy Atkins," she said. "My sister Hope is the driver of the other car. I have her information here and wanted to get your information for her."

"All right," the man said. "I'm JD—Joseph Daniel—Johnson." He rattled off his phone number and then gave Joy the name and number of his insurance agent.

Joy entered the information in the notes app on her phone.

Then she gave him Hope's name, phone number, and insurance information.

Joy realized she hadn't gotten the name of the woman. The insurance company would need that too.

She turned to the woman and squinted a little against the lowering afternoon sun that had slipped out from behind a cloud. "I need your name too."

Joy lowered her head to put the information in her phone. "Belina," the woman said.

Joy's head shot up. Blond hair. Brown eyes. Slim, tall build. "Belina?"

The woman's face reddened.

"Are you Belina Fleury?"

The woman took a step backward. Her voice was even deeper than before. "Do I know you?"

Joy shook her head. "But I know Abrielle Fleury and Claire Walter. You look just like them. Are you their sister?"

The woman turned around and started walking through the crowd. Once she reached the sidewalk, she began to run.

"Did you think she was a Fleury sister when you saw her?" Joy asked Evelyn as they walked back to the hospital.

"I can see the resemblance now," Evelyn said. "But that wasn't at all what I thought when I saw her. I've never seen Abrielle or Claire wear jeans and a T-shirt before."

Evelyn handed Joy the tow truck driver's card. "Here's all the information you'll need. He said both the car and trailer will be in a locked facility."

"Thank you," Joy said. "I really appreciate your help." Her hand trembled a little as she slipped both her phone and the card into the pocket of her sweater.

As they entered the hospital, Evelyn said, "I'm going to get back to work, but call if you need me. And I'll check in before I go home."

"Thank you," Joy said. "I really appreciate your help."

As Evelyn veered down the hall toward the records department, Joy headed to the Emergency Room. She stopped at the counter. The receptionist was a young woman named Krisnan, who sometimes came into the gift shop.

"Hi, Krisnan," Joy said. "My sister just arrived via ambulance. I need to be with her."

Krisnan's eyes filled with compassion. "Oh, I'm so sorry." She typed on her keyboard and a moment later said, "She's just now being admitted, in room three." Krisnan pressed the button. "You can go on in."

"Thank you." Joy hurried through the open doors. Room three was on the left, and the door was open a crack. When she knocked on it, Hope asked, "Joy, is that you?"

Joy pushed the door open. "Yes, I'm here."

The paramedics were transferring Hope onto a bed, and a nurse stood at the computer.

"This is my sister," Hope said to no one in particular—or perhaps to everyone.

The paramedics completed the transfer, and the nurse stepped away from the computer. She elevated the head of Hope's bed, took a white blanket from the counter, and spread it over her.

As the paramedics left the room, Joy put the overnight bag on the floor and stepped to Hope's side. Her forehead and the side of her face were still bloody, but the wound didn't seem to be bleeding now.

The nurse stepped back from the computer again and started asking questions. "Where is your pain?"

"My head and left foot, mostly."

"On a scale of one to ten, how bad is it?"

Hope answered, "I'd say a seven."

Joy placed her hand on her sister's arm.

The nurse asked a few more questions and then said the doctor would be in soon.

After she left, Hope asked about her car and trailer.

"They'll be stored until we can take care of things," Joy said.

"Do you think the car is totaled?"

Joy shrugged. "Let's see what the insurance company says."

"I think it is." Hope looked down at her lap. "Are you going to ask me what happened?"

Joy wasn't sure what to say. Was Hope worried she'd be judgmental of her?

"I ran the red light." Hope's dark eyes were full of fear. "Why am I so spacey? Am I going to be able to start work on time?"

"Call them," Joy said. "People get in accidents. Everything will work out." But she thought of the job Hope lost when she broke her ankle. "Where is the job?"

"The College of Charleston. As the grounds crew supervisor."

"What a fun job," Joy said.

"Right? It's a dream job for me."

"Maybe you should call now. Just so they won't expect you in the morning."

"But what if I'm okay? Maybe I'll be released soon."

"Maybe, but…" Joy pointed at Hope's head and then her foot. "I doubt you'll feel like starting a new job in the morning."

Hope's eyes filled with tears again. "You're probably right, like always."

Joy grimaced inside. Had she portrayed an "always right" persona to Hope?

"Where's my purse?" Hope asked.

Joy retrieved it from the chair against the wall and placed it on the bed beside Hope just as a man walked in. Chad Barnhardt, a doctor Joy knew well.

"What are you doing here?" he asked Joy.

"Hope is my sister."

He smiled at Joy and then turned to Hope. "Nice to meet you, although I'm sorry for the circumstances. Can you tell me what happened?"

Hope was briefer than she usually was with a story. "I was broadsided in the intersection over there, on Magazine Street. They had to cut me out of the car. I have a gash here." She pointed to her forehead. "I hit my head pretty hard and, you should know, I'm recovering from a concussion, from just a couple of weeks ago. I fell down the last two stairs at my apartment complex and whacked my head on a concrete step."

Joy winced. That sounded awful.

Hope pointed to her left foot. "My foot was trapped under the brake pedal—it doesn't feel right."

The doctor washed his hands, pulled on gloves, and checked her head wound and her eyes.

Next he examined her foot.

"Any other pain? In your abdomen? Legs?"

"My right leg is sore but not like it's broken or anything. And I have some pain in my chest, but I think it's from the seat belt and airbag."

"All right," he said. "I'm going to order X-rays of your foot and chest and a CT scan of your head to make sure there's nothing more than the wound. But first I'll clean up and stitch that gash."

He took off the gloves and threw them in the trash. As he washed his hands, he said, "The nurse and I will be back in a few minutes."

After he left, Hope said, "You don't have to stay."

"Of course I'll stay," Joy answered. "But I should go check on the shop. Then I'll be right back."

As she left the ER, her phone dinged. She expected it to be Evelyn or Anne, but it wasn't. It was Claire. CAN YOU TALK? ABRIELLE IS DRIVING ME NUTS.

When Joy reached the gift shop, Anne said she needed to pick Addie up from after-school care but could then come back to the hospital. They sometimes ate supper in the cafeteria when Ralph's work as a chaplain kept him at the hospital late.

Joy sent Hope a text, saying she'd be back in the ER in about an hour. After waiting on a couple of customers, once the shop was empty, she called Claire.

Instead of saying hello, Claire blurted out, "I got absolutely nowhere with Abrielle about the insurance. She's as stubborn as can be."

"I'm sorry. Hopefully you'll still get the information you need," Joy said. "Listen, I have some surprising news."

Claire had a hint of a whine in her tone. "I hope it's good."

Joy said, "I saw Belina. At the intersection of Magazine and Logan Streets, behind the hospital."

"What?"

"My sister, Hope, just arrived in town and was in an accident that involved a man named JD Johnson," Joy said. "Belina was in his pickup with him."

"Goodness." Claire gasped and then said, "I need to sit down."

Joy asked, "Are you all right?"

"No."

"Where are you?"

"At home. Daddy isn't with me. I don't want to tell him about Belina and get his hopes up until we know more."

"When she told me her name was Belina, I guessed she was your sister. She looks so much like you and Abrielle. When I asked if she was Belina Fleury, she took off through the crowd and started running."

Sadness filled Claire's voice. "Oh no."

"What are you thinking?" Joy asked.

"I don't know." Claire paused a moment. "Is it a coincidence that Belina showed up now? Or does she have something to do with the missing painting? And why was she with JD? They were friends in high school, but I had no idea they kept in touch. Not that I have any idea about Belina's life anyway. Was she hurt in the accident?"

"She didn't seem injured and neither did JD," Joy said. "He was driving a big pickup, and I think it protected them."

Claire asked, "How about your sister?"

"She's in the ER. She needs stitches in her head and then X-rays and a CT scan."

"Oh dear," Claire said. "Are you with her right now?"

"I was. I'm back in the shop until I close."

"I'll come right now," Claire said. "I can be there in five minutes."

"You don't need to," Joy said. "You have enough to deal with right now."

"No. I want to. I need to. Lloyd is staying in Savannah another night. I'll see you in a few minutes."

A couple came into the shop and looked at the teddy bears. Joy showed them the one with a blue South Carolina palmetto sweatshirt on it. "This is one of our best sellers," she told them, thinking it might also be a nice gift for Hope.

"Our first grandchild just arrived," the woman said. "Two months early. All of our gifts are at home. We were so worried, we just jumped in the car and headed here."

"Where are you from?"

"Myrtle Beach."

"How is the baby?"

"Good," the grandfather said. "A little boy, a real fighter. He's in the NICU, but he's just over three pounds and is doing as well as expected."

Joy's hand flew to her chest. "I'll pray for him."

The woman reached for Joy's hand. "Thank you."

The grandfather held up a stuffed Peter Rabbit with a blue jacket. The grandmother laughed, clapped her hands together, and said, "Perfect."

After the couple purchased the stuffed animal and left, Joy bought the teddy bear with the South Carolina sweatshirt for Hope. Then she sent Sabrina a text. Aunt Hope was in a car accident. She's in the ER here at Mercy. She's okay but needed stitches for a head wound and injured her foot.

Joy flipped the Closed sign on the front door and then busied herself with tidying up the shop. More than ten minutes passed, but Claire didn't show up. Twenty minutes passed and still no Claire.

When thirty minutes passed, just as Joy was about ready to give up and head back to the ER, Claire appeared at the door with Belina—who had a scowl on her face—trailing behind her.

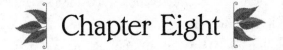# Chapter Eight

After Joy unlocked the door and Claire stepped inside, Belina turned back toward the lobby. "I'm leaving."

Claire stepped back through the door and grabbed her sister's arm. "Not until you properly meet Joy. And then let me buy you a sandwich."

Belina groaned. "I need to call JD."

"Come on in, and I'll let you use my phone. Then we can get something to eat." Claire stepped back into the gift shop, dragging Belina along.

"Joy," Claire said. "I'd like you to meet Belina, officially."

Joy extended her hand. "I'm so pleased to meet you."

"Likewise," Belina said. "Sorry for running earlier. I was feeling overwhelmed."

"With good reason, I'm sure," Joy said.

"Is Anne back yet?" Claire asked.

Joy shook her head. "But I'm expecting her any minute. You two should go get something to eat."

"But don't you need to be with Hope?"

Joy shrugged. "It's all right. I can wait."

"We have a minute." Claire pulled her phone from her purse and held it out to Belina. "You can use my phone."

"Thanks." Belina took it and stepped away.

Claire moved closer to Joy and said, "Sorry I took so long. After I parked, I headed to the intersection where the accident was. Belina was standing on the corner."

"I was hoping JD was still around," Belina said.

Claire turned her attention back to Joy. "This time she didn't run."

"You two should go get something to eat," Joy said again, just as Anne and Addie came to the shop door. When Anne saw all of them inside, she waved, and Addie pushed the door open.

"I couldn't find my backpack," she said. "That's what took us so long."

Anne rushed in after her granddaughter. "Sorry to interrupt." She smiled at Claire and then noticed Belina. She said quietly, "How nice to see Belina."

Claire nodded.

Belina's voice grew a little louder. "Please come get me."

Claire took a step toward her sister. "I can give you a ride, Belina."

Ignoring her, Belina faced the wall and said, "I'll call you in a little bit." She ended the call and walked to the door. "How about that sandwich?" she asked Claire.

"After I introduce you." Claire put a smile on her face. "Anne and Addie, I'd like you to meet my sister Belina."

Addie giggled. "You two look like copies of each other, even though you're wearing different clothes."

Claire laughed. "Well, thank you. Belina is the most beautiful person I know."

Belina scowled.

"I'm pleased to meet you," Anne said. She didn't mention that she'd seen Belina at the accident scene.

"Well," Claire said, heading toward the doorway. "Let's go get that sandwich." She glanced back over her shoulder. "We'll sit out in the Grove if anyone wants to join us."

"We'll join you," Anne said. "After Addie has a chance to tell Ralph hello."

Addie led the way out of the shop, followed by Anne. Joy collected her purse and the teddy bear for Hope from her office and then headed back to the ER.

The receptionist buzzed Joy through, and when she arrived at the room, Hope had just returned from her X-ray, and Ralph was with her.

Joy gave him a hug. "I heard you're working tonight."

Ralph hugged her back. "From?"

Joy stepped back. "Anne and Addie, of course. They're looking for you."

He held up his phone. "I just texted them to meet me in my office in a few minutes. And I heard your sister was in the ER."

Joy played along. "From?"

"Anne, of course." Ralph smiled. "I was just checking in with Hope. What a way to spend her first day in Charleston."

Joy nodded. "I'm just glad it wasn't worse."

Joy turned to her sister. The wound on her forehead was stitched. "How was it to get the stitches?" she asked.

"Not too bad," Hope replied.

"I brought you something." Joy handed her the teddy bear. "It's a welcome-to-South-Carolina gift, along with a get-well wish."

Hope took it from her. "Thank you."

Suddenly Joy second-guessed the gift. Was that a stupid thing to give her fifty-four-year-old little sister? "What's next?" Joy asked.

"My CT scan. Someone will come get me in a few minutes." Hope propped the bear up beside her. "Everyone's so nice. I can see why you like working here so much."

A wave of gratitude swept over Joy. It was true. The people who worked at Mercy were exceptional, including Ralph.

A transportation aide appeared with a wheelchair. He smiled and said, "Time to get that scan."

"Nice to meet you, Hope," Ralph said. "Call me if you need anything."

"Thank you." Hope smiled at him. "Go get some dinner," she said to Joy. "I'll text you when I'm back."

"No," Joy said. "I'll walk along with you."

"You'll just be in the way, ma'am," the aide said. "Go get something to eat."

Joy headed to the coffee shop, looking out at the Grove as she did. A few of the tables were occupied, but she didn't see Claire or Belina.

She decided to forgo the coffee and went back to the gift shop to do some paperwork while she waited.

Fifteen minutes later, her phone dinged. Hope was back in the ER, and she had gotten a boot for her foot. Joy left the shop, expecting that she'd be walking home to get her car and give Hope a ride back to her house. When she arrived, Hope was still in the wheelchair. "They're going to keep me overnight for observation because of my previous concussion," she said. "I'm headed up to the third floor."

"What do you need?" Joy said. "I can go by your trailer."

"I have everything in my overnight bag. Would you carry it for me?"

"Of course."

Joy walked behind the transportation aide as he wheeled Hope into the elevator. Hope's room on the third floor was at the end of the hall with a view of the harbor.

Once Hope was settled in the bed, Joy found her toothbrush and toothpaste in her overnight bag and put those out. "Did you call the college to let them know you won't be in tomorrow?"

Hope nodded. "I hope this won't be like that time I broke my ankle, when I lost the job at the nursery."

"I hope not too," Joy said. "There's no reason to think it will be."

"Why am I so accident-prone?"

"Accidents happen all the time," Joy said. "To everyone." But they did seem to happen more disproportionately to Hope.

Hope wiggled down a little in the bed. "They gave me pain meds in the ER. I think I'll sleep for a while."

Joy took Hope's phone out of her purse and put it on the table. "Text me if you need anything. I'll check in on you before bed and first thing in the morning."

Hope reached out and took Joy's hand. "Thank you. You've always been the best big sister."

Joy wasn't so sure about that, but she squeezed Hope's hand and said, "I love you. I'm glad you're here." Hopefully good things would come from having her close.

Joy pulled the sheet and blanket up around Hope's chin, tucking her in. "Sweet dreams," she said.

"Mama always said that too," Hope murmured.

"I remember." Joy patted Hope's shoulder. "I'll see you in the morning."

When Joy reached the lobby she glanced toward the Grove. Through the window she saw Claire and Belina at a table, along with Anne and Addie, not far from the angel statue. All were eating. Claire saw Joy and beckoned for her to join them.

Joy decided to do just that. She bought a salad from the coffee shop and headed out to the Grove, darting under the canopy of the eastern redbud tree.

The lights strung around the perimeter of the Grove and in the trees were on, creating a magical setting. As she reached the table, she said, "I thought you'd be long gone."

Claire shook her head. "Belina is waiting for JD to pick her up. He had some errands to do first."

Before Anne could reply, she saw Evelyn coming toward the group, holding up a file and calling out, "You won't believe what I found."

Evelyn plopped down at the head of the table, with Claire on one side and Anne, with Addie beside her, on the other. Belina sat next to Claire and Joy sat at the end of the table.

"What did you find?" Anne asked Evelyn.

"It could be the mother lode." Evelyn pulled on a pair of archival gloves. "Or maybe just a vein. But it's interesting and may help us figure out what Arthur Fleury was doing in France in 1871." She opened the file. "Claire and Belina, you probably know all about your family history."

"I don't know anything," Belina said.

Claire frowned at her. "I know a little. I've never been that interested. But I should sit down with Daddy before it's too late."

That seemed to get Belina's attention. She sounded alarmed as she asked, "What's wrong with Daddy?"

"Nothing. But, you know, he's getting older."

Belina's brow wrinkled, but she didn't say anything more.

Evelyn picked up a piece of paper. "I'm guessing some of the documents in Dr. Fleury's office ended up in the archive room at some point, because a lot of this has nothing to do with the hospital." She held up the piece of paper. "For example, this document is the charter for the Fleury family business, Fleury Shipping, in Charleston. It was established in 1680—no surprise that the family was on the ship, the *Richmond*, that arrived in Charleston that year, with forty-five French Protestants aboard. Soon, more Huguenot refugees arrived and in 1687 a church was built on the corner of what is now Church Street and Queen Street. By 1700 there were around four hundred and fifty Huguenots in the area."

Belina yawned, covering her face halfway through it, and Anne pulled a notebook and crayons from her purse for Addie.

Joy drizzled balsamic dressing on her salad.

Evelyn put the piece of paper down and picked up another one. "Here's a contract between Fleury Shipping and a man by the name of Louis Joubert dated March 14, 1787, for one hundred bolts of silk, shipped from Port Le Havre."

"Interesting," Joy said. "Do you think he's related to Theodore Joubert?"

"I don't know if it's the same branch or not—yet." Evelyn picked up another piece of paper. "But I found something that indicates that Dr. Fleury knew Theodore Joubert's family and may have even been related to them."

Claire rubbed her hands together. "That sounds promising. Maybe the paintings were gifts."

"Or," Joy said, "to play devil's advocate, Doc Fleury could have stolen from someone he knew and was related to."

Belina pushed her plate away. "I'm going to go use the restroom."

Joy watched her go.

"I hope she comes back," Claire said.

"Should one of us follow her?" Joy asked.

Claire shook her head. "That will just make it more likely she'll run. I asked her to come home with me tonight because Abrielle is going back to her apartment. Belina's old room is always ready for her."

Anne spoke in a low voice. "Do you think she has something to do with the missing painting? She seemed uncomfortable when the topic turned toward the possibility that Dr. Fleury may have stolen it all those years ago."

Claire glanced at Joy. "Do you think she took the painting?"

Joy shrugged. "That's the $64,000 question, right? That's what we need to figure out."

Belina returned a couple of minutes later and said to Claire, "Can we go home now? I'd like to see Daddy."

"Sure." Claire stood, slinging her bag over her shoulder, and grabbed her tray. "I'll see you all soon."

"I have some more information for you," Evelyn said.

Belina wrinkled her nose.

"I'll stop by in the morning," Claire said. "Can you tell me then?"

Evelyn nodded. "All right."

After everyone told Belina and Claire goodbye, Anne put her hand on Joy's arm. "We need to go tell Ralph good night and then get home and get this little one into her bath and then to bed."

Addie wrinkled her nose. "Can't I stay up late tonight?"

"Certainly not," Anne said. "It's a Monday, not a Friday."

After they left, Joy asked Evelyn, "What's the other information on the Fleury family?"

"It's actually more about Theodore's branch of the Joubert family," Evelyn said, "and how it intersects with the Fleury family."

"I'm all ears," Joy said. When she glanced up she noticed that Garrison Baker, the hospital administrator, had sat down at the next table with a sandwich and magazine. She still needed to ask him about using the mezzanine level for the auction. She'd forgotten all about it once Hope was in the accident. She'd ask him in a few minutes.

Evelyn took three items from the folder. Two were newspaper clippings in plastic sleeves and the other was a sheet of copy paper with a paragraph of print on it. She held up one of the clippings. "I have no idea what newspapers these are from, but they're written in French and dates are written at the top. Although it's quite faint, I think the date is October 7, 1871."

Joy asked, "Do you know French?"

Evelyn nodded. "I studied it. I wouldn't say I'm fluent, but I think I was able to translate the article."

Joy smiled. "What do you have?"

"One article is about Dr. Fleury traveling to France in 1871 to inquire about selling Fleury Shipping to a company out of Le Havre. He traveled there first. The reason for selling the business was that his medical practice didn't leave him the necessary time to devote to the shipping business, which needed a lot of work after the war, and his only son, who was a lawyer, also didn't have time for it." Evelyn placed the clipping on the table. "However, there's the possibility that the business wasn't doing that well. The economy of South Carolina was still depressed after the Civil War, and there wasn't that much discretionary income. People didn't have the money to buy European imports."

Joy nodded. That made sense.

"That both Dr. Fleury and his son, Alexander, had chosen professions other than the shipping business was a big turning point for the family. The shipping business had been lucrative up until the war but tanked during the fighting because of the blockades and then never fully recovered afterward, although Doc Fleury did build it back up some."

"What about the second clipping?"

"The article is about Theodore Joubert, but it mentions Doc Fleury."

"What exactly does it say?"

"Well." Evelyn smiled. "I can't say that I'm going to get this exact, but I did my best." She picked up the sheet of copy paper and cleared her throat. "'Theodore Joubert entertained Dr. Arthur Fleury, a relative—'"

"So they were related?"

"So it seems," Evelyn said and then continued to read, "'...who is visiting Paris from South Carolina. The two visited a gallery, where Joubert had his first show.'"

"Do you think the Jouberts were Huguenots too?"

"Perhaps," Evelyn said. "Some of the Huguenots who stayed in France converted to Catholicism over the years but not all."

"Is there any mention of Arthur buying Theodore's paintings at the gallery?"

"No," Evelyn said. "Just of his visit to the gallery."

"So that puts him in France, in Paris in particular in 1871, which corroborates the clipping from the newspaper in Charleston about his trip. And it also establishes that the Fleury family and the Joubert family were related."

Evelyn nodded. "I'll do some more research and see what else I can learn." She put the clippings and the piece of paper back in the folder and pulled out another sheet of paper. "I've also found some other documents about Dr. Fleury's involvement in the founding of the hospital and his contributions to its operation."

Joy peered at the document. It was a list from 1829 of donors to the hospital fund, and Fleury Shipping was at the top of the list.

Evelyn took a couple of other documents from the file. "It appears that after Arthur completed medical school, he convinced his father to invest in the hospital. That was a better time for commerce than after the war, and it appears the business was doing quite well then." Evelyn pulled out another document. "Arthur's office was around the corner, on Magazine Street, and he did rotations at the hospital every day. It also appears he stayed involved with the shipping business too."

"Interesting."

"Dr. Fleury moved his office into the surviving wing of the hospital during the war, which is why all of these papers exist today. He lost most of his fortune because his patients could barely pay him. Thankfully the house and property were paid for and all he needed to come up with were the property taxes each year. But the trip to France to sell the family business was necessary to keep his practice afloat and also the estate, which cost quite a bit for the upkeep."

"Did he get what he needed for the business?" Joy asked.

"I'm not sure," Evelyn said. "I haven't found anything to confirm if he did or not."

"So he could have had motivation to take the paintings?"

Evelyn shrugged. "I have no idea if he had motivation to take the paintings or not, but I'm not sure what good they would have done him. How would they have made him any money? He obviously didn't sell them."

"Maybe he was afraid to," Joy said. "Maybe word got out that they were missing."

"Perhaps…"

Joy shivered. Was someone watching them? She looked over her shoulder.

Garrison Baker was staring at them.

His face reddened.

"Sorry," he said. "I didn't mean to be eavesdropping—but I was." He stood and took a step toward them. "Mind if I join you?"

"Of course not," Joy said. "I need to ask you a question."

"All right." He sat down.

She explained about the Belina House Gallery being closed. "Which means we might not be able to hold the auction there Saturday night. Could we hold it on the mezzanine, here?"

"I need more information," he said. "How many people? Who are the vendors? Exact hours. That sort of thing."

Joy nodded. "Abrielle Fleury could answer all of those questions."

"I'll give her a call." He took out his phone. "Tomorrow. I just need to put it on my calendar…" It took him a moment. When he was done, he put his phone away. "The auction raises a significant amount of money each year. It would be a shame to have to cancel the event. I'll see what Abrielle says."

"Thank you," Joy said.

"Now I have a question for you," Garrison said. "I saw the article in the paper this morning about Doc Fleury. I've always felt such an affinity for him. He helped found the hospital and then ensured its survival after the war. He was a determined man who provided medical care for thousands and thousands in Charleston throughout his fifty-year career. I was shocked to learn someone was accusing him of stealing a painting and maybe more than one."

"We were too," Joy said.

"It appears, from what I overheard, that you are researching him. Do you hope to prove him innocent?"

Evelyn exhaled. "It's more like we're searching for the truth."

"Well," Garrison said. "Thank you. And please prove him innocent. The reporter from the *Dispatch* called me today to ask for a comment about Doc Fleury, and I declined. I imagine it looks as if I'm trying to preserve the public image of the hospital, which I am. But I truly hope Doc Fleury didn't do something like that."

Joy agreed emphatically. "And yet," she said slowly, "there's a chance he could have. Right?"

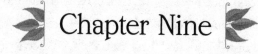# Chapter Nine

As Joy left the Grove and started through the lobby, someone yelled, "Mom!"

Even though she didn't believe the call was directed toward her, she turned, instinctively.

But the call *was* for her. Sabrina, her dark hair bouncing on her shoulders, headed across the lobby, straight at her.

"What are you doing here?" Joy asked as she hugged her daughter.

"I came to see Aunt Hope. She told me you went home, but that she was up to having me visit." Sabrina's hazel eyes, so much like her father's, brimmed with concern.

"Oh." Joy stopped focusing on Sabrina's eyes and felt a pang of jealously. Hope had sent Joy on her way, but she was happy to have Sabrina visit.

She changed the subject and asked Sabrina, "How was your class today?"

"Good. It's great to be back in college, especially in a literature class, although it was a tight squeeze getting back in time to pick up Eloise from school."

"I can imagine," Joy said. "How are the girls?"

"Good. Currently, mostly just excited about their great-auntie Hope. They're thrilled she's moving here." Sabrina lowered her voice. "I am too, but I was a little shocked that she didn't tell us sooner. Why do you think she didn't?"

"I don't know," Joy said. "I haven't had a chance to ask her, in particular, but she did say she fell and got a concussion a couple of weeks ago. Maybe that affected her."

Sabrina winced. "Maybe so. I was concerned she was afraid you wouldn't want her to move here."

Joy's hand flew to her chest. "I hope she doesn't feel that way." Inside, Joy cringed. Was she that obvious?

Sabrina took a step toward her mom. "I shouldn't have said that—I'm sure she doesn't. It's just that you two are so different. Actually, Eloise and Mallory remind me of the two of you. Serious and free spirited. You know how Eloise acts as if she's responsible for every little thing Mallory does, especially anything embarrassing."

Joy tried not to give away her growing angst. Did Sabrina think Joy had been embarrassed by Hope all of these years? The truth was, Joy *had* been embarrassed with Hope at times, long into adulthood.

Sabrina flipped her hair over her shoulder. "I'm probably over-thinking all of this." She nodded toward the elevator. "I'll go up and see how Aunt Hope is doing."

Joy hugged Sabrina a second time. "Call me after your visit, would you?"

"I will," Sabrina said. "Are you walking home?"

Joy nodded.

"Mom." Sabrina winced. "Hurry, before it gets dark."

Joy smiled. "I will. Don't worry about me. Visit your auntie and then give me a call." As Joy waved to Sabrina, someone called out, "Joy! Sabrina!"

Both turned. Amanda Taylor, Sabrina's best friend from college and now a doctor who worked at Mercy, came toward them across the lobby. "What are you two doing here so late?" Amanda had been part of the family since their college days and had been a godsend while Wilson was ill and after he'd passed.

After Amanda gave Joy and then Sabrina a hug, Sabrina said, "Do you remember my aunt Hope? She was in a car accident this afternoon. I'm on my way up to see her."

"Of course I remember Hope. Mind if I go with you? For just a minute."

"Of course not." Sabrina smiled. "I'd really like that."

"I'll let you two go." Joy gave a little wave. "See you soon."

"Thanks, Mom," Sabrina said, giving her another hug.

"Bye, Joy." Amanda gave her a hug too, warming Joy's heart. Thanks to Amanda, Joy had her job at Mercy. She loved her like a second daughter.

She watched as the two young women headed to the elevator, their shoulders so close they practically touched as they walked. Sabrina didn't have a sibling, but thank the Lord she had Amanda. She was nearly as close as a sister could be, minus the angst from growing up together.

Five minutes later, as Joy walked down Queen Street toward Meeting Street, she remembered a time when she came home from college for summer break. Hope was in high school and had a job at a drive-in. Joy had an internship at the American Cancer Society in the fundraising department.

Hope would come home all giddy about who she'd seen at work and how much fun she was having. Joy would give her a sideways look and then tell their parents about all the great things the Cancer Society was doing for people. Raising money. Providing treatment. Saving lives. Looking back on it, Joy saw how she'd minimized Hope's work, which was also important. Hope was serving people. Making connections. Making people feel as if they belonged.

Joy turned onto Meeting Street and headed north. All those years ago, she'd played the role of the righteous big sister so well. The next year, when Joy was a senior in college and Hope was a senior in high school, Joy was too busy to go home for Hope's birthday, and then when Hope left a message with Joy's roommate, she forgot to call her little sister back. She'd gone out with Wilson and stayed up until two in the morning working on her senior project.

She was surprised when Hope decided not to go straight to college. Why wasn't she following in Joy's footsteps when she'd paved the way?

Soon after graduation Wilson proposed to Joy and they became engaged. Joy moved back home to plan the wedding while Hope moved to Corpus Christi to work as a receptionist for an oil company.

She came back to be Joy's maid of honor and then moved to Chicago and took a job making sets for a theater company. Then she moved to Seattle and took a job with a landscaping company.

Joy worked for the American Cancer Society after she married but quit when she was six months pregnant with Sabrina and became a stay-at-home mom.

Soon she was enthralled with her baby, along with being in love with Wilson, and dedicated herself to being a good wife and mother and creating the best home possible. She became oblivious to Hope and her life way out west.

Joy called Hope when she thought of it, but it was Hope who called faithfully to talk with Sabrina. It was Hope who sent a new picture book once a month. It was Hope who began a drawing exchange with Sabrina when she was four, sending sketches back and forth across the states.

It was Hope who moved back to Houston so she could be a full-time auntie to Sabrina, and the two ended up with a beautiful relationship.

But Joy had never been as appreciative of Hope as she should have been.

Joy was a mother and a wife. Hope jumped from job to job. Yes, she came back to Houston—but she didn't end up staying long. After she lost the job because she broke her ankle, Hope moved to Dallas. A couple of times Sabrina went and stayed with her for a week. Another time, Hope took Sabrina to Galveston.

Those had been fun trips and good memories for both of them. And yet, Joy feared she'd never showed Hope the appreciation she should have. However, she was sure Sabrina had.

Joy reached her house, unlocked the door, and let herself in. After she put her bag away, she made herself a cup of mint tea and took it out to the patio as darkness fell.

She thought about Sabrina spending time with Hope, which—for some reason—made her miss Wilson more than usual.

But it also made her miss Hope. Or, more accurately, regret that she hadn't put more effort into being a better sister. Especially a better big sister.

If only she'd poured as much into Hope as Hope had poured into Sabrina.

Her phone rang. Joy answered it. "Hello, sweetheart."

"Hi, Mom. I just left Aunt Hope."

"How's she doing?"

"Good. Tired. She's so thankful for your help today. She said she didn't know what she would have done without you. She hopes she didn't stress you out too much."

Joy winced. "Of course she didn't."

"Well, she said she's looking forward to seeing you in the morning. Will you give me a call? And let me know how she is?"

"Yes, ma'am," Joy said.

"I've got to go and get home to the fam."

"Give everyone a hug," Joy said. "I love you."

"I love you too, Mom. Bye." The call ended and Joy leaned back against the chair, tipping her head up to look at the night sky. The stars were just coming out.

Her phone dinged. She checked it, expecting a text from Sabrina with something she forgot to say. It was from Claire. BELINA ONLY STAYED LONG ENOUGH TO GET MONEY FROM DADDY. SHE'S DISAPPEARED. NO SURPRISE. I LET DETECTIVE OSBORNE KNOW TO ADD HER TO THE LIST OF SUSPECTS.

Joy stared at her phone. What a shame. She texted back, I'm sorry.

She thought of Hope alone in the hospital and had a strong urge to go back up and see her.

But Hope probably didn't want that.

Joy stood and began watering her plants. Sabrina was busy with school and her family. Joy, although she had made friends with Evelyn and Anne and Shirley, and Claire too, still battled loneliness.

Could she forge a friendship with Hope, one like Claire and Abrielle had? Or was she destined to have a relationship with Hope like the two sisters had with Belina? She guessed she'd find out.

Joy woke early the next morning, drank two cups of coffee as she got ready for the day, and then headed to the hospital even earlier than usual, giving herself plenty of time to see Hope. But when she reached her sister's room, Hope was sound asleep. Joy guessed she'd been woken up several times during the night. She decided to go down to the lobby, buy a pastry, and put some more thought into the Fleury family and their missing painting. Then she'd come back and check on Hope before it was time to open up the shop.

As she started out the door of the coffee shop, she saw Evelyn at a table under a large potted palmetto tree. The morning was warm but not hot, and the Grove smelled of freshly watered plants.

The atmosphere was so different than at night. The greenery and morning sun were as different as could be from the enchanting darkness punctuated by the strings of light, but just as inviting.

"Mind if I join you?" Joy asked Evelyn as she approached.

"Please do." Evelyn's face lit up. "I was just thinking about the missing Fleury painting."

Joy sat on the chair across from Evelyn. "So was I. Tell me what you've been thinking."

"More about the history of the family. I talked with James about them last night, and he had some information he's come across through the years. The Fleury family played a big part in the building of all the Huguenot churches in Charleston, up until the last one. They and others would sometimes travel from their homes to the churches by boats because this area—the high ground between the Ashley and Cooper Rivers—sometimes flooded when the tide came in. Gradually creeks and marshes were filled in, taking care of most of the flooding. Unless, of course, there's a bad storm."

Joy nodded. She'd heard all about how the city flooded during tropical storms, including hurricanes. Of course, Houston had its fair share of hurricanes and flooding too.

"There was a pond close to the Fleury property that was filled in sometime in the early 1700s. Gradually the whole area was. But before that, tropical diseases thrived in the marshy areas. It's a wonder people survived at all." Evelyn took a sip of coffee and then said, "That seemed, according to James, to be a reason Arthur Fleury chose medicine."

Joy cocked her head. "Oh?"

"His mother and sister both died from the 'agues.'" Evelyn made air quotes. "Which was most likely malaria."

"How horrid." Joy knew that malaria, tragically, still killed hundreds of thousands of people a year.

"Right around the time he began studying medicine, French chemists discovered that quinine could treat fevers, and it was soon used to treat malaria. Dr. Fleury was one of the first in the area to use it to treat the agues."

"Interesting. Did he travel to France to get the medicine?"

"Perhaps," Evelyn said. "I can't find anything that supports that theory, but other documents might. The South Carolina Historical Society has his papers—letters and that sort of thing."

Joy nodded. "I've heard that before." Could she squeeze some time out of her day to see what she could find?

Evelyn took another sip of coffee and then said, "I'm changing the subject. Have you come up with a list of people who might have taken the painting Saturday?"

Joy took her notebook from her bag. "I've jotted down a few ideas."

Evelyn lowered her voice. "Mind if I ask who might be on it?"

"Well, I hate putting anyone on it. But none of these people have been ruled out." She opened the notebook. "Abrielle hasn't been ruled out entirely, and I haven't heard anything definitive as far as if she was current on the gallery insurance payments. If she wasn't, that would rule out her motivation being to collect the insurance money. Of course, she could have sold it on the black market—or even be planning to. Marshall was adamant about not selling the painting, and Abrielle said she wouldn't do so without his consent."

Evelyn pursed her lips.

Joy continued. "Grey Monte has an alibi—he was at his parents' cabin with his sister and her friends. There's a chance he could have snuck out in the middle of the night though. Detective Osborne is looking into security tapes from other nearby businesses, because the tape at the Belina House Gallery was erased."

Evelyn said, "So that's two."

"Yes," Joy said. "Claire is also on the list—she could have left home in the middle of the night. And now Belina Fleury is also on the list." She told Evelyn about Claire's text from the night before and Belina's suspicious disappearance.

"Oh, that's too bad," Evelyn said.

"Because Belina is staying at JD's and didn't let her family know she's in town, it makes him a suspect too, by association," Joy said.

Evelyn nodded. "Everyone needs to be investigated."

"I don't know that these people are suspects, but they could be people of interest. The art seller, Patrick Ray, from Manhattan. The Belgian art collector, Jacque De Villiers. And the art authenticator, Pamela DePass, who lives in Savannah."

As Joy said Savannah, she thought of Claire's husband, Lloyd. Was it a coincidence that he was in Savannah? He kept "staying another day." Was he really there to help his elderly aunt? Or for another reason?

Without saying anything to Evelyn, Joy added him to the list too.

This time, when Joy stopped at Hope's open door, her sister was awake.

"How are you, Hopey?" Joy used her sister's childhood nickname before she realized what she was doing.

"Much better," Hope said. "I even slept a little."

"I stopped by earlier, but you were asleep," Joy said.

Hope smiled. "That's good to know. Honestly, it feels as if I was awake most of the night. I'm looking forward to going to Sabrina's and getting a good night's sleep."

Joy froze. "Sabrina's?"

Hope nodded. "She invited me to stay with her. She said since you're at work all day, I wouldn't be as lonely."

"But she has classes and the girls…"

"Right. I told her of course not at first. I don't want to get in the way of her studies and all that. But she said she's only gone for a few hours each day, she won't neglect her studies, and I'll be a help with the girls." Hope raised the head of her bed a little more. "Besides, I heard back from the college about my job. They said to let them know when I can come in and of course they'll hold the job. They're not concerned that my foot is in a boot—or that I found out I have a hairline fracture."

"Great." Joy knew her voice was flat. "What about your head?"

"I won't know the results of the CT scan for a couple of days, but I'm feeling better. I'll stay away from screens for the next couple of days."

"What about transportation?"

"I'll need to rent a car until mine is repaired or I can buy a new one. I'll need help moving into my apartment on Saturday, but Sabrina said she and Rob will do it. She'll recruit a couple of their friends to help."

Joy swallowed hard and then said, "It sounds as if you have it all figured out."

"Oh, I didn't do anything. Sabrina did it all. I was feeling overwhelmed, but she quickly talked me through everything." Hope smiled again. "Young women these days are amazing, don't you think? They're so assertive, so on top of things. Sabrina's a superwoman if I ever saw one."

Joy nodded. "She is amazing. That's for sure."

"You raised her to be that way," Hope added.

"Oh, I don't think I can take credit for Sabrina. She's always been amazing…" Joy's voice trailed off.

"I'm guessing I'll get out of here around eleven or so. Sabrina said to text her, and she'll swing by on her way home from class."

"Great," Joy said. "Well, call me if anything comes up before then. If you get out before Sabrina is out of class. That sort of thing."

"I will."

Joy stepped forward, leaned down, and gave Hope a hug. "I'm so thankful you're all right. And so glad you've moved to Charleston."

"So am I," Hope said. "Thank you again for everything you did for me yesterday. I hope I didn't embarrass you too much."

"What are you talking about?"

"Oh, causing a wreck so close to your workplace. Having your friends see your sister as such a mess, and then join in the crowd of gawkers."

"You weren't 'such a mess,'" Joy said. "You were in an accident. Evelyn and Anne came out to help—they certainly weren't gawking."

Hope shrugged.

Joy sat down on the side of the bed. "What is this all about?"

Hope shook her head. "Nothing. I'm sorry I said anything."

Tears stung Joy's eyes as she stood again.

Hope lowered the bed again. "I think I'll try to rest more before the doctor comes in."

"All right," Joy said. "Goodbye."

"Bye."

Joy hurried from the room. She wanted to call Sabrina, but she was afraid her voice would give away her emotions. It appeared that Hope had moved to Charleston to be close to Sabrina and her family—not Joy.

A decision Joy couldn't fault her sister for. Sabrina had always been one of Hope's biggest fans and, obviously, much more accepting of her than Joy had ever been.

Joy felt a little sick to her stomach. Had she had too much coffee already? Not enough?

Or was she paying the consequences of not being a good big sister to her only sibling?

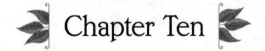

Chapter Ten

Just before eleven, as Joy finished wrapping a silver jewelry box for a young woman visiting her grandmother who'd just had surgery, Garrison Baker came into the shop.

He waited until the woman left, glanced toward the door, and then took a step closer to the counter. "Have you found out anything more about Doc Fleury?"

Joy shook her head. "But I hope to go to the Historical Society later today."

"For?"

"To look through his collection of letters," Joy said. "I'm hoping he mentions his trip to France in the early 1870s and the paintings in the letters from that period."

"Any other ideas?"

Joy pursed her lips together. "Evelyn is looking in the hospital's archives for more documents that belonged to Doc Fleury."

He exhaled. "The reporter who wrote the article called me a couple of minutes ago asking—again—for a statement about Doc Fleury."

"What did you tell her?"

"No comment." He exhaled. "I've put the media relations director on this, but you should communicate directly with me if you find anything."

"All right."

"When are you going to the Historical Society?"

"At noon, when Lacy comes in."

"Can you go sooner?"

"Not without closing the shop down."

"All right." He took a step backward. "Call me this afternoon."

"I will," Joy said.

After he left, she busied herself with straightening up the teddy bears. One, just like the bear she'd given to Hope, had been knocked to the floor. Joy picked it up and held it. If Hope thought Joy's friends were gawking at her, perhaps she also felt Joy had been patronizing to give her a bear as a get-well gift. She hadn't seen it this morning. She should have given her a dozen flowers instead. Or a box of chocolates.

Her phone dinged just as two young women came into the shop. They were laughing and then one of them said, "I can't wait for Shelby to find out how hard being a mother really is."

Joy put the teddy bear back on the shelf and gave the women a broad smile. "Hello," she said.

The other woman gave Joy a wave.

"What should we get her?" the first woman asked.

The other woman held up a gift bag. "I already got her oils and lotions. And a sleeper for the baby."

"You're always on top of things." The first woman yawned. "I was up half the night with Bobby. Shouldn't he be sleeping through the night?"

"Not necessarily," the second woman said.

Joy took her phone from her pocket. The text was from Sabrina. CAN YOU TALK?

In a minute, Joy texted back.

The first woman headed to the teddy bears. She picked up a blue one with a bow tie. "This is cute."

The other woman nodded. "It's darling."

The first woman walked up and down the middle aisle of the shop and said, "You know, I think I'll pick something up and drop it off once they're out of the hospital. Let's go up and see the baby."

"All right." The second woman waved to Joy. "Thank you."

"Have a wonderful day," Joy said.

The two women hurried out of the shop, and Joy quickly stepped into her office, keeping one eye on the door. She dialed Sabrina's number, but no one picked up.

Joy slipped her phone back into the pocket of her sweater and stepped back into the shop just as Sabrina came through the door.

"Hi, sweetie," Joy said. "I just tried to call you."

"Oops." Sabrina held up her purse. "I didn't hear it. I'm here to get Hope, so I thought I'd just talk with you in person—if you don't have any customers."

"I'm free at the moment," Joy said with a grin.

"Last night, Hope said she felt she was imposing on you, with you working all day, to stay at your place. I said she was always welcome at our house too. But now I feel as if maybe I overstepped."

"No, it's fine," Joy said. "Hope is really looking forward to staying with you."

"Are you sure? You're not upset that she's not staying with you?"

"Of course not," Joy said.

"Mom," Sabrina said. "You'd tell me if you were, right?"

"Yes, sweetheart," Joy said. "I worry because you're so busy. But if you feel like it won't be too much, I think it would be really nice for Hope to be with you and your family."

"If you're sure…"

"How about if I bring dinner over tomorrow evening?" Joy put her hands in her sweater pockets. "How about lasagna?"

"That would be great." Sabrina brushed a strand of hair away from her face. "I'm going to get Aunt Hope, go home, put fresh sheets on the spare-room bed, and then get the girls from school." She smiled. "It's a good thing I don't have any exams yet."

Joy nodded in agreement. "Tell Hope I'll see her tomorrow."

"All right." Sabrina stepped forward and gave Joy a hug. "See you then."

Joy watched as Sabrina left the shop and hurried across the lobby toward the elevator. Had she wanted Joy to insist Hope stay with her? Joy felt stuck in the middle, between her daughter and her sister, a place she never expected to be.

After Sabrina left, Joy called the Historical Society to find out if she needed an appointment to access Doc Fleury's letters. It was a good thing she inquired because the letters were in the society's archive, which was housed on the third floor of the Addlestone Library at the College of Charleston.

She made an appointment for twelve thirty.

Joy walked the seven blocks to the college, heading north on Coming Street. She stopped at the corner of Wentworth for a horse-drawn carriage with a family of tourists inside to go by, a mother and father and a little girl with dark hair who looked like Sabrina when she was little.

Joy thought of all the fun vacations she and Wilson had taken Sabrina on. They visited Charleston when Sabrina was ten and then went on to Savannah that same trip. They'd taken Sabrina to Disney World when she was six and then again when she was twelve. And they'd gone to Washington DC for Sabrina's fifteenth birthday. Joy didn't remember, not once, considering asking Hope to go with them. Should she have? Sabrina probably would have enjoyed it, and it would have meant a lot to Hope.

The *clippity-clop* of the horse faded as it headed east. The little girl turned around and glanced behind quickly and then turned back around. Joy's heart lurched. There was no way her mother and father had any idea how quickly that little girl would become a woman.

Just before twelve thirty she arrived at the college, which was nestled in the heart of Charleston. She found the rectangular white library building, and then the office on the third floor. She introduced herself to the woman behind the desk. "I'm Joy Atkins, here to look through the Fleury letters."

The woman smiled. "Right on time." She directed Joy through a door into the back of the office and then pointed at a table as she said, "I'm Amy. Make sure and ask me if you have any questions. I have the collection of photocopied letters ready for you along with a notebook and pencil." The letters were bound in five volumes, which Joy hadn't expected. It appeared Dr. Fleury had been a prolific letter writer. "Dr. Fleury wrote thousands of letters over his lifetime, starting when he was twenty-six, not long after he started practicing medicine. He dictated the majority of his letters to an assistant—there were many over the years—who made a copy of each one. It's really a remarkable collection. The originals are quite fragile and are stored offsite in a secure area." Joy guessed a bank vault somewhere. Amy continued. "We're grateful that the Fleury family donated them to the historical society, over a hundred years ago now." She gestured toward the volumes. "Wear the archival gloves at all times, please, even though they're photocopies. We need them to last as long as possible."

"Of course," Joy said. "Thank you, Amy."

She sat down, put her bag on the table, and pulled on the gloves.

She opened the first volume. As much as she wanted to, she wouldn't have time to read through all the letters, but she needed to see when they started and then skim through the letters and stop when the information seemed important. The first one was dated May 23, 1827, and was addressed to Dr. Fleury's father concerning the funding of the hospital. The next one was to another business-man in town, but the third one was to a Joseph Bienaimé, at an address in Paris of an apothecary. The letter was dated December 6, 1828, and written in French. Thankfully there was a translation. Monsieur Bienaimé was the pharmacist who helped isolate quinine to treat malaria. Dr. Fleury wrote about malaria in the Low Country of South Carolina and that it was a contributor to the area's high mortality rate, particularly in pregnant women, infants, and young children. He added that his own mother had died when she was pregnant and Dr. Fleury's younger sister had also succumbed to the disease a decade earlier. Joy kept reading. Dr. Fleury was writing to tell Monsieur Bienaimé that he was going to visit Paris in six months and hoped to consult with him.

Joy flipped through the next several letters. Finally, there was a reply from Monsieur Bienaimé who wrote that he would attempt to fit in a meeting with Dr. Fleury.

Six months later, Dr. Fleury was in Paris and wrote a letter home to his father. He'd been able to meet with Monsieur Bienaimé, who shared a supplier contact of cinchona, the plant quinine was made from, in Peru.

I have one other important happening to share with you, Arthur Fleury wrote his father. *Actually two more. First, I was able to meet Monsieur Jules Joubert last week. He is in Paris on business with the family shipping business, the one your aunt inherited from her father.*

I believe he and I may have a long friendship. I've invited him to visit us in Charleston, along with his wife.

Which brings me to my last item of information. Jules's wife, Suzanna, has a sister Estelle, whom I've been spending quite a bit of time with. In fact, I will be bringing her home as my wife.

"Oh my," Joy said out loud. There was now a romance, along with the mystery. And now the Joubert and Fleury families were related distantly from over a century before but also through the two sisters, Suzanna Joubert and Estelle Fleury. Joy found the letters to be quite intriguing.

She kept reading. Many were addressed to Jules and Suzanna, others to businesspeople, and some to hospital patrons in Charleston. Some were to Arthur's father if one of them was out of town on business.

Joy marveled at the endless letters. With no phones, no email, and no texting, letters were what kept people connected. And it was obvious that Arthur was a man who was connected. Of course, having an assistant probably helped him to be so prolific.

His letters had become a sort of diary, including his work schedule, the building of the hospital, patients he'd seen, and the relationship between the Jouberts and Fleurys. The Jouberts had a large family—the four youngest were Abrielle, Theodore, Belina, and Claire.

Joy felt as if she'd struck gold.

It was two o'clock, and Joy needed to get back to the hospital. She closed the second volume and took off the gloves, placing them on the table.

On her way out she stopped at the counter and asked Amy for an appointment at the same time the next day.

"Of course." Amy jotted the time on the piece of paper in front of her and then looked up. "How did it go?"

"Great! I found some of what I was looking for, a connection between the Fleury family and a family in France. I'm looking forward to reading—well, skimming—the rest of the letters."

Amy smiled. "I love to hear that sort of thing."

The rest of the afternoon continued without incident until Garrison came into the gift shop. "Any luck?" he asked without saying hello.

She'd been meaning to call him. "I didn't have time to go through all of the letters, but there's a connection to a Theo Joubert's family, which most likely is *the* Theodore Joubert's family. If so, the two families were related, both through Arthur Fleury and his wife, Estelle."

"That sounds promising that the paintings were a gift. Why didn't you finish going through all of the letters?"

"I had to get back here, to the shop."

"Oh." He exhaled.

"I'll go back tomorrow," she said.

"I had a half dozen phone calls from that reporter again," he said.

Joy's eyebrows shot up.

"I know," Garrison said. "I'm afraid of what she might be digging up on Doc Fleury."

"I can't imagine she has access to any information that we don't."

"I hope not," Garrison said. "What do we do about the unveiling of the portrait on Saturday?"

"We have a few days to figure it out," Joy said. "Let's see what happens."

He started to leave as Shirley came into the shop. "Garrison. Hello!"

He gave Shirley a smile. "How are you doing?"

She covered a yawn and then laughed. "Excuse me. I'm tired, but other than that, just fine."

Garrison gave her another smile and said, "I hope you can get some rest, sooner or later." With a wave, he left.

Shirley turned to Joy. "What brought Garrison to your shop?"

"Did you see the article in yesterday's newspaper?"

Shirley nodded. "I did. So did Mama."

"So did Garrison. And the reporter has been hounding him ever since. He's worried about the upcoming unveiling of Doc Fleury's portrait and how the community will respond if it turns out he stole a Joubert painting that's gone missing again."

"I see," Shirley said. "How are things going as far as trying to figure out who stole it Friday night?"

Joy grimaced. "I have a list of suspects. I need to do some research on the ones who live out of town. The Belgian art collector and the New York art dealer, in particular." She hoped to find some extra time this evening to do that.

Joy then updated Shirley on the Fleury family happenings, followed by, "Yesterday my family intersected with theirs."

"What happened?"

Joy explained about the accident. "Hope ended up spending the night in the hospital last night."

"Where is she now?"

A hint of sadness swept through Joy. "At Sabrina's house."

Shirley cocked her head. "She's not staying with you?"

Joy shook her head. Her voice caught a little as she said, "I'll take dinner over there tomorrow evening." She tried to smile, but her voice gave away her hurt. "Which means I need to go shopping tonight."

For a minute Joy was afraid Shirley was going to press her on how she was feeling, as Nurse Shirley could so skillfully do, but she didn't. Instead she patted Joy's shoulder.

The letters had been a distraction from thinking about Hope, but going through the whole story had stirred it all up again.

After a moment, Shirley asked, "What are you going to fix for dinner?"

"Lasagna," Joy said. "I used to fix it for Sunday dinner back home fairly often. It's Sabrina's favorite." It was one of Wilson's favorites too, but Joy didn't want to say that out loud.

"Sounds delicious," Shirley said.

"What are you doing here?" Joy asked. "Picking up a shift?"

Shirley shook her head. "Mama had a doctor's appointment at the clinic. She's still there, but I'm getting a prescription at the pharmacy for her."

"How she's doing?"

"She had a bad spell this morning. Her blood pressure shot up." Shirley looked weary. "But she's doing better now."

"I'm sorry," Joy said.

"I'm just so glad she's still with me." Shirley's brown eyes filled with tears, but then she smiled. "You should have heard what Mama said when she read the article about the missing painting."

"What did she say?"

"'That Fleury family. There's always something going on with them.'"

Joy laughed. "Did she give any more information, such as how she knows so much about the Fleury family?"

"Knows so much?" Shirley asked. "Or thinks she knows so much?"

Joy laughed again. "I'm thinking she knows something. I'm a believer in Regina."

Shirley laughed too. "And she's a believer in you. But that doesn't mean her memories can be trusted."

Joy shrugged. "I'm still betting on her."

Shirley glanced at the clock on the wall. "I've got to run."

"Thank you for stopping by," Joy said. "You cheered me up."

Shirley stepped forward and gave Joy a hug. "Hang in there about your sister. And remember, everyone's family is complicated in one way or another."

"You're right about that," Joy said.

As Shirley left the shop, Joy tried to figure out her emotions about Hope. Her sister was probably happier staying at Sabrina's. And having her there meant Joy didn't have to worry about Hope being by herself. She was able to do the research today instead of rushing home over her lunch hour to check on Hope. On the other hand, there was definitely a part of her that felt rejected by Hope, and yet she knew she shouldn't take her sister's decision to stay with Sabrina personally.

Her phone dinged, and she slipped it from her pocket.

It was from Abrielle, to both Joy and Claire. I JUST SPOKE WITH GARRISON. HE SAID WE CAN USE THE MEZZANINE, WHICH MEANS THE AUCTION IS BACK ON! HOW ABOUT A PLANNING MEETING TONIGHT? AT THE CAFÉ ACROSS THE STREET FROM THE GALLERY? 6:30?

Chapter Eleven

AFTER WORK, JOY HURRIED HOME, got her car, and drove to the grocery store to shop for ingredients for the lasagna, her famous chopped Italian salad, and torta caprese, a chocolate cake made with almond flour, which she knew Hope loved. Once she'd finished the shopping, she hurried home.

As she put the groceries away, Joy thought through her schedule. After dinner with Abrielle and Claire, she'd brown the hamburger, grate the cheese, and boil the pasta. Then she'd assemble the lasagna and bake it, so all she'd need to do tomorrow was reheat it. While it was baking, she'd mix up the cake and pop it in the oven. It would be a late evening for her, but worth it. While the lasagna reheated the following day after work, she would mix the salad.

She had a few minutes before leaving for dinner, so she grabbed her laptop and sat on her sofa to see what she could find about Jacque De Villiers. Entry after entry popped up about the De Villiers family. They owned properties in Brussels and were involved in financing. Jacque was fifty-seven. It was clear he was a wealthy man from the articles about him. There were photos of him in Paris, London, and New York City, mostly in art galleries and museum events. His wife died three years ago, and he had no children.

It appeared the family had deep roots in Brussels, from the late 1600s. The De Villiers family had a shipping business into the late 1800s but after that invested primarily in property.

A shipping business. Could there be a connection to the De Villierses and Fleurys? Or was it pretty common for families to make their wealth in shipping?

The first reference to an art collection was from 1912 when the family purchased a Monet. Other artists mentioned over the next century included Pissaro, de Belleroche, Sisley, Cassatt, and Morisot. Interesting that the last two were both women.

Joy kept reading. The family had a gallery at one time but sold it in the 1980s, moving the collection to a mansion built in a suburb of Brussels.

Next, Joy googled LLOYD WALTER, CHARLESTON, SC. Fleury and Sons, Law Firm popped up, as well as several volunteer board positions Lloyd held in Charleston. There was nothing nefarious. Next she logged onto one social media site after another. There was nothing on the first two, his name and business information were on a third, and then a profile on a fourth that wasn't secure. He hadn't posted for four years, but he was tagged in a post from two days before. *A big thank you to Cousin Lloyd for all of his help with Mama. I don't know what we would do without him.* The photo was of an elderly woman sitting in a rocking chair. It appeared he'd been telling the truth about why he was in Savannah.

Next Joy googled JD JOHNSON, CHARLESTON, SC. He was in a news story about a fire at a neighbor's house. JD called 911 and then saved his neighbor before the firefighters arrived. There was also a small article about him volunteering with Habitat for Humanity. That warmed Joy's heart.

She found one charge of petty larceny from twenty-five years ago—he found a wallet and hadn't returned it, although in the article he claimed he planned to and just hadn't gotten around to it. There was nothing about him breaking the law since, not even a traffic infraction.

She couldn't rule out any of the three as suspects, but she hadn't found anything incriminating either. She closed her laptop and headed downstairs.

The evening had a hint of coolness to it, so Joy put on a sweater before she walked the six blocks to the café. There was a light on in the Belina House Gallery but the sign, of course, said CLOSED.

It was 6:28 when she stepped into the café, the first to arrive. The hostess led her to the table and distributed three menus. And then Joy sat and waited. 6:35. 6:40. She tried to not think of everything she needed to still get done before bed.

She texted Sabrina to check in with her. And then Hope. Neither texted her back. Six forty-five came and went.

Just as she was ready to text the sisters, Claire appeared on the sidewalk outside the window of the café. She held her phone and spoke into it, her expression tense. Finally, she slipped her phone into her purse. Then she hurried into the café.

"Sorry I'm late," she said to Joy. "Lloyd called."

"How's he doing?"

"Still in Savannah."

Joy noted that Claire had given his location in response to the question of *how*, not *where*.

Claire sighed as she hooked her purse on the back of her chair and sat down. "His aunt isn't doing well. I think he should come home, considering everything that's going on, but he said if he does he'll most likely just have to turn around and return." She put her elbows on the table and leaned forward. "The truth is, we haven't been getting along that well. Isn't that weird? You can be married for thirty years and think you've got everything figured out and then, bam"—she clapped her hands together—"you hit another rough patch, for seemingly no reason."

"I'm sorry," Joy said.

Claire frowned. "I shouldn't be telling you this. Not when you've lost your husband. At least I still have mine."

Joy smiled. "Of course you should tell me this. Wilson and I hit plenty of rough patches—thankfully we always got through them—but I certainly understand."

"That makes me feel better," Claire said.

"Any word from Belina?" Joy asked.

Claire shook her head. "I spent all day worrying about her, when I wasn't trying to figure out what's going on with Lloyd. It feels like everything is falling apart." She glanced around. "Where's Abrielle?"

"She hasn't shown up yet," Joy said.

Claire pulled her phone out of her bag. "I'll call her." She placed the call and then left a curt message. "Where are you?"

Just as she finished, Abrielle came through the door to the café, waving at them as she did. "Sorry," she called out. "I was on the phone with Pamela. She has some information about the painting."

"What did she say?" Claire asked.

Abrielle sat down between Claire and Joy as she said, "There's been chatter about it online."

Joy asked, "On the Theodore Joubert appreciation website?"

"I'm not sure," Abrielle said. "Pamela's going to send me the link." She held up her phone. "At least she said she would…" Abrielle turned to Claire. "Is Lloyd back?"

Claire shook her head.

"Wasn't he supposed to come back Sunday morning? And here it is Tuesday evening?"

"Aunt Mae isn't doing well." Claire's voice was low. "He's working on getting her into an assisted living place."

Abrielle's voice was louder. "What about her children?"

"Would you keep your voice down, please?" Claire grimaced. "I don't want the whole city to know our business."

Abrielle shrugged. "What about Mae's children?"

"Only one still lives in Savannah," Claire said. "Betsy. She's the oldest—in her sixties now—but she has some health issues."

"You know what's odd?" Abrielle asked.

Claire gave her a puzzled look.

"When Pamela was in town last Thursday, taking a last look at the paintings, I saw her speaking with Lloyd in the alley behind the gallery."

Claire's expression changed from puzzled to alarmed. "What?"

Abrielle nodded.

"Lloyd doesn't know Pamela."

"That's what you think."

"Perhaps he bumped into her in the alley."

"What would Lloyd be doing in the alley at all?" Abrielle asked. "It's blocks from the law office."

"Well, the law office oversees the gallery. Maybe he had some questions. I'm sure there's a logical answer."

"Doesn't it seem odd to you that he's gone now? Gone for the baptism? Gone right when the paintings were stolen? Gone when the church was set on fire? Gone to Savannah, where Pamela lives?"

"No." Claire crossed her arms. "What are you insinuating? You're jumping to ridiculous conclusions. Besides, he wasn't gone when the paintings were taken. He was here through brunch on Saturday morning. And remember, he's taking care of Aunt Mae."

"Why didn't you go see to her?"

Joy was growing more and more uncomfortable. Besides the bickering, Abrielle seemed to think it was Claire's job to take care of everyone.

Claire's expression shifted to hurt. "I didn't go, because Aunt Mae is Lloyd's aunt. And I'm taking care of Daddy, remember? And seeing to everything else too, including the auction."

Abrielle shook her head but didn't say anything more.

"How about Jacque De Villiers?" Claire asked. "Have you tracked him down?"

"Actually…" Abrielle glanced at her phone. "I'm expecting a call from Patrick any minute. He's been trying to find Jacque too." She placed her phone on the table, faceup.

The waiter approached the three to take their order.

"Oh, I'm so sorry. We haven't even looked." Abrielle picked up a menu. "Could you give us another minute please?" She gave the waiter a charming smile.

"Of course. Take all the time you need."

As he left, Abrielle's phone rang. "Patrick." She hit ACCEPT and put it on SPEAKER.

After they greeted each other, Abrielle asked, "What did you find out?"

"Jacque is in Richmond, looking at a painting he's been interested in, along with visiting the old Huguenot Church in Manakin, just outside of Richmond."

"Did you ask him to give me a call?"

"I did," Patrick said. "He will—later this evening."

"Thank you," Abrielle said. "I'll talk to you soon. Bye."

"Goodbye…" Patrick's voice faded as she ended the call.

"There you go," she said to Claire. "Jacque has an alibi."

Joy wouldn't call it an alibi, exactly. She decided not to share what she'd found about Jacque De Villiers online—it might not be relevant to the case.

"How about Patrick Ray?" Joy asked.

"He was at an opening in Manhattan until after midnight the night of the theft," Abrielle said. "And that's been confirmed by the owner of the gallery and social media posts with photos. It would have been impossible for him to catch a flight down here in that short amount of time."

Joy said, "I see," and then decided to share what she'd found at the South Carolina Historical Society's archive at the College of Charleston. She filled them in. "I'll go through the rest of the letters tomorrow, but there definitely was a connection between the Fleury and Joubert families and more than just distant relatives. Doc Fleury was Theodore's uncle. His wife and Theodore's mother were sisters."

"That's a helpful piece of information," Claire said. "Hopefully the paintings were given to Doc Fleury." Her phone rang as she spoke. She pulled it from her bag.

"Lloyd?" Abrielle asked.

Claire shook her head. "I don't recognize the number."

"You'd better answer it," Abrielle said. "In case it's a request for a ransom."

Claire looked horrified. "Ransom?"

Abrielle nodded. "For the painting."

"Oh." Claire answered. She listened for a moment and then said, "We're at the café, across from the gallery." After a pause she said, "See you soon."

As she ended the call Abrielle asked, "Who was that?"

"Belina." Claire slipped her phone back into her bag. "She wants to speak with us. It'll take her about a half hour to get here."

The three ordered their food. A grilled shrimp Louie for Claire, a club salad for Abrielle, and a Southwestern salad for Joy. Their food came out quickly, and they were nearly done when Belina arrived.

She wore jeans, sandals, and a frilly blouse. It was unbelievable that she was in her early fifties. She looked much younger. But when Belina sat down, Joy could see that she had lines around her eyes and a few faint age spots on her tanned face.

Belina said hello to Claire and Abrielle and then turned to Joy. "What are you doing here?"

"Belina," Claire chastised, "we were having a planning meeting for the auction on Saturday."

"I need to get going," Joy said, pushing back her salad. "I still have a lot to do tonight."

"But we've hardly talked about the auction," Abrielle countered.

"It seems y'all might have more pressing—" Joy was interrupted by JD coming through the door.

"What's he doing here?" Abrielle asked.

Belina waved toward him. "He brought me."

"Oh." Abrielle leaned back while Belina pulled up a chair for JD, trapping Joy.

"Hi, JD," Claire said. "How have you been?"

He rubbed the back of his neck. "All right, except for my neck from the accident yesterday."

Claire gave him a sweet smile and then asked Joy, "How's your sister?"

"All right."

JD seemed confused.

"I met you yesterday," Joy said. "My sister is the one who ran the red light."

He nodded. "That's right." He spoke softly and seemed shy.

Joy took twenty-five dollars out of her purse, which was more than what was needed to cover her meal and tip, and placed it on the table.

"No," Claire said. "We'll split yours. We invited you to a planning dinner and didn't get any planning done."

"Let's do lunch tomorrow," Abrielle said. "We can come to the hospital."

Joy shook her head. "I'll be at the college library."

"Dinner?" Claire asked. "Unless Lloyd is home."

"He won't be," Abrielle said.

Belina tilted her head, causing her long blond hair to flow over her shoulder. "Where's Lloyd?"

"Don't ask," Abrielle answered.

Joy cleared her throat. "I'm having dinner at my daughter's house tomorrow."

"That leaves the committee meeting dinner on Thursday evening at Claire's," Abrielle said. "We might need to take some time after dessert to see to any last-minute details, with only two days before the event."

"We'll make that work," Claire said.

"Let's do that." Joy was relieved. "Shoot me an email with anything that needs to be done before then." Although she wasn't sure when she'd do it, but right now she just wanted to get home and start cooking for her family. She gave everyone a wave. "Nice to see you, Belina and JD."

Claire waved back. "See you tomorrow."

"Tomorrow?"

"I'm volunteering. I'm supposed to come in at noon, but is it all right if I come in earlier?"

"Sure." Joy hadn't remembered that Claire was volunteering the next day. She volunteered more than anyone Joy knew, even more than Anne. "See you when you come in."

Joy turned toward Abrielle, who said, "Bye. See you Thursday."

They called out farewells as Joy stepped away from the table. She'd been so impressed with Claire and Abrielle when she first met them. Had they shown their true colors tonight? Or their high levels of stress?

"Have you heard of a Theodore Joubert appreciation website?" Belina asked. "It's all over social media."

Joy stopped.

"I have," Abrielle said. "Although I haven't looked at it yet."

"I started it."

"You started it?"

Joy turned back to the table.

Belina nodded.

"Why?" Abrielle asked.

"He's always been my favorite artist. I did a research paper on him in school," Belina answered. "I wasn't surprised at all when people started claiming he'd painted *Belina in the Garden*. That's what brought me home." She motioned to JD. "And JD was nice enough to let me stay with him. But then I found out the painting had been stolen, and yesterday I guessed you two would blame me. That's why I ran."

JD shifted on his chair.

"I decided I needed to come clean about the website and why I came home. But I didn't steal the painting. I never would have figured out the security code nor would I have had any idea how to break into the church."

Joy became acutely aware that she was eavesdropping. As she took another step away from the table, JD shifted again and stretched his leg out to the side. Joy turned and headed to the door. Belina might not know how to break into the gallery and the church, but would JD?

If Belina headed home because of the painting, had she told JD that people suspected it was a Theodore Joubert and worth a boatload of money?

Joy yawned as she poured herself a cup of coffee in the gift shop the next morning. Everything had gone well the night before with her cooking and baking. She found great fulfillment in preparing food, especially for those she loved most, but it was eleven thirty by the time she cleaned the kitchen.

Not even the brisk walk to the hospital had woken her up. A cup of coffee—or two—should soon do the trick.

Just the smell of the coffee opened her eyes a little more. After another sip she cradled the cup and headed to her desk.

As she booted up her computer, her phone dinged with a text. Sorry I didn't return your text last night. Things were a little crazy, but we're all doing fine. Looking forward to seeing you tonight.

Joy stared at her screen. She wondered what Sabrina meant by "things were a little crazy." Did that have to do with the girls?

Or Hope?

She texted back, What happened? She waited a long minute for a response and then texted, Looking forward to tonight too! Joy guessed she'd find out soon enough what was going on.

She turned her attention to the glassware order she needed to place. A half hour later, just before it was time to open, she refilled her coffee cup.

A rapping on the door startled her, and she started toward it. Claire waved through the glass.

Joy unlocked and opened the door. "What are you doing here so early?"

"I've been awake for hours," Claire said. "I need to apologize for last night."

Joy took a step backward. "Whatever for?"

"How Abrielle and I went on and on, acting as if we were teenagers. Although we never actually acted like that way back then." She sighed. "We're both under a lot of stress."

"Of course you are," Joy said. "Don't worry about last night."

Claire shook her head. "We were horrible. And it got even worse with Belina."

"Oh?" Joy motioned for Claire to come into the shop and then she closed and locked the door behind her.

"She's the one behind that website."

"I overheard that as I was leaving," Joy said.

Claire lifted her arm up, making her purse swing back and forth. "You should have stuck around. It was all pretty intense."

Joy could imagine. She lifted her eyebrows, wanting to hear whatever Claire wanted to tell her.

"Belina wondered years ago if the painting might be an early Joubert, and she said she even asked Abrielle about it but that Abrielle disregarded her question. She says she's the one who posted her hypothesis on the website with a photo of *Belina in the Garden*, which is what caught Pamela's attention in the first place."

"Really?"

Claire shrugged. "Who knows? That's just what Belina said. Maybe she posted the photo—although I can't find the post—but it was Abrielle who contacted Pamela after Patrick Ray suggested she do so. He saw the painting and thought it had some similarities to Joubert's early work. It feels like another con by Belina."

"What do you mean?"

"She was always—" Claire wrinkled her nose. "*Fanciful* is the word Mama used to use. Yes, Belina was always creative, and she had a gift when it came to drawing and then painting but also when it came to telling stories. Mama said she had a vivid imagination, while Abrielle called it downright lying."

Joy poured Claire a cup of coffee while she talked.

"Belina was the prettiest of us and the most clever. She was devastated by Mama's death, probably because Mama was the only one who really understood her—or at least catered to her. Once Belina flew the coop she never came back. She studied art in Savanah and then Paris. Then worked as a model. Later she did voice work for commercials."

Joy could see that. Belina had a distinct voice. Low and a little husky. Perfect for voice-overs.

Claire continued. "Eventually, Belina ended up in LA and worked as a fashion designer. To have her come back here, staying with JD, is surprising. Does she have a job? Is she in dire straits? Through the years, Daddy has given her money because she always lived beyond her means, but I have no idea what's going on with her now. This website seems to be her main concern."

Joy handed Claire the coffee and couldn't help but think of Claire living in the family home and Abrielle living on the top floor of the Belina House. They had certainly been helped by their father too. Of course, Joy didn't bring that up. Instead she said, "What does Belina think of the other two paintings?"

"That they're counterfeits. That someone tried to copy Theodore Joubert's style, which is exactly what Pamela thinks. So it's nothing new." Claire took a sip of her coffee and then said, "This is good. What is it?"

"A French blend, from Raphael's, in Houston. Everyone seems to love it." Joy gestured toward the shelf with coffee by the pound.

Claire took another sip and then said, "Anyway, I'm sorry we were all such a mess last night. We usually have better manners than that."

"Don't give it a second thought," Joy said.

"Oh, I will." Claire laughed. "I can't help it."

"So how are you doing today?" Joy asked.

"I had a long talk with Lloyd last night, and he assured me Abrielle is wrong about why he's in Savannah. I even spoke with Aunt Mae. Lloyd found a place in an assisted living community for her, and she'll move in two weeks." Claire took another sip of coffee. "As far as Pamela, he said he met her in the gallery last week when he stopped by with a check to pay her—it was more than what Abrielle had in the gallery account."

That didn't sound good.

"So I'm not as stressed out about that, but I am about the auction. Are you sure you can't meet for lunch today?"

"Positive," Joy said. "But let's talk through some things while we work. Then we can meet tomorrow to finish up the planning. We can start with the flowers, and then I'll order them."

Joy pulled her notebook out of her bag, making sure not to open it to her list of suspects.

She'd already put quite a bit of thought into the flowers, hoping to use rich shades of dahlias, burgundy and dark red, night butterfly and *chat noir* dahlias, with succulents for accents, along with silver dollar eucalyptus and dusty miller. As she and Claire readied the shop for opening, Joy explained her ideas.

"That sounds perfect," Claire said. "We'll need fourteen bouquets. Ten for the cocktail tables we're renting, two for the food tables, one for the beverage table, and the last one—a larger one—for the auction table."

It sounded as if the mezzanine might be crowded with so many tables.

Once the shop opened, Joy went into her office and pulled the card for Gwen, the owner of the Flower Farm, out of her wallet. She'd befriended her at the City Market a couple of weeks earlier. Gwen had a farm outside the city. Joy had quizzed her about her flower raising, dahlias in particular, and then Gwen had given her a card and said, "Call me if you want to place a special order sometime. I'd love to help you out."

Gwen answered after the third ring.

When Joy identified herself, Gwen said, "Joy, great to hear from you! How can I help?"

"I want to place an order, for this Saturday. For an auction."

"Nice," Gwen said. "What do you need?"

"To start with, dahlias," Joy answered. "Night butterfly and chat noir dahlias."

"I know we have the first one, but let me check about the chat noir. Hold on a sec." Gwen's voice was muffled but Joy could clearly hear her say, "Belina, do we have any chat noir?"

The husky voice that answered "There's a whole row left" unmistakably belonged to Belina Fleury. Had she really just shown up in Charleston two days before?

Chapter Twelve

CLAIRE CONFESSED SHE HAD NO idea Belina was working at the Flower Farm. "It does make it seem as if she's been in town longer than she said." Claire stood with both of her palms flat on the checkout counter. "What's the number to this Flower Farm?"

Joy handed her the card.

Claire took it. "I'm going to grab my phone."

Joy could hear her in the back room, asking, "May I please speak with Belina?"

There was a pause and then, "I heard you were working at the Flower Farm. When did you start?"

A customer came into the shop, and Joy quickly closed the door to the back room and greeted the elderly man. "I'm looking for a card," he said. "For a friend."

Joy directed him to the rack to the side of the counter. "We have a good collection," she said. "Both humorous and sentimental."

It didn't take the man long to choose a funny one with an illustration of two old men playing golf on it. By the time he'd paid, Claire had come out of the back room.

After the man left Claire said, "Belina claims she got the job yesterday, but I don't believe her." She sighed. "Do you think you could ask your friend when Belina started?"

Joy pursed her lips together and then said, "You've already asked Belina. If I ask Gwen and she says something to Belina, it could put her on the defensive."

"True," Claire said. "I just hate it when she lies to me."

Joy nodded, sympathizing with Claire. Thankfully, Hope had never been a liar. In fact, Hope was always very honest—about how much she enjoyed spending time with Joy and her family, about how much she loved being Sabrina's aunt, about how much she valued having Joy as a sister. Hope had always been positive about Joy.

But had Joy been as affirming to Hope? Was that why she was so worried Joy would be annoyed with her for causing an accident? Was that why she preferred to stay at Sabrina's instead of with Joy?

The shop was busy for the rest of the morning. Joy sent Claire on a break at eleven. She returned a half hour later. When Lacy arrived at noon, Joy asked Claire if she'd like to tag along to the College of Charleston to go through the rest of Arthur Fleury's letters.

"Oh, goodness, no, I'd much rather help Lacy," Claire answered. "I have no desire to read a bunch of old letters. Just give me the highlights."

When Joy arrived at the college, Amy had the entire collection of five volumes on the table. "Just in case you need to double-check something in an earlier letter," she said.

"Thank you." Joy pulled on the archival gloves and opened the third volume.

In the late 1850s, before the war started, the Fleurys' only daughter, Susie, stayed in France with her Joubert cousins, spending time in the village of Itteville, where the Jouberts had a farm, besides their home in Paris. She wrote home that Theodore and Belina were the two Joubert children who showed the most artistic talent. Susie loved France, especially the village of Itteville. She wrote of hiking above the village, of the church, and of the garden on the farm. While in France, Susie came down with typhus and died, breaking her parents' hearts. She was buried on the Joubert family farm in Itteville.

Two years later, during the first year of the war, Estelle passed away.

The next letter was dated in 1871, from Belina Joubert, to Doc Fleury inviting him and his son Alexander to visit. Doc Fleury responded, accepting the invitation for himself but wrote that Alexander had recently opened a law firm and had too many responsibilities to travel at that time.

There were no letters after that until one from Alexander dated July 25, 1874 announcing the birth of his daughter, Belina Estelle. Alexander wrote, *I named her after Mother and your favorite niece.*

Doc Fleury responded with a note posted from the Fleury estate in Charleston, dated July 30, five days later. *It's with much joy that I received your notice of the birth of Belina Estelle Fleury. I know the perfect gift for your Belina—someday. I will pay my respects to the young lady—and her parents and brother Michael—as soon as possible.*

That was the last item in the book. Joy stood and headed through the door, stopping at the counter. She asked Amy, "Are there any other documents? Papers from the shipping business? Receipts for purchases? Anything from his last trip to France?"

Amy glanced toward her computer. "I don't see anything in the inventory, but I'll double-check when I put the letters away. I'll give you a call if I find anything."

"Thank you," Joy said. "One more question. When did Arthur Fleury die?"

"I can't remember the exact date, but I'll look it up." She turned toward the computer and opened a file. "There he is. July 31, 1874."

The entire trip back to the hospital, Joy thought of Arthur Fleury. Did he see his granddaughter before he died?

She had so many questions. Why, when he'd been a prolific letter writer most of his life, were there no letters during 1871 and very few after that? Perhaps it was due to his advancing age or maybe he could no longer afford an assistant.

She also couldn't help but think of the many relationships in the story of the Fleury family from the 1800s. Arthur's love for Estelle. Susie and her cousins. Estelle and Suzanna.

She thought of Hope again. The Fleury and Joubert families had managed to survive and thrive in their relationships back and forth across the Atlantic with only letters and a rare visit.

How fortunate Joy was to have a sister who wanted to live in the same town with her. This would be a turning point for her relationship with Hope, she was sure.

Her thoughts fell to the paintings. Did Arthur bring them back from France as stolen merchandise? Or were they given to him? The paintings were of Susie's favorite places—from above the village, of the church, and in the garden. She was buried on the Joubert family property in Itteville.

Why wouldn't Theodore give the painting of *Belina in the Garden* to Arthur? And, it made sense that Alexander would name his daughter Belina Estelle. Was Doc Fleury's reference to a "perfect gift" the painting?

All of that was interesting—but none of it helped solve the mystery. Had she wasted her time going through the letters? It was all fascinating, but it did nothing to prove Doc Fleury innocent or to solve the present-day mystery of who stole *Belina in the Garden*. Surely there was more evidence, somewhere. Hopefully Evelyn would have better luck in the hospital archives.

As she pushed through the door into the hospital lobby, her head down, a voice said, "Joy. Are you all right?"

Her head popped up. Roger Gaylord. His brown eyes gazed down at her.

She smiled up at him, feeling as if she'd been lost in a riveting story. Which she had been. "I'm fine," she answered. "Just deep in thought. How are you?"

"Good. Looking forward to the auction on Saturday."

She smiled again. "So am I."

"It's one of my favorite events of the year," he said. "I've always had great admiration for the Fleury family—their deep roots in Charleston, their love of the hospital, their love of art."

Joy could relate. And yet, the family also had a secretive side. If only she could figure out what had gone on in the past—and what was going on in the present too.

"Good to see you," Joy said. "See you on Saturday."

Roger nodded. "See you then."

When she reached the shop, Claire was waiting on a little boy and his mother. "Grandma's sick," the boy said. "But I think she'll like this plant." It was a calla lily with extra greens.

"I think she will too," Claire said. "I'm a grandma, and I know I'd love it."

The boy smiled, and his mother tousled his hair.

Joy continued on to her office, and when Claire finished, she stepped to the open doorway. "You look exhausted. How did it go?"

"Good." Joy did feel drained, emotionally. "The letters are beautiful. They imply that Arthur went to France in 1871, although there aren't actually any letters from him to anyone during that time. Perhaps he wrote his son Alexander, and those letters were never added to the collection." Joy went on to tell Claire about the Joubert family, Susie and her death, the invitation to Arthur to visit France in 1871, and then the birth of his granddaughter, Belina Estelle, and Arthur's death.

"Oh my." Claire rested her hand on her chest. "How sad."

Joy jotted down a note to herself to send Garrison an email about what she'd found—and hadn't found—in the rest of the letters. She raised her head and said, "What was really interesting was that the garden at the Joubert family property outside of Itteville, the village church, and the view of the village from the hillside were all Susie's favorite places in France—and those are the settings of the paintings."

"Interesting," Claire said. "But it still doesn't prove anything."

"Yes." Joy exhaled. "I realize that."

"So what now?"

"I'll talk to Evelyn and see if she's found anything more in the hospital's archives."

"Good idea," Claire said. "I wish I could stay longer and cover for you while you talk to her, but I had a call from Daddy. Belina is stopping by soon, and I want to be there."

"Of course," Joy said. "We can talk more tomorrow, when we meet with Abrielle."

"Perfect." Claire smiled. "I can't tell you how much I appreciate all of your help trying to sort through the history of the paintings and the present-day thief. And your help with the auction too."

"It's my pleasure," Joy said. "Really. I'm enjoying getting to know you and Abrielle better, and I certainly don't want one of the founders of Mercy Hospital to be falsely accused of stealing from a world-renowned artist, even if the young man was his nephew."

"Yes, ma'am, there's that," Claire said. "But after my talk with Lloyd last night, I think the more pressing issue is whether the current theft will put the Belina House Gallery out of business. He said the finances are much worse than what Abrielle has been admitting."

Leaving Claire in charge of the shop, Joy sat at her desk and sent Garrison an email. Then she texted Evelyn to see if she'd found any more information on the Fleury family. NEGATIVE, Evelyn texted back. BUT I'VE BEEN REALLY BUSY TODAY.

Joy took out her notebook with the list of suspects. She couldn't rule out any of the Fleury sisters nor Claire's husband, Lloyd. Abrielle was suspicious of Lloyd being in Savannah. Add that Belina had come back to town without letting Abrielle or Claire know. What if a combination of the sisters—or Lloyd—were working together to trick the other ones out of their share of the painting?

And then there was JD.

"Knock, knock."

Joy lifted her head. Rebekah stood at the door, which was half-way open.

"Do you have a minute?" Rebekah asked.

"Sure." Joy closed her notebook. "Come on in."

"I just had a few questions for Claire—she told me to come speak with you, that you had some information about the case."

Joy nodded. "I've jotted down some notes."

"Do you mind if I close the door?"

"Go ahead," Joy said. Clearly Rebekah didn't want Claire to overhear the conversation.

Rebekah stepped into the office and gently pushed on the door until it latched. She turned back toward Joy. "Do you mind sharing your notes?"

"Not at all. I was just looking at them." She opened the notebook to the right page and placed a sticky at the top. She handed it to Rebekah and then pointed at the chair on the other side of the desk. "Please sit."

Rebekah sat and studied Joy's notes. After a few minutes, she said, "That's quite a list of suspects. Any special concerns about any-one on the list?"

"Well, it is a little awkward to be working with Claire and Abrielle to figure out who stole the paintings when they're both on the list, and when Lloyd and Belina are too, along with JD Johnson."

Rebekah handed the notebook back to Joy. "How about Patrick Ray and Jacque De Villiers?"

"Abrielle seems to think De Villiers has an alibi, but I'm not convinced. Patrick Ray was at an opening in Manhattan that night—which has been confirmed—so it's improbable he could have been here."

Rebekah stood. "Thanks for showing me."

"Was it helpful?"

Rebekah shrugged and smiled. "Time will tell."

Joy found it odd that Rebekah had sought her out to talk to. She waved to the detective as she left. Maybe she needed confirmation from a neutral source.

As soon as the shop closed and she'd cleaned up, Joy hurried home. She popped the lasagna in the oven, assembled the salad, and then prepared the bread and slid it in the oven too.

Once everything was heated, she covered it in foil and placed the hot dish and bread in one box and the cake and salad in another. Then she loaded everything into her Mini Cooper and headed to Sabrina's house, determined to show Hope how much she loved and valued her.

She arrived at five forty-five to the sight of Eloise and Mallory playing with Hula-Hoops in the driveway.

"Mimi!" Mallory yelled as Joy parked on the street. "You're here!" The Hula-Hoop fell to the cement and the five-year-old jumped out of it. As Joy climbed out of her car, Mallory ran to meet her.

Eloise, who was nine, carefully put her hoop on the grass and started walking toward the car. Sabrina opened the front door, and the family's Cavalier King Charles spaniel came dashing out too.

"Mopsy!" Sabrina yelled.

As the dog raced by, straight for the street and Joy, Eloise grabbed her collar.

Sabrina hurried to Eloise and took the dog from her. "I've got her," she said. "I'll be right back to help, Mom," Sabrina called over her shoulder.

Joy opened the back of her car and took out one of the boxes. Eloise stepped up. "I can take that."

"Are you sure?"

Eloise nodded and took the box with the salad and cake.

Sabrina came back out of the house and as soon as she saw Eloise, she said, "Let me take that."

Joy waited to grab the second box, watching her daughter and granddaughter. Eloise didn't seem to want to give up the box, but then Mallory skipped up the sidewalk and bumped into Eloise. Sabrina grabbed the box as it began to tip.

"Mallory," Eloise wailed. "Watch what you're doing."

"Be kind," Sabrina said to Eloise as she headed to the house, carrying the box with one hand.

Joy grabbed the second box and called out to Eloise. "Would you close the hatch for me?"

Eloise turned toward her, a pout on her face. But she did as Joy asked.

Mallory held the door open with a flourish and Sabrina led the way, followed by Eloise. As Eloise reached the door, Mallory jutted out her foot as if she was going to trip her. Eloise stepped wide and stuck out her tongue at Mallory, which wasn't like her at all.

Proving that mothers do have eyes in the back of their heads, although sometimes selectively, Sabrina snapped, "Eloise, that's enough. Go to your room until it's time for dinner."

"Mom," Eloise whined, "she tried to trip me."

"You're older. You know better. You've been trying my patience all day."

Eloise shuffled down the hall to her room while Mallory darted in front of everyone and plopped down beside Hope on the couch. Hope put her arm around her great-niece. "Hello, Joy," she said.

"Hi," Joy answered. "How are you doing?"

Hope lifted her boot a little. "Great. I really couldn't be better, considering—"

"Come on you two," Sabrina said to Hope and Mallory. "We'll eat as soon as we get the food on the table."

"Where's Rob?" Joy asked.

"Working late."

Joy followed Sabrina through to the dining room. The table was set with Sabrina's china and crystal water glasses.

"It all looks so fancy," Joy said. "I don't think the food quite lives up to the setting."

"Are you kidding me?" Sabrina laughed. "You know how much I love your lasagna. And I've been too busy to make it lately."

They continued into the kitchen, which connected to the family room. Mallory raced ahead, turned on the TV, and plopped down on the plush couch. Joy was surprised when Sabrina didn't ask her to turn it off.

Sabrina and Joy soon had the food on the table.

"I'll go get Eloise," Joy said.

"Thanks." Sabrina turned to the family room. "Mallory, turn off the TV and wash your hands."

"Yes, ma'am, Mommy," Mallory called out, but the TV continued to blare.

Families, Joy thought as she headed back through the living room toward the hall. And sisters in particular. She'd avoided the conflict between siblings by only having Sabrina. Being around Eloise and Mallory brought back all sorts of memories from her own childhood though.

She'd been aware for several years that she identified most with Eloise and felt Sabrina overlooked Mallory's indiscretions while punishing Eloise too harshly. Now she wondered if Hope identified most with Mallory and felt Eloise deserved being chastised for reacting to Mallory.

She thought of the Fleury sisters and their dynamics, complicated even more because there were three of them instead of just two.

The tension remained high through dinner. It seemed Eloise hadn't gotten past her earlier frustration with her little sister, and Mallory continued to be loud and disruptive.

But when dinner was almost over, as she took her last bite of lasagna, Mallory said, "Yum. Lasagna is my favorite."

"Mine too," Eloise said.

"Mine three." Sabrina smiled at her daughters. Joy was happy they could all agree on something.

Sabrina said to her girls, "I remember my grandmother making it when I was little."

"It's her lasagna recipe," Joy said.

Hope smiled at her. "Yours is better."

"No." Joy chuckled. "I'm sure it's not."

Hope nodded and took another bite.

Joy leaned back, content for the moment. "I made torta caprese. I hope everyone saved room."

Hope gushed, "That's my favorite."

"I know," Joy answered.

"Really?"

"That's why I made it."

"You're kidding."

Joy shook her head. "You deserve your favorite cake this week, of all weeks."

"Well, thank you," Hope said.

Maybe all Joy needed to do was reach out to Hope. To be kind.

"If it's Auntie Hope's favorite dessert, then it's mine too." Mallory grinned at her grandmother.

Joy smiled back. Mallory was a doll with her dark hair and big brown eyes.

Eloise pointed at Mallory. "You don't even know what torta caprese is."

"Yes, Eloise, I do."

"What is it?"

Mallory grinned and looked up at Hope, batting her eyes.

"Chocolate cake," Hope whispered loudly.

"Chocolate cake," Mallory repeated.

Eloise leaned forward in her chair. "That's cheating."

"That's enough," Sabrina said—once again. So much for the moment of calm.

Joy stood and started clearing the table, not wanting to involve herself in the girls' dispute. Next, she served the torta caprese, giving Hope the first piece and then Mallory hers. When Joy tried to serve Eloise, she said, "No thank you."

Joy held the plate in midair. "Are you sure?"

Eloise nodded. "May I be excused?"

Sabrina answered, "No. You can sit here and visit with us while we enjoy dessert."

Eloise crossed her arms and slunk down in her chair.

Sabrina sighed. "Go to your room."

Eloise stood, pushed in her chair, and slipped out of the dining room without saying anything.

Once she left, Sabrina said, "This is a repeat of last night. I don't know what's gotten into her. We were having such a nice dinner. She's so moody."

"And mean," Mallory chimed in.

Hope patted Mallory's arm and then said, "She reminds me of your grandmother when she was growing up."

Joy had just cut into her cake with her fork. "Ouch." So much for the moment of charity from Hope earlier—it had flown away with the moment of calm between the girls.

Hope laughed. "In fact your grandmother was moody for years, if I remember right."

There was an awkward moment of silence. Joy's plan to show Hope love and appreciation wasn't going as she'd hoped. Instead she felt defensive and had to caution herself not to respond lest she say something unkind.

Finally, Sabrina said, "What's going on at the hospital after that article about the Fleury family?"

"Fleury?" Hope asked. "As in Belina Fleury?"

"That's right," Joy said. "The family owns an art gallery, and three paintings were stolen from it on Friday night or Saturday morning. Two were found but the other one is still missing."

Sabrina added, "The missing one is most likely an early Joubert."

Hope's eyes grew big. "As in Theodore Joubert?"

Sabrina nodded.

"Wow." Hope took a bite of cake.

"It gets more complicated," Sabrina said. "One of the founders of the hospital may have stolen it from Theodore Joubert in the early 1870s."

Hope shook her head. "One of the founders of Mercy Hospital?" She turned her attention toward Joy. "Your hospital?"

"Yes," Joy said. "Doc Fleury is the great-great-great-grandfather of the Fleury sisters."

"There's more than one?" Hope asked.

"Yes, ma'am, there are three. Abrielle, Claire, and Belina."

"And they're named after the paintings, right?" Sabrina asked.

Joy nodded. "I spent some time yesterday and today going through letters of Doc Fleury's, trying to figure out how he acquired the paintings."

"What did you find out?"

"That the Fleury family was related to the Jouberts, several generations back, through Arthur's family and then as first cousins through Arthur's wife, Estelle."

"Fascinating," Hope said.

"It is," Joy said. "Belina, Theodore's younger sister, wrote Arthur inviting him to visit the Joubert family in 1871, but there were no letters confirming that he did, although there are articles that confirm he went. I need to research Arthur's son, Alexander, who became a lawyer, and his children, Michael and Belina Estelle."

"Sounds as if the name Belina has been passed down through the generations," Hope said.

"So have the names Abrielle and Claire." Joy took another bite of cake.

"Claire and Abrielle live in Charleston, right?" Sabrina asked.

Joy nodded, her mouth too full to speak.

"Where did Belina live?" Hope asked. "Before she came to Charleston so I could hit the pickup she was riding in?"

Joy swallowed and then answered, "California, the LA area."

"Does she have a good relationship with her sisters?" Hope asked.

"It's a little strained," Joy answered.

Mallory, who had chocolate smeared around her mouth, sat up straight. "What does that mean?"

Hope quickly said, "That they don't get along."

"Like me and Eloise?"

"No," Joy said. "It's an adult thing—not a kid thing. You and Eloise are fine."

Mallory giggled. "Not really. She's mean."

Sabrina shook her head at Mallory. "Usually your sister is very nice to you, even when you try her."

Mallory's smile melted into a frown, and she leaned back against her chair.

Joy was pleased that Sabrina had spoken up for Eloise.

Hope patted Mallory's arm and said, "I'm guessing Belina has a reason for her strained relationship with her sisters. Is she the youngest?"

Joy shook her head. "Middle."

"Aww, that's probably even worse."

Joy felt another stab to her heart.

Hope didn't seem to notice. "I could help with the research on the Fleury family to try to figure out what's going on," she said. "I have my laptop."

"I'm focusing on the historical mystery," Joy said. That wasn't entirely true. She wanted to figure out the present mystery too, but she didn't want Hope to get involved in that.

"All right," Hope said. "What did you say their names are, the ones from the past? Alexander, Michael, and Belina Estelle Fleury?"

Joy nodded. "Yes. Alexander was Arthur's son, and Michael and Belina Estelle were Alexander's children."

Hope placed her fork on her empty plate. "You want to know if there's any information that connects them to the paintings?"

Joy nodded again. "But I doubt you'll find anything online."

Hope shrugged. "It won't hurt to look. I'm not going to start work until next Monday now, and I can't move into my apartment until Friday."

"I can help you," Joy said. "With the move."

"That's all right. Like I said, Sabrina and Rob and a couple of their friends are going to do it."

"Oh, that's right." Joy tried to look on the bright side. She really didn't have time, what with the auction and all, but she still felt excluded.

Maybe Sabrina sensed Joy's discomfort. "Guess what?" she said.

Joy smiled and shook her head.

"Rob's work gave him tickets to an auction on Saturday night." Sabrina smiled.

"The hospital fundraiser?"

She grinned. "Three tickets, so Hope can come with us. I've already found a sitter."

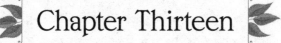

Chapter Thirteen

JOY WOKE UP IN THE middle of the night thinking about Hope. Her statement about Joy being moody all those years had hurt. But was she right? Joy had always been aware of Hope's flaws. Had she been unaware of her own?

It wasn't like Hope to be critical. Was it because of her wreck and injury? Or did she feel safe enough at Sabrina's to criticize Joy?

Would she act that way at the auction on Saturday? In front of Claire and Abrielle? In front of Roger?

Joy slept fitfully until her alarm rang at five thirty. Exhausted, she climbed out of bed.

An hour later, as Joy walked down King Street toward the hospital, her phone dinged. She expected a text from Sabrina. But it was from Hope. I FORGOT TO SAY THANK YOU FOR THE TORTA CAPRESE. THAT WAS VERY KIND OF YOU TO MAKE MY FAVORITE.

Joy stopped walking and read the text again. Then she texted back YOU'RE WELCOME. THANK YOU FOR THE THANK YOU. ☺ I HOPE YOU HAVE A GOOD DAY.

When she reached the hospital, she checked her phone. There was nothing more from Hope.

Joy slipped her phone back into her purse. It was nice of Hope to thank her for making the torta caprese, but it seemed obvious that she had moved to Charleston to be near Sabrina and her family—not near Joy.

How had Joy gone from, four days ago, feeling as if Hope was being intrusive to move to Charleston to feeling neglected that her sister's motivation hadn't been to be closer to her?

She thought of Belina Fleury coming home and not telling her sisters. And of Hope saying that there was probably a reason Belina had a strained relationship with her sisters. Belina had left Charleston; they had stayed.

Hope had left Houston; Joy had stayed—until she moved to Charleston. But by then her husband had passed away and so had her parents.

Joy unlocked the door to the shop, slipped inside, and breathed in the scent of coffee brewing. After she'd poured herself a cup, she retreated to her office. Feeling melancholy, she took a sip of coffee.

How would having Hope in Charleston impact her relationship with Sabrina and Eloise and Mallory? How would it affect her relationship with Hope?

"Joy?"

Someone had come into the shop. Had she forgotten to relock the door?

"Back here," Joy said, putting her coffee down and heading into the shop.

Claire, wearing a navy skirt and jacket with a bright yellow blouse and yellow pumps, stood in the middle of the store. "Why was the door unlocked?"

Joy grimaced. "I forgot to relock it." She must be more preoccupied than she thought.

"Daddy needed a prescription filled, so I said I'd pick it up for him, but I forgot the pharmacy doesn't open until eight," Claire said. "Mind if I grab a cup of coffee?"

"Of course not," Joy answered.

As Claire poured herself a cup, she said, "Lloyd came home last night."

"How is he?"

"Good." Claire turned to Joy, who leaned against the counter. "Aunt Mae is doing better. I'll go back with him next week and we'll get her moved."

"I'm so glad he's home," Joy said.

"So am I." Claire hesitated a moment and then said, "Abrielle's suspicion of Lloyd made me suspicious too. But once he was home, I knew he wasn't involved in anything nefarious. I think Abrielle is deflecting." She sighed. "He did tell me something interesting though."

"What's that?"

"That the gallery has been losing money for quite some time. Abrielle didn't want him to tell me—she kept saying she'd turn things around. When Patrick told her *Belina in the Garden* might be a Joubert, she thought all of her problems would be solved."

"Did you ask him if the painting was insured?"

"Yes, ma'am," Claire said. "He thought so but said he needed to speak with Abrielle about it. She handled the insurance."

Knocking on the window turned their attention toward the door. Belina peered into the shop, one hand shading her eyes. She wore jeans and a sweatshirt and had a messenger bag strapped across her chest.

"I wonder what she's doing here," Claire said.

Joy wondered too.

Claire unlocked the door and let her sister in.

Abruptly Belina asked, "Where's Abrielle?"

"I don't know," Claire said. "But she's not here, and there's no reason she would be."

"She told me she'd meet me here. Daddy said you were going to be here."

"In the shop?"

"No, at the hospital. The pharmacy. I called Abrielle and she said she'd meet us here. I saw you through the window."

Claire crossed her arms. "All right."

Joy imagined they'd all go to the Grove to talk, but just then Abrielle came into the shop too. "There you both are."

"Joy, is it all right if we talk in here?" Belina asked. "Where no one can hear us."

"Sure," Joy said. "If you'll be done by eight."

"It won't take long," Belina said.

"I'll go into my office and give you some privacy." Joy took a step away from the counter.

Belina crossed her arms. "I'd rather you stayed," she said.

Joy stopped and glanced toward Claire, who shrugged.

"All right," Joy said.

"I didn't see the article in the newspaper until last night. So what's up with the insurance?" Belina exhaled, sharply.

Neither Claire nor Abrielle responded.

Belina pulled a newspaper out of her bag. "What's this line about?" She read, "'The Belina House Gallery insurance policy is in question.'" She looked up, her gaze falling on Abrielle and then Claire. "Daddy hasn't read the article and knows nothing about all of this." She took a deep breath. "Are you two keeping secrets again?"

"No," Claire said.

"Then what's going on? Were the paintings insured?"

Claire turned her attention toward Abrielle, who suddenly was very interested in her fingernails.

"Abrielle?" Claire asked. "Do you have any answers? Lloyd said you handle the insurance."

"I have so many questions," Belina said. "They range from, did you stage the theft to collect the insurance money? To, did you let the insurance policy lapse because you planned to sell the painting on the illicit market?"

Abrielle raised her head. She first looked at Claire and then Belina. Finally she said, "Neither."

"Then what's going on?" Belina asked. "Is there an insurance policy on the painting?"

Abrielle shook her head.

Claire gasped.

"Why not?" Belina asked.

"We couldn't afford it," Abrielle said. "I let the policy lapse six months ago on our collection and only kept it on the building and the paintings we didn't own. My plan was to renew the insurance once the painting was authenticated and the word was out. Once that happened, I figured traffic to the gallery would increase and so would our sales. Plus, we could lease the paintings to art museums for exhibits and make money that way. Our money problems would be over. But I didn't have time to renew the insurance after the painting was authenticated and before it was stolen, considering it was stolen before I knew for sure it was authentic."

"How could you let the insurance on the collection go?" Claire asked.

Abrielle shook her head. "We have a good security system, or so I thought. I believed I'd planned for everything. And then when it seemed we might have a masterpiece in the gallery, the only people who knew the painting might be a Joubert were Pamela, Patrick, and Jacque. Besides me, Lloyd, and you. I didn't anticipate that any of those people would steal it."

Joy wondered if perhaps Belina had stolen the painting, hoping to collect the insurance money, since that clearly couldn't have been Abrielle's motivation. It seemed, now, that Abrielle was innocent of taking it.

Belina stepped to Abrielle's side and, to Joy's surprise, put her arm around her older sister. "More people than you think knew, or at least suspected, the painting was a Joubert. I had no idea the problems I might be creating by starting that website and posting a photo of the artwork on it. I'm sorry."

Abrielle reached out and took Belina's hand.

"The important thing now…" Belina paused.

Joy was impressed with how gracious Belina was being.

"Is to figure out who took the painting, where it is—and get it back." Belina stood up straight. "Not for the money but because it belongs to our family and it should remain with our family. It's far more important than the gallery."

Joy couldn't help but recall that Marshall had said the same thing on Sunday. She was tempted to delete Belina's name from the suspect list, but she knew better than to do so. Perhaps Belina was putting on an act. At this point there was no way to know.

Ten minutes later, the Fleury sisters long gone, Joy was opening the shop, going over the revelation that Abrielle had let the insurance lapse.

Abrielle hadn't apologized to her sisters for doing so, seeming to think she had no other choice. Surely Marshall or Claire and Lloyd would have covered the payments, if necessary. Why hadn't Abrielle asked for help, especially when Claire had a share in the gallery? And it seemed Belina did too.

Anne interrupted Joy's thoughts with a warm, "Hello! How are you?" She held a small box in one hand and held her other hand behind her back.

"I'm all right." Joy gave her friend a smile. "How are you?"

"Great!" Anne held the box up. "I brought you something." She pulled her other hand from behind her back and waved a fork.

"Hmmm," Joy said. "Something to eat?"

Anne nodded.

"It's too small to be a pecan pie."

Anne laughed. "Close enough." She handed the box and the fork to Joy. "A mini pecan pie."

"Yum. Thank you." Joy took both items. "How about a cup of coffee?"

"I wish I could," Anne said. "But I need to get to the discharge desk. I'll stop by later."

Joy held up the box and fork. "Thank you. You really brightened my morning."

Anne smiled. "See you soon." Anne was the epitome of Southern hospitality.

Joy poured herself another cup of coffee and went into her office with the mini pie. She sat down at her desk, powered her computer on, and googled BELINA FLEURY.

Joy knew Belina had studied art in Paris, worked as a model, and done voice-over work. A young French actress with the same name popped up. Joy scrolled down as she took a bite of the pie, looking for someone Belina's age. There was a photo of a younger Belina, posing for the camera. Then an article about her work with a fashion designer in California. That was all.

Joy searched for Theodore Joubert's appreciation site. The website Belina started popped up. Photos of Joubert's paintings lined the top of the site, excluding *Belina in the Garden.* Joy scrolled down and saw the photo of *Belina in the Garden* posted on a blog post three years ago.

Joy took another bite of pie and then a sip of coffee as she stared at the pale pink dress and the dark hair of the model. The pink of the rose on the trellis was darker than the dress, and the roses in the background were red. Lavender filled the right corner of the painting and there were both poppies and daisies in the garden, to the left. The setting was most likely early summer. The model wasn't smiling, but her expression had an element of playfulness.

Joy scanned the comments and then the replies. BEF was responding to all the comments. Surely the *B* and *F* stood for *Belina Fleury.* What was her middle name? Estelle?

Why didn't the Fleury sisters know the history of their family? It made no sense to Joy.

She took the last bite of the mini pecan pie and then quickly sent Anne a thank-you text. YOU MADE MY DAY. BEST PIE EVER! THANK YOU!

Then she thought of Grey being a seventh-generation Charlestonian, and yet he didn't know that much about his history either.

But Daniella Hattel, who'd only visited Charleston as a girl, already knew quite a bit and was determined to learn more about the city.

Life often worked that way. The familiar became unknown while the unfamiliar was cherished.

Joy read through some of the comments about *Belina in the Garden*. One person wrote, *It's definitely a Joubert* while another wrote, *My five-year-old could have painted this*.

That certainly wasn't true. The painting was beautiful.

Another commenter posted a painting of Joubert's from 1879 of another garden scene. *Note the poppies in both paintings and the daisies. Very similar.* The latter painting had a little girl in it, not a young woman, and the colors were bold and the shapes more pronounced than in the earlier painting. But the styles seemed similar to Joy too.

Lacy came in, and Joy closed her computer to greet her. Several customers came through the shop in the next hour, and then just after eleven Joy slipped out for a break. First she stopped by the exhibit Abrielle had hung in the hallway and examined the three properties associated with the Fleury family. The Gothic Revival Huguenot Church. The Italianate-style Belina House Gallery with the flower boxes filled with white angel's-trumpet. And the Fleury

Estate, with its lovely gardens. It must have been painted in the summer, because both poppies and daisies were in bloom.

The next painting was the one of the Old Exchange building. Who was the artist? There was no signature. She went back to the first three paintings. There was no signature on them either.

She went to the fifth and final painting. It was of a cottage set back on a property in a grove of trees. Joy didn't recognize it. She went back to the Colonial-style Old Exchange building. There were pots of dahlias on the outside. Joy was sure there weren't pots of any flowers in real life.

She glanced at the painting of the Huguenot Church again. There were flowers in front of it too, pink and red pentas planted in black pots.

There were five paintings all together but no signatures on any of them. And no sign with a description of the artist. Just labels under each painting of the building.

Joy took her phone out of the pocket of her sweater and composed a text to Abrielle. WHO PAINTED THE PAINTINGS IN THE HALLWAY AT THE HOSPITAL? She hit send and waited a moment, hoping Abrielle would reply with a quick answer. She didn't.

She decided to walk through the lobby and up the stairs to the next floor. She felt tired and hoped the activity would perk her up. It was that or another cup of coffee.

She passed the mezzanine exit from the staircase and continued on to the second floor. She walked to the parking garage and then through the double doors into the sticky heat. Then she took the stairs down to the first floor of the garage and stepped out onto the sidewalk and headed back to the front door of the hospital.

As she approached the lobby doors, someone called out her name. She turned around.

Hope came toward her, hopping along on her boot. "There you are."

"Here I am," Joy said. "How did you get here?"

"Sabrina dropped me off to pick up a rental car this morning, and I decided to come have lunch with you. We need to talk."

It was eleven thirty by the time Hope and Joy got their salads and chose a table in the far corner of the Grove. It was humid, yes, but the scenery was so beautiful that sitting outside was worth it.

Joy pulled her sunglasses from her bag and slipped them on. Then she asked, "What's going on?"

"It turns out I can't move into my apartment until Monday. Can I stay with you until then?"

"What about staying at Sabrina's?"

"I think I've overstayed my welcome."

Joy lowered her sunglasses. "What do you mean?"

Hope winced. "Sabrina hasn't said anything to you?"

Joy shook her head as she took a bite of salad.

"I'm surprised…" Hope took a bite of her salad too and met Joy's gaze.

Joy swallowed and asked, "What's going on?"

Hope put her fork down and sighed. "I think I'm making things stressful for them. It's Mallory. She seems to have really bonded with me, but she's not very nice to Eloise."

"Oh?"

"Have you noticed that before?"

"I did last night."

"But not before?"

"Perhaps a little."

Hope picked up her fork. "Sabrina didn't seem to notice it until bedtime last night, but when Mallory insisted I read her a story but that Eloise couldn't hear it too, Sabrina put her foot down and told Mallory she couldn't tell people what they could and could not do."

"Mallory's behavior is probably developmentally on target." Joy had read about age-appropriate physical, mental, and emotional expectations to keep abreast of what to expect from her granddaughters. "She just started kindergarten, which is a big transition. She's gaining more independence but is also pushing boundaries. And she's trying to determine her place in the family and world—so when someone visits, it's understandable she would react in some way."

Hope nodded. "Wow, that helps." She paused a moment but then said, "I'm afraid I encouraged her behavior though."

"How's that?"

Hope lifted her eyebrows. "Eloise can be bossy, and I remember clearly how it feels to be the little sister. I may have been—" She shook her head. "No, I *was* too sympathetic toward Mallory, and I ended up hurting Eloise."

"Well," Joy said. "If you sympathized with Mallory because I was bossy—"

A stricken expression fell on Hope's face.

Before Hope could say anything, Joy continued, "Then that's understandable. I *was* bossy."

Hope's expression relaxed a bit.

"And if you feel you were unfair to Eloise, you can apologize to her. She's good at accepting apologies."

Hope smiled. "Just spending time with them makes me more understanding of you when we were little. Mallory can get annoying—always asking questions, talking nonstop, helping herself to other people's belongings. She opened my laptop this morning." Hope shook her head. "Back when I was five, the stakes weren't as high, but I remember using your colored pencils without asking. And then I broke most of them."

Joy didn't remember that particular incident—although she did remember a few years later Hope using her makeup and mixing pots of eyeshadow, ruining all of them.

"Anyway," Hope said, "what do you think I should do? Stay at Sabrina's? Or come to your place for the next few nights?"

"If you stay, maybe you can encourage Mallory and Eloise to get along better."

Hope took a deep breath. "Maybe…" She took another bite of salad. After she swallowed, she said, "I'll think about it."

"You're always welcome to stay with me," Joy said. "The spare bedroom is waiting for you."

"Thanks." Hope took another bite of salad. Then she said, "I found some information on the Fleury family."

"Really?"

She nodded. "My foot was hurting, and I couldn't sleep, so I did some research. The doctor cleared me for some screen time. The college has an expansive database that includes South Carolina historical documents that I'm able to use."

Joy smiled, encouraging Hope to continue.

"Alexander Fleury had the two children, Michael and Belina Estelle," Hope said. "Sadly, Belina died when she was thirteen…" Hope took a piece of paper from her bag. "In 1886 from consumption." She kept reading from the paper. "Michael graduated from the College of Charleston in 1892 and then went on to law school at Harvard."

Joy's eyebrows shot up. "Impressive."

Hope nodded. "But he came back to Charleston and joined his father's law practice." She continued to read. "Michael had three children, two boys and a girl. Jon, Edmond, and Claire."

"A Claire. Any Abrielles?"

Hope held up a finger. "There's more." She consulted her notes again. "Jon died as a toddler, but Edmond—who was born in 1903— had a daughter, Abrielle, plus a son named Marshall, born in 1937."

Joy smiled again.

"Sadly, this Abrielle died from leukemia, in 1960."

Joy's smile disappeared. "That would have been before Abrielle Fleury, the current one, was born."

"That's right," Hope said. "She was born in 1966." She kept reading. "Belina was born in 1968 and Claire was born in 1970."

"Interesting." Joy thought about all the girls and young women who had died in the Fleury family. The current generation was the first who had lived to adulthood. "Here I thought the Fleury sisters were named after the paintings, but they were most likely named after their deceased relatives."

Hope frowned. "It's sad, isn't it?"

Joy nodded. "It makes me thankful for you and for Sabrina. It also makes me think of Marshall saying he was thrilled to have three daughters. That it was meant to be." Joy had thought it was interesting at the time, for a man who didn't have a son to carry on the family name that had been going strong in Charleston since the late 1600s. But that wasn't what mattered to Marshall.

"Thank you for doing that research for me," Joy said.

"I hope it will help." Hope slid her notes across the table. "I can see why the Fleurys fascinate you. They seem like a really special family."

"An interesting family, certainly," Joy said. "But I don't think they're any more special than any other family."

Hope shrugged. "You could have fooled me by the way you keep going on and on about them."

"What's that supposed to mean?" Joy's phone buzzed, and she glanced down at it. "It's Abrielle," she said.

She read the text. Don't forget dinner tonight at Claire's. 6:30. See you then.

Nothing about the paintings. Joy read the text again and then replied, See you then.

Formal dress, Abrielle texted back.

Joy winced. Thankfully Abrielle had remembered to tell her.

She turned her attention back toward Hope, who was now standing.

"You need to get back to work," Hope said.

Joy tucked her phone into her bag. "I have a few more minutes before my volunteer's shift is done."

"I'll let you know about staying with you." Hope leaned down and picked up her tray.

Joy stood. "Let me take your tray."

Hope shook her head. "I've got it." Then she shuffled away.

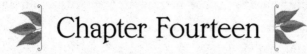

Chapter Fourteen

SOON AFTER JOY RETURNED TO the gift shop, Evelyn came through the door carrying a ratty cardboard box. "I found this in the very back of the corner cupboard in the archive. I haven't gone through it yet, but from what I picked out, a few of the things had the Fleury name on it. Don't get rid of anything." Evelyn smiled.

Joy smiled back. "Never."

Evelyn dipped the box so Joy could see inside. "I've included a couple pairs of gloves."

"If I don't get through the box today, should I leave it in my office or take it back to the archives?"

"Keep it here," Evelyn said. "I'm not going to get to it today or tomorrow. I'm buried in work. I'll go through it next week, but hopefully there might be something in it that can help you now."

"All right." She took the box from Evelyn. It had that musty, bookish odor to it. "If I don't have time this afternoon, I'll come in early tomorrow morning and see what I can find."

Not long after Evelyn left, as Joy dusted the blown glass on the shelf near the front of the shop between customers, she saw Shirley walking beside Regina, holding her mother's arm. Joy waved, but they didn't see her. She hurried to the door.

"Shirley! Regina!"

Shirley turned to her and smiled.

Joy motioned for them to come into the shop.

Shirley shook her head and mouthed, "Mama's tired."

Regina turned her head, "What?"

"Wave to Joy," Shirley said. "And then I'm getting you home to rest."

"No, no, no." Regina turned toward Joy. "That's my friend. I want to say hello."

Joy grimaced and shrugged apologetically. Then she said, "I'll make some coffee. Come sit down for a few minutes."

Joy held the door open for the two women. Regina, still holding on to Shirley's arm, flashed her a smile as she walked into the shop.

Regina wore a brown pantsuit with a light pink scarf around her neck and carried a darker pink bag on her arm. Her hair and makeup were perfectly done. She was always put together.

Joy directed them back to the two comfy chairs and said, "I'll start a new pot."

"Better make it decaf," Shirley said.

"All right." Joy remembered that Shirley said sometimes Regina couldn't sleep and would wander the house.

As Joy made the coffee she said, "Regina, you mentioned you had contact with the Fleury family years ago. I'd love to hear your story."

"Oh, I didn't really have contact with them, not all of them. I took a class with one of them."

Shirley made a face. "What are you talking about, Mama?"

Regina gave Shirley a sassy look. "Listen and I'll tell you." She folded her hands in her lap. "I was working and keeping busy with church. I had my two girls, but I wanted something just for me. So I signed up for one of those community classes, you know." She smiled a little. "One of those 'find yourself' art classes."

"When exactly was that, Mama?"

"Oh, I don't know. Late eighties or so." She adjusted the scarf around her neck and folded her hands back in her lap. "There was a man in the class I recognized right away. Marshall Fleury."

"Really?" Shirley shook her head. "Are you pulling our legs?"

Regina chuckled. "No. I am not. Just listen." She continued with her story. "I was as surprised as you are now that he was in that class. He was a bigwig lawyer in town with his own practice. His wife had just passed away, sadly. I didn't think he would have time to spend on a little art class. But there he was. We chatted now and then. Of course I didn't let on that I knew who he was. One time I mentioned I was a nurse, and he told me about his support for the hospital. The next week I told him I had two daughters and he asked me for advice about parenting girls. Over time he told me his oldest daughter had just returned to Charleston to run the family art gallery, while another daughter was studying art in Paris. His youngest daughter was at Duke for her first year of college. Another time he told me his oldest was smart but controlling and his second daughter was a talented artist but blamed herself for her mother's death. The girl was wild her senior year and thought it was her fault their mother died. She felt so guilty she wouldn't go to her high school graduation and ended up withdrawing from her family." Regina paused for a moment. "That made me so sad." She shook her head and continued. "The youngest girl felt she couldn't live up to her sisters' brains and talent and felt invisible. She believed she had something to prove and ended up trying to be perfect—always dressing just so and acting just so and caring what everyone thought of her, just so."

Joy put her hand to her chest. Did Claire still feel that way?

Regina kept talking. "All families are fragile," she said, "but Marshall's was more fragile than most, at least at that time." Regina shook her head. "All families have conflict, but what's important is how families repair that conflict. Marshall tried, but sometimes it's impossible." She sighed. "He was such a nice man. He still is. I still hope the conflict in his family can be repaired. I tell him that when I see him from time to time."

Shirley tilted her head. "Where do you see him?"

"Around town. At the grocery store. A fundraiser now and then. That sort of thing. He always remembers me. He asks about you." Regina nodded toward Shirley. "And I ask about his girls. I even ask about a young man he was trying to help back then. A friend of his middle daughter." She shook her head and laughed a little. "I can't remember his name though. Marshall arranged for him to work at their church."

Joy was pouring the coffee but stopped. A friend of the middle daughter's? Who worked at the church? "Any chance the young man's name was JD?"

"Come to think of it, it was an initial name." She wrinkled her nose. "I can't remember if it was JD or not. Could've been AJ or JC or DJ." She laughed.

Joy handed a cup of coffee to Regina as she said, "Well, your memories about everything else have been wonderful."

As Joy handed Shirley a cup of coffee, she wondered if JD had been the young man Marshall helped and if so, would JD still have a key to the church? That would have been thirty years ago. It was highly unlikely—but plausible.

The conversation shifted to Regina's health. She'd been to an appointment at the clinic next door to the hospital, and they'd just picked up another new prescription from the pharmacy when Joy saw them.

"Her blood pressure has been high," Shirley explained. "The doc is hoping this new medication will take care of it."

Fifteen minutes later, the cups of coffee drained, Regina and Shirley were on their way, leaving Joy to think about the Fleury sisters. How could Claire feel invisible? She was so noticeable with her dark eyes and blond hair, perfectly assembled outfits, and important positions. And yet Joy could see Claire's desire for perfection in the way she dressed, in her many volunteer tasks, in her garden.

It made Joy think of Hope. Did she feel invisible? It wasn't as if Joy was gorgeous or a genius, but she had been good at school and had a solid group of friends, both things that Hope never had.

At a quarter to two, Joy had a text from Abrielle. I'm on the mezzanine. Can you come up?

Sure, Joy texted back. See you in a few.

Once she checked with Lacy, her volunteer, Joy took the stairs to the mezzanine level. Abrielle, who wore a flowing dress with a floral scarf around her neck and held a clipboard in her hand, waved from the far end. She said, "I'm trying to figure out where to put everything. The food tables. The cocktail tables." She snapped her fingers.

"I need to call and have them delivered here instead of at the gallery."

"Do you want me to do that?"

"I have the number on my phone," Abrielle said. "I'll do that right now."

She handed Joy the clipboard and a file. "Would you hold this? You can look in the file. It has photos of all of the paintings."

As Abrielle made the call, Joy slipped the file out from under the clipboard. She opened it and zipped through the photos, wondering if the artist who did the paintings in the hallway downstairs had contributed any of their work to the auction. But there was nothing.

When Abrielle ended her call, Joy said, "You never answered my text about the paintings down in the hallway. Who's the artist?"

"Anonymous," Abrielle answered.

Joy stared at her. "But surely you know."

"The artist doesn't want to be identified."

"Why not?" Joy asked.

Abrielle shrugged and reached for the clipboard as she pulled a pencil out from behind her ear. The two began talking through where to put the food tables, the drink table, the cocktail tables, and the auction table. It was going to be crowded. "We'll put the photos of the paintings on the auction table, next to the bid sheets," Abrielle said.

Abrielle marked the table locations on her clipboard. She'd already mapped out the arrangement of the paintings. "The artists will drop them off tomorrow, between two and four. I'll hang them after that," Abrielle added.

Joy looked up and saw Garrison and Roger Gaylord coming toward them. "We've been looking for you," Garrison said. "Have you found anything more about Dr. Fleury and the paintings?"

Joy shook her head.

Garrison looked as sad as a dejected puppy dog. "I've heard from the reporter a couple more times," he said. "It sounds as if she's written another story that's going to run Saturday. I asked her to wait until Sunday so it doesn't hurt the auction."

Joy grimaced. She doubted Daniella would cooperate.

"Just ignore her," Abrielle said. "This will all blow over sooner or later. We don't have proof Arthur didn't steal the paintings and no one has proof that he did."

"That we know of," Garrison said. "It's likely someone, some-where, has proof of something. And at this rate, Daniella Hattel is going to figure it out before we do."

As if on cue, the reporter appeared at the top of the stairs. "Did I hear my name?"

Garrison groaned.

"If one of the founders of this hospital was an international thief, don't you think the city of Charleston has a right to know that?" Daniella asked.

"No one cares," Abrielle said. Joy knew she was bluffing, but Daniella didn't seem to realize it.

Her eyebrows arched. "Of course they care. Here's a man who's been revered all of these years. Idolized, practically. People deserve the truth."

Abrielle shook her head.

"Don't think everyone thinks the way you do," Daniella said to Abrielle. "Because they don't."

"Well," Abrielle said. "Don't think they all think the way you do either."

"Ladies." Roger stepped forward. "There's no use discussing this." He directed his gaze at Daniella. "When we find information that clears Arthur Fleury's name we'll let you know. I promise." Roger nodded back toward the staircase. "Garrison has to get back to work, but I would love to buy you a cup of coffee and answer any questions, if I know the answers, that you have."

Daniella wrinkled her nose, but said, "All right."

Garrison headed to the staircase without saying goodbye.

But Roger turned to Joy and said, "See you tonight."

She smiled. She was looking forward to it.

After they left, Joy remembered the other thing—besides the mystery artist—she wanted to ask Abrielle about. "Shirley and Regina stopped by the shop earlier this afternoon." She relayed Regina's story about a friend of Belina's being hired at the Huguenot Church. "She said the friend had an 'initial name.'"

"JD," Abrielle said. "I remember when Daddy got him the job. He worked there for several years."

"Any chance he would have kept a key?"

"To that side door?"

Joy nodded.

Abrielle exhaled. "I doubt it. We can talk about it at dinner tonight with the others, but I'll let Detective Osborne know now." She took her phone from the pocket of her dress. "I hadn't thought of JD working at the church all those years ago—and I doubt anyone else remembered either."

After she arrived home from work, Joy showered, styled her hair, and put on her makeup. Then she dressed in her silver dress with the matching shawl that she'd worn to a work dinner of Wilson's a few years ago. It fell just below her knees, and she had a pair of navy pumps to go with it.

She put on lapis earrings and a lapis necklace and checked herself in the mirror. She was definitely a few years older than the last time she wore the outfit, but she didn't look bad. She smiled at herself. In fact, she looked good.

She took a ride share to the Fleury estate so she wouldn't have to worry about parking. When she arrived, Lloyd was at the gate to the driveway, letting a luxury sedan drive onto the property. He motioned for Joy to walk through the gate. The driver of the sedan parked in front of the garage door and then climbed out. It was Roger, wearing a black suit with a navy tie.

He waved and then strode toward her. "Joy." His eyes sparkled. "You look lovely."

"Thank you." She smiled. "You look quite dashing."

He smiled and together they walked to the patio, where lights were strung through the trees bordering the patio.

As Roger and Joy neared the group, Marshall waved. "Joy," he called out, "it's so nice to see you." The patio door was open to the house, where another group gathered around a food table.

When Joy reached Marshall, he gave her a hug and a kiss on the cheek. The gesture warmed her heart. Then he shook Roger's hand. "How are you, Roger?"

"Joy!" Claire stood in the open doorway. "Come in!"

Anne and Ralph and Evelyn and James were all inside. As Joy stepped into what looked like a library, she noted Abrielle and Belina standing over by the fireplace deep in conversation—a rather tense one by the looks of it.

"What a beautiful dress," Claire said to Joy.

"Thank you. So is yours."

Claire's three-quarter sleeve emerald-green dress had a full pleated skirt. It was darling, and the sort of style Claire pulled off with a flourish.

"Drinks are over there." Claire pointed to the table to the left and then to the right. "And hors d'oeuvres there."

"Sounds good," Joy said.

After greeting Anne and Evelyn and their husbands, Joy examined the pot of warm spiced olives and then the cheese plate, which was labeled *Bleu d'Auvergne. Camembert. Vieux-Boulogne. Cantal.*

Joy thought of the cheesemonger saying that Wilson used to quote. *"Something old, something new, something stinky, and something blue."* She could identify the bleu cheese, for sure. And she recognized the Camembert, which was from Normandy and had always been a favorite.

She took a plate from the stack and dished up a bit of each cheese, keeping them in the order of the labels, and then dished up a few olives and a slice of the baguette.

She sniffed the plate. The Vieux-Boulogne was definitely the stinky one.

Roger stepped to her side. "Cantal cheese." He reached for a plate. "Did you know it's one of the oldest cheeses in France? I believe it dates back to the Gauls and became popular when it was served to Louis XIV."

Joy took a bite. It had a soft inside and a tangy taste. "It's good," she said.

Roger dished some olives onto his plate. "It's one of my favorites. I'm not sure if it's the history or the taste, or maybe a combination." He smiled, warming Joy's heart.

Joy tried one of the olives as she looked around the room. The walls were lined with shelves, filled with books, except for the area of the fireplace, where Abrielle and Belina still stood.

There was a leather couch in the middle of the room that was back to back with a desk.

Anne and Evelyn joined Joy as Roger drifted toward Ralph and James.

"This is such a lovely room," Joy said.

"Wait until you see the rest of the house," Evelyn said. "Claire renovated each and every room."

Claire overheard them and said, "It only took me twenty years."

"Only." Evelyn shook her head. "You researched every detail. It would have taken anyone else a hundred."

Claire laughed. "Oh, I doubt that. But you know, I do like things to be done right. It was the perfect project for me." She stepped to Joy's side and touched her elbow. "I'll give you a quick tour of the first floor." There were three floors altogether.

From the library, Claire led Joy through a hallway and into a dining room. The massive table was set for twelve with china and silver. A bouquet of dahlias sat in the middle.

"Belina brought the flowers," Claire said.

"Lovely," Joy murmured, knowing they came from Gwen's farm.

A wall of windows faced the backyard but the curtains were drawn. A chandelier, casting soft light across the room, hung over the table.

"The kitchen is through here." Claire pointed and led the way. "Do you remember Brooke?"

Joy answered, "Of course."

Claire's daughter stood in the middle of a completely modern kitchen with a breakfast nook on the far side. Brooke wore an apron tied around her waist. "Hi, Joy." Her hair was piled on top of her head. "Mom," she said. "We should serve the soup soon."

"Right," Claire said. "I'll call everyone to the table in just a minute. I'll show Joy the living room and then call the others."

As Joy followed her out of the kitchen, Claire said, "Brooke is my sous chef and helps serve dinner. She's been helping me since she was ten."

"Nice," Joy said as they stepped into the living room.

It was grand and featured another fireplace with a carved mantel and bookcases on either side. A large area rug covered a portion of the wood floor. There was a beautiful painting of the home over the mantel. It reminded Joy of the paintings in the hallway of the hospital.

"Who painted that?" Joy asked.

"Belina did." Claire turned toward her. "Isn't she good?"

Joy nodded.

"She did that years ago, when she was in Paris and homesick. She hasn't painted in years."

"What a shame." Obviously Belina had painted the pieces in the hallway at the hospital too.

Joy stepped closer to the painting. There was a blond woman at the patio gate. "Who's the woman?"

"Our mother." Claire said, hurrying back toward the dining room. "I'm going to grab my apron. Would you go tell the others it's time to eat?"

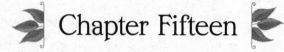

Chapter Fifteen

TEN MINUTES LATER, EVERYONE HAD gathered around the table, where Claire had seated Joy and Roger next to each other. Lloyd said a blessing over the food, adding a request for a blessing over the auction. "You know we want to help fund Mercy Hospital," he prayed. "May our work help in the healing of others, but also in the good of our own souls."

Several people, including Joy, echoed his amen. Lloyd didn't sound like someone who'd orchestrated a theft. Joy tried to put those thoughts aside. She liked Lloyd's idea of the work they all did helping others but also helping to grow themselves too. That was the way the Lord worked.

She added a prayer for healing among the Fleury sisters—and healing between Hope and herself too.

Brooke and Claire served the French onion soup, which was delicious. Once everyone finished it, Brooke cleared the bowls and then she and Claire served the chicken confit. It was delicious too. Joy could taste juniper berries in the fresh diced tomatoes, plus garlic and thyme. The dish was served atop mashed potatoes with steamed green beans on the side. More baguettes, freshly made, were also served.

As they ate, Marshall said to Belina, "I thought JD would be joining us. I was looking forward to seeing him."

Belina shot a look at Abrielle, who simply shrugged.

"He planned to come," Belina said, "but Abrielle scared him away."

Marshall dabbed at the corners of his mouth with a napkin. "What happened?"

"A vague memory from thirty years ago," Belina said. "Remember when you got JD the job at the church? Abrielle thinks he still has a key to the side door and used it to enter the church on Sunday morning."

"Oh." Marshall had a confused expression on his face. "Why would he have a key from thirty years ago?"

"Exactly," Belina said. "A detective came to talk to JD right before we were supposed to leave. He was too embarrassed to come."

Joy's face grew warm, knowing she was the source of the disagreement between the sisters.

"That's a shame," Marshall said. "But I can see why the detective needed to ask him. All possibilities must be explored, correct? Reverend Martin gave the detective a list of everyone who might have a key, from years back. But he wouldn't have known about JD, and I forgot about him working at the church. If I'd remembered, I would have said something."

Claire remained silent on the topic and a moment later stood and started clearing the entrée plates. Brooke joined her.

Joy leaned forward a little and addressed Marshall, who sat across the table from her. "I've enjoyed researching Doc Fleury this week. I read through his letters at the college library."

"I haven't read those since I was a young man," Marshall said. "I'm afraid I don't remember much."

"They're fascinating. The collection includes copies of letters he sent to people and letters from those he corresponded with—up until 1871. After that, until his death in 1874, there are no letters. Just two notes right before he passed away. I was wondering if you have anything here at the house, specifically from his nephew and nieces in France?"

Marshall tapped his chin with his index finger. "Let me think. Since I've moved into the cottage, I can't always remember where things are." He looked around. "Where's Claire?"

She stepped to the kitchen door. "Here I am, Daddy."

"Do you know where the carved box is that we found during the remodel? It used to be in the library."

"It's still there," she said. "On the top shelf."

Lloyd stood. "I'll get it."

As Lloyd left the room, Marshall said, "If I remember correctly there are a couple of postcards in the box, from France, sent not too long after postcards were first fashionable."

When Lloyd returned, he handed a box, about eight inches by six inches, to Marshall.

"Thank you." Marshall took it and placed it on the table. As he opened it, Joy could see both a fleur-de-lis and a palmetto carved on the top.

"Hold on just a second, Daddy," Claire said. "We're going to serve dessert and coffee. Then you can open the box."

Belina groaned while Abrielle laughed. "Leave it to Claire to have her dessert usurp a century-old mystery." Abrielle wagged her finger at her sister. "No, ma'am. Dessert can wait."

Marshall winked at Abrielle and said, "Waiting a few more minutes won't hurt anything."

Claire sighed. "No, Daddy. Abrielle's right—dessert can wait." She turned and flashed a smile at Lloyd. "And you thought I couldn't be flexible."

He laughed.

Claire put a hand on her hip and said, "Go ahead, Daddy. Let's see if there's anything in that box to help exonerate Doc Fleury."

Marshall opened the box and lifted out a small stack of postcards. He counted them. "There are six." He held up the first. "They're all hand-painted." He flipped it over. "Ah, now I remember. They're all written in French." Belina sat next to him, and he met her eyes. "Would you translate them for us?"

"After I wash my hands." She glanced up at Claire. "Do you have any gloves?"

"Not archival," Claire said. "But I have some cotton ones."

A few minutes later, Belina was back at the table pulling on a pair of white gloves.

Marshall slid the box toward her. She picked up the postcards and thumbed through them as she said, "Why didn't you show these to me before?"

"We only found them a couple of years ago," Claire said. "During the remodel. They were in the attic. Daddy's kept them in the library, trying to decide what to do with them." She shook her head. "I forgot all about them."

Belina muttered, "I suppose they'll be donated to the same place that all the other family documents have been…"

"We'll see," Marshall answered.

Belina shuffled the postcards around. Joy assumed she was putting them in chronological order. "They're all written by the same person, but none of them are signed. They're all addressed to Uncle Arthur Fleury and dated between September 1872 and August 1873." She held up the first two, showing the fronts. The first was of a field of golden wheat with an oak tree in the middle. The other was of a trail through a forest, flocked with snow.

Belina said, "I'll do my best to translate, although my French is rusty." She cleared her throat. "'Dear Uncle Arthur, I think often of your visit and how it blessed us. We will always miss our dear cousin Susie, but having you with us again soothed our souls. I will write more soon but wanted to inform you that *Maman* and Papa have agreed, based on my recent work, to let me live in Paris with T and to finally study art.'"

The second postcard was a Christmas greeting. The third was an update about art school. Belina read, "'I am only one of two women in the program, and the instructors are not happy that we've been allowed to study at their school. Many still do not think we should study human anatomy, in particular. Please tell Cousin Alexander hello and that we long to see him and his family, along with you, dear Uncle Arthur.'" Belina looked up.

The next was written before Easter and the painting was of a field of daffodils. "'As you celebrate the resurrection of our Lord, we pray for renewal in your own life. We will all be together on the farm for Easter and will remember how much Susie loved it there.'"

The front of the fifth postcard was of a field of lavender. "'We will all meet at the farm next week and spend the summer together. T and I will paint. Maman and Papa will rest and garden. Wish you were joining us, dearest Uncle Arthur.'"

Belina held up the last postcard, dated the first of August, 1873. It was of the garden at the farm and looked very similar to the painting *Belina in the Garden* but without Belina. "'Dear Uncle Arthur,

T painted this card. Our thoughts are still on Susie and the places she loved most in the village. With affection, CSJ.'"

Belina looked up. "That's it. It all seems pretty vague."

Claire frowned. "Except T painted a card that looks like the setting for *Belina in the Garden*."

Abrielle nodded.

Joy said, "It was Belina who invited Doc Fleury to France in 1871, and a note from Alexander to Doc Fleury, sent a few days before the doctor died, indicated that he named his daughter Belina Estelle after his deceased mother and Doc Fleury's favorite niece."

"Is there any correspondence between him and his other nieces?" Abrielle asked.

Joy shook her head. "But Susie Fleury, when she was staying in France, wrote to her father that Theodore and Belina were the most talented artistically out of the four youngest children."

"Well, there you have it, y'all." Abrielle's voice sounded strained. "Another Belina was a favorite of a Fleury patriarch." She laughed, but it didn't come off as funny.

"All of my daughters are my favorite," Marshall said, a worried expression on his face.

"Of course we are," Claire said. "Abrielle was joking." She glanced at Belina. "If appears as if there were two Belinas, more than a century apart, who were gifted painters."

Joy couldn't help but note that Claire used past tense—who *were* gifted painters.

Before anyone responded, Abrielle's phone buzzed. She pulled it from her pocket. "It's Jacque De Villiers. He's in town. He wants to meet with me."

Claire clapped her hands together. "Invite him for dessert."

"Good idea," Abrielle said. "And then I'm going to text Detective Osborne. Maybe she can 'show up.' It might be her best chance to talk with him."

Fifteen minutes later, Abrielle led Jacque De Villiers into the dining room and introduced him to everyone. He greeted each person with an accent, but it sounded more nasal than French to Joy, although she certainly wasn't an expert. He was a dashing man with a slim build, a thick head of dark hair with a hint of gray at his temples, and vibrant brown eyes. He wore a tailored jacket and trousers, a button-up white shirt, and expensive leather shoes.

"What a delight to be included in your dinner party for dessert," he said. "I feared I'd be crashing the party, but Abrielle assured me no." He smiled. "But I'm not sure I can believe her."

"*Au contraire*," Belina said. "We're happy to have you join us."

"Well, I must say, I'm pleased to meet Abrielle's papa and her sisters, because I want all of you to know how devastated I was to find out about the missing Joubert." He shook his head. "Unbelievable."

Abrielle directed him to the chair beside hers that Lloyd had added to the table.

He sat and so did Abrielle.

"I was worried about you," Abrielle said to Jacque, "when you didn't answer my texts or Patrick's either."

"*Oui, mademoiselle*, that does look odd, doesn't it?" He grimaced. "I was on a sort of pilgrimage, one my papa sent me on, and completely disconnected. I do that every once in a while. It does wonders for one's soul. I knew Patrick had my back when it came to the painting and would take care of any details that came up. Anyway, there's a Huguenot artist who lives outside of Richmond that Papa and I are interested in."

Abrielle turned toward him. "Oh?"

"To add to our Huguenot collection. That's why we're interested in the Joubert—why we hoped all three were Jouberts."

"Interesting," Abrielle said. "I didn't realize you were Huguenot."

"I'm not." He smiled. "But Father still claims the connection, from our family's past. It's all fuzzy for me."

Claire interrupted the discussion by carrying out the dessert, which was displayed on a large crystal cake plate.

"It's a *Paris-brest*," she said. "A choux pastry ring filled with custard. Think of it as a giant chocolate éclair." She put it on one end of the sideboard, cut it with a flourish, and began placing slices on dessert plates. Brooke poured coffee into dainty cups on the other end of the sideboard.

Once the pastry and the coffee were distributed, Claire sat at her place at the end of the table and took a bite. All the others followed suit.

The Paris-brest was delicious. "Did you make this?" Joy asked Claire.

She nodded, demurely.

"She made everything we ate tonight," Lloyd said. "Even the baguettes."

Claire shook her head. "I didn't make the cheese."

Lloyd laughed. "But you probably could if you put your mind to it."

As everyone finished dessert, the doorbell rang again. "I'll get it," Claire said.

A minute later she escorted Detective Osborne into the dining room. "Look who's here!" she exclaimed.

Rebekah looked as poised as ever with her straight posture and her hair piled high on her head. "Oh, you have guests," she said to Claire and then waved to Abrielle. "Why didn't y'all tell me? I'm so sorry to interrupt."

"No, you're just in time for dessert." Claire addressed Lloyd. "Sweetie, I think we can squeeze in one more chair, by Joy."

He headed into the library while Claire poured another cup of coffee and placed another slice of dessert on a plate.

Within a couple of minutes, Rebekah had a place at the table, a slice of Paris-brest, and a cup of coffee. She grinned. "Well, this is a sight for sore eyes. My evening just got much better."

"What's going on?" Abrielle asked.

"Oh, the usual." She picked up her fork. "But I do have some good news. We're done with our investigation at the gallery, so you can hold the auction there."

"Wow," Abrielle said, glancing at Claire.

"We can do it," Claire said. "This means we won't need to have a post-dinner planning meeting. We'll just do what we always have. Email all of the artists tonight. Tell them to drop their work off at the gallery instead of at the hospital. And send a text to the cleaners right now. See if they can come in the morning. If not, I'll do it."

"All right." Abrielle took out her phone.

Jacque smiled at her. "That's wonderful news. I'm so glad I'll be in town for the auction. Perhaps I can make some other acquisitions in Charleston before I have to return home."

Rebekah touched her forehead. "I just put it together. You are *the* Jacque De Villiers. The one interested in buying the Joubert painting."

"The one and only," he said. "I'm guessing you have some questions for me, since I saw the painting on Friday and it disappeared soon after."

Rebekah nodded as she took a bite of the dessert.

Jacque pulled a piece of paper from the pocket of his jacket. "I suspected so. I was going to ask Abrielle to give this to the lead investigator, but now I can give it to you. It's a list of the people I've seen in and around Richmond this past week, going through today." He passed the piece of paper to Claire who passed it to Evelyn who passed it to James who passed it to Anne who passed it to Ralph who passed it to Rebekah.

"My alibi, if you will," Jacque said.

If Jacque De Villiers was guilty, he clearly believed he couldn't be proven so.

"Thank you. Where are you staying?"

"The Spectator Hotel."

Rebekah slipped the piece of paper into her pocket. "I'll be in touch tomorrow if I have any questions."

Jacque nodded. "I put my number on the paper too, and I promise to answer my phone." He wagged his finger as he smiled. "No more electronics holiday for me."

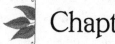 Chapter Sixteen

As they stood from dinner, Roger said, "I saw someone drop you off. Will they be picking you up too?"

Joy held up her phone. "It was a ride share. I was just going to arrange for a ride home."

"May I take you?" he asked.

"Oh, I don't want to inconvenience you."

"Not at all," he said.

After they said their goodbyes and thank-yous to Claire and her family and the others, Joy walked with Roger to his car. It was only a few minutes to her house. On the way, Joy's phone buzzed. *Hope.*

"I'm sorry," she said to Roger. "It's my sister. I should answer it."

He turned onto Wentworth Street. "Of course."

Joy spoke softly. "Hi, Hope."

Without even saying hello, Hope said, "I need to stay with you tonight."

"Everything all right?"

"Kind of," Hope answered. "I told Sabrina I was missing you and thought I should give you a turn."

"All right." Joy glanced at Roger as he stopped at the curb in front of her house. "Come on over. I'll be ready for you."

She put her phone back in her purse. "Thank you for the ride."

"You're welcome. See you on Saturday."

Joy unbuckled her seat belt. "See you then."

Roger came around the car and opened her door. He extended his hand, and she took it, stepping out of the car. It had been a long time since someone had opened a car door for her.

"Good night," she said as she started up the walk to her house. When she reached the door, she unlocked it and then turned. Roger still stood on the sidewalk. She waved and he waved back. She stepped into the house and closed and locked the door behind her, touched by Roger's thoughtfulness. He seemed liked a kind and caring man.

She guessed she had just enough time to change her dress before Hope arrived. But by the time she'd slipped her shoes off and started for the staircase, the doorbell rang.

She opened the door to find Hope on her doorstep, her bag slung over her shoulder.

Joy chuckled. Hope must have been around the corner when she called. "That was fast," she teased.

Hope shrugged. "I was counting on you saying yes."

"Of course I'd say yes." Joy motioned for her to come inside.

Hope shuffled inside. "I saw someone drop you off. And you're all dressed up."

"A friend working on the auction brought me home. And we were at a dinner for the planning committee."

"Sounds like fun," Hope said.

"Is everything okay with you and Sabrina?"

"Like I said before, I think I outstayed my welcome." Hope leaned against the newel post of the staircase. "And, honestly, I need a break. Hanging out with a five-year-old is more tiring than I remembered."

Joy smiled. It had been a long time since Sabrina was five.

Hope yawned, which was a relief to Joy. She was happy to have her sister stay with her, but she didn't want to stay up much later.

Joy showed Hope the living room, kitchen, and patio and then grabbed Hope's bag. "I'll carry it for you."

Hope said, "Your house is lovely."

"Thank you. I'll show you your room." She motioned toward the staircase. "Will you be all right going up the stairs?"

Hope nodded.

A half hour later, Hope was settled down for the night and Joy was in her pajamas and headed to bed. Once her head hit the pillow, she fell asleep immediately. But three hours later she was wide awake. If Belina Joubert had painted five of those six postcards, what happened to her painting career? Had it ever taken off?

And what about the story of the De Villiers family's interest in Huguenot artists? Was that legit or just a ruse for Jacque going missing all week?

She got up, grabbed her laptop, and climbed back in bed with it. She would start by researching female artists in France in the 1870s. There weren't many. Up until that decade, female artists stuck with painting landscapes, but starting in the early 1870s a handful were allowed to study art, including anatomy. That aligned with the information from the postcard.

Joy researched Belina Joubert but didn't come up with anything. She did find a book titled *Les Femmes Artistes, au Début* by Deborah Bernard. Joy found a website for the author and then clicked on the contact button. An email window popped up and Joy quickly wrote, *I'm looking for information on a sister of Theodore Joubert, Belina Joubert. She may have attended art school in Paris in the early 1870s. Have you come across any information about her? Thank you, Joy Atkins, Charleston, SC.*

Joy yawned. She wasn't sure she'd found anything helpful. Hopefully something in the box Evelyn had dropped off in the gift shop would corroborate that Belina Joubert was an artist. But how could they prove, even with that information, that she was the one who created the other two paintings?

Apparently Jacque hadn't suspected that Belina Joubert was the artist of the other two paintings. Wouldn't he have wanted them if he had? Belina Joubert was also a Huguenot artist.

Joy googled Huguenot artists and found paintings from the late 1500s to the early 1800s but nothing after that, except for an artist in New York State from the 1900s who did western scenes. She googled female Huguenot artists but nothing turned up at all.

None of it made any sense to her, including why a millionaire art collector would steal a painting.

It made more sense that Belina and JD took the painting.

Or could Patrick Ray and Jacque De Villiers be working in cahoots? Or perhaps Abrielle made a pact with one of them so that she could keep all the money to herself? Maybe Belina appeared to be the black sheep of the family, but really it was Abrielle.

Joy put the laptop on her desk and climbed back under the covers. She was no closer to figuring out who had stolen the paintings—and then put the two in the custodian's closet and set it on fire—than she'd been on Sunday afternoon. She closed her eyes, doubting sleep would come.

She awoke with a start to the smell of bacon frying and coffee brewing. She was pretty sure she didn't have bacon in the house—although she definitely had coffee. She reached for her phone. 5:40. She'd overslept. She slid out of bed, shuffled to her closet, picked out an outfit, and headed to the bathroom for a quick shower.

Once ready, she headed downstairs, where Hope sat at the kitchen table with a mug in front of her, looking at something on her phone. "There you are, sleepyhead."

"What do you mean?" Joy headed straight for the coffee. "I'm ready and rarin' to go."

"Aww, that's what Dad used to say." Hope smiled. "I made bacon."

"I smelled it," Joy said. "Where did you find it?"

"The freezer," Hope said.

Ah. Now Joy remembered stashing half a package there, after using the other half to make a hot potato salad earlier in the summer.

"I made biscuits too," Hope said. "And I can fry you some eggs."

Joy shook her head. "Biscuits and bacon will do. Thank you." She grabbed a plate. "Want to go sit out on the patio?"

"Sure."

As they stepped outside, Hope said, "This area looked great last night but it's even more amazing in the daylight. It's so you, Joy, with all the plants and flowers."

Joy put her cup and plate on the table. "Nothing will replace the fields of bluebells in Texas or the wide open spaces, but this little bit of heaven makes Charleston a perfect place for me."

Hope nodded. "I can see why. What a great spot to start your day."

Joy smiled. "It is. And I pretty much end my day here too, generally."

Once Joy finished her breakfast and coffee, and thanked Hope again, she asked, "What are your plans for today?"

Hope shrugged. "I might drive around and see what I can see, get acclimated with the area. Take a look at the college and the office where I'll be working."

Joy thought of the research Hope had done on Alexander Fleury and his children. Perhaps she'd be willing to help again. "If you want a project, I have a box of documents that might have something to do with the Fleury family. Evelyn doesn't have time to go through them, and I'm not sure how much time I'll have either."

"That sounds like fun," Hope said. "I'll get dressed and come down to the hospital."

Ninety minutes later, Joy had the gift shop open and was waiting on a customer buying a stack of get-well cards when Hope came through the front door. Joy gave her a wave and said, "Coffee's on. Help yourself." She nodded toward the counter in the back.

Hope poured herself a cup. When Joy finished with the customer, she said, "The box is in my office."

She led the way and told Hope to sit down at the desk and put on the archival gloves that Evelyn had provided. "The thing to do is sort everything. One pile for everything that has nothing to do with the Fleurys. One pile for anything that has to do with Doc Fleury's business. Another that has anything to do with Doc Fleury's personal life. If there's anything written in French, put that in his personal file—unless you can be sure it's business."

"Great." Hope rubbed her hands together. "I love this sort of thing."

Joy met her sister's gaze. "Thank you. I really appreciate it."

Hope smiled in return. "You're welcome."

Joy helped one customer choose a vase for a friend and then another one choose a plant for a neighbor. Then, with no one in the shop, she returned to the office.

"This is fascinating," Hope said, pointing at the piles on the desk. "The majority don't have to do with the Fleury family." She pointed to the largest pile. "But I have found a few things that have to do with them. A few business letters. And some bills. Plus three letters written in French." She pointed to the third pile.

"Oh, good. I'll see if Claire can ask Belina to come and translate them."

"Will that be awkward?" Hope asked. "Since I caused the accident."

"I don't think so," Joy said. "I'll tell Claire you're here."

A customer came into the shop, and Joy returned to the counter. When she had a spare minute, she texted Claire to see if she'd ask Belina to stop by, adding that Hope was helping to go through the box of documents.

Joy felt odd asking Belina to translate the letters, when she was still one of the top suspects for the theft of the painting. But she had seemed to do such a good job with the postcards the previous night. It was worth a try.

Belina arrived just after eleven. Hope had finished going through the box but hadn't found any more letters and only a few more business documents.

"How are you?" Hope asked Belina as Joy led her into the office.

"I'm fine," Belina said, a concerned expression on her face. "How are you?"

"Better, thank you for asking." Hope held up the letters and a second pair of archival gloves. "Thank you too, for coming to translate the letters."

"Of course," Belina said. "We need to know whether Doc Fleury was a thief or not. Both mysteries need to be solved."

Belina took the gloves and pulled them on. Then she took the letters from Hope.

"They're in chronological order," Hope said. "They're all dated after Arthur Fleury died although the first two are addressed to him."

"Interesting..." Belina scanned the first letter and then looked up. "The ink is pretty faded..." She started reading silently. When she finished, she said, "It's the same handwriting again and dated September 8, 1874, and they're signed *BJ*."

"That is interesting," Joy said.

"She said that she was sending three 'articles' to him, as gifts. Then she gives news of the family, that her mother's health isn't good, that her father is walking with a cane, that her older brothers and sisters are busy with their families, that her sister Abrielle has a beau, and that her sister Claire is working as a tutor for the De Villiers family."

"What?"

"They lived in Brussels. BJ goes on to say the Jouberts have done business with the De Villiers family before and that they purchased one of Theodore's paintings and wanted more. She writes, 'I wish they would be interested in buying one or two of mine. I haven't sold a single one.'"

"Wow," Joy said. "The letter connects the De Villiers family to both the Jouberts and to a desire for Theodore's work."

Belina nodded. "I wonder if she used BJ professionally, so buyers wouldn't suspect she was female. Perhaps she decided to use her initials for personal correspondence too." She handed the letter back to Hope and picked up the second.

"This one is dated December 6, 1874," Belina said, "and is addressed to Arthur too."

Joy clasped her hands. "How odd that Alexander didn't let them know that Arthur had passed away by then."

"Yes," Belina answered and then silently read the letter. "This is from BJ too. She's concerned that she hasn't heard from Arthur and says that she's been ill and is returning to the farm to recuperate. She asks Arthur to write to her there as soon as possible." She handed the letter to Hope, who turned over the third letter to Belina.

Again, Belina read it silently. Then she exhaled. "This is so sad. This one is from Abrielle Joubert and dated January 28, 1875. It's addressed to Alexander Fleury. First, she writes how sorry she was

to hear of Arthur's passing, saying the entire Joubert family is griev-
ing. Then she wrote, 'We have tragic news as well. Both Belina and
Maman passed away the third week of December of influenza. Papa
is beside himself, but I know you well know the grief he is feeling, as
we all are.'" Belina paused a moment. Perhaps she was thinking
about the loss of her own mother. Then she kept reading. "'Papa is
so despondent, in fact, that the business is suffering and so are our
finances.' She closes the letter with, 'We are missing a painting of
Theodore's, along with two of BJ's, as she preferred to be called.'"

This seemed to be proof that only one of the paintings was
by Theodore Joubert—and the other two were most likely painted
by Belina Joubert.

Belina kept reading. "They were painted in Susie's memory.
We've been offered a sum of money for Theodore's from the
De Villierses that will help our family immensely in our time of
need. Do you know anything about these? Theodore said that BJ, at
one time, hoped to ship them to you.'"

"Wow," Joy said. There definitely was a connection between the
Joubert family and the De Villierses, who wanted the paintings.
Could they have been the three "articles" that BJ sent to Arthur?

Belina looked up. "No matter what, it's sad that there was conflict over the paintings between the Joubert family and Alexander."

Joy thought so too. "But it looks hopeful, doesn't it, that the
paintings came to the Fleury family as gifts?"

"Unless the 'items' weren't the paintings. Whatever the circumstances," Belina said, "it's sad that the Jouberts wanted the paintings
back, and clearly Alexander never returned them. We never heard
about any French relatives growing up, so I'm guessing the rift was

never repaired." She sighed. "It seems both families were in a lot of pain."

"Yes," Joy said. "It also seems, even way back then, that the De Villiers family wanted Theodore's painting. I think that's information that Rebekah needs."

Belina nodded. "So do I."

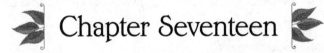

Chapter Seventeen

HOPE HAD GONE HOME AND Lacy arrived soon after for her shift in the gift shop, so Joy readied herself to walk to the gallery to help set up for the auction. But first she needed to return the box of documents to Evelyn. As she thought about the Joubert family, she thought of the email she'd sent in the middle of the night. Had she dreamed all of that? Or had she really sent an email?

She checked her phone and found the sent message but no response.

When she arrived at the records department, Evelyn was talking with Anne at the counter.

"How are you doing?" Anne asked Joy.

Joy started to yawn and covered her mouth. Then she laughed. "Sorry. I wasn't yawning because of the two of you." She told them about Hope showing up the night before and then her own middle-of-the night research.

She put the box on the counter. "There are three letters in here that are important." She relayed the content of the letters as translated by Belina, explaining the vague use of the word *article* instead of painting. "So it's still unclear whether Doc Fleury could have—or did—steal the paintings or not."

"Is there a copy of a letter to Belina from Arthur about the paintings?" Anne asked.

Joy shook her head. "It seems he stopped copying his letters by then."

"It would be nice to have something more to exonerate Doc Fleury," Anne said. "To know he didn't try to cheat the Joubert family out of those paintings. Alexander too."

"I agree," said Joy.

Evelyn pulled her pencil from her bun and made a mark on the ledger in front of her. Joy knew she was checking the box back in.

"I'll keep looking this afternoon and see if I can find anything else," Evelyn said.

"Aren't you coming to the gallery?"

Evelyn shook her head. "I'm too busy to take time off. Besides, since the auction will be at the gallery now, Abrielle won't need much help. She has the entire process down."

"What about you, Anne?" Joy asked.

"I need to head back to help with a couple of discharges and then pick up Addie. We'll stop by and see if any errands need to be run."

"All right." Joy patted the box. "Thank you. I'll keep hoping something more definitive appears. And that we can find the present-day thief."

As Joy headed toward the gallery, she thought of JD and Belina. They certainly had the motivation to steal the painting. Jacque De Villiers had the motivation but not the need. He could afford the painting if he wanted to buy it. Belina couldn't, and her sisters wouldn't have ever given it to her, even if she asked.

Joy arrived at the gallery and paused for a moment on the sidewalk, admiring the white angel's-trumpet blooms in the black window boxes.

The gallery was closed in preparation for the auction, and Claire told Joy the front door would be locked, for security reasons, but to knock and Grey would let her in.

She hurried up the steps and knocked. Immediately the door popped open. Grey stood in front of her with a smile on his face. He swept his arm in a wide arc, welcoming her inside.

"Isn't it great that we can have the auction here?"

"Yes, sir," Joy said. "How are you?"

"Great. And innocent. I mean, I knew all along, but even Detective Osborne agrees that I am after questioning my sister and her friends and looking at the security footage at the gas station close to our cabin that shows I didn't leave the area that night." He grinned. "I *am not* the thief."

Joy smiled back. "I'm so happy to hear that."

"Abrielle's in the back room." Grey pointed to the counter, which was covered with paintings wrapped in brown paper. "As soon as she's done back there, we're going to start hanging these."

"I'll go check in with her." Joy doubted she'd be any help hanging the paintings but hopefully she could help with other things.

As Joy neared the back room, she heard voices. Abrielle's and one she didn't recognize. She stopped at the doorway. Abrielle was talking to a woman wearing jeans and a work smock. Reading glasses were perched on her nose, and her gray hair was piled on top of her head.

"Hello," Joy said.

Abrielle turned to her. "Oh, hi, Joy." She motioned to the woman. "This is Pamela DePass. She's the art restorer from Savannah. Thankfully, she had time to come work on our two." Abrielle turned to Pamela. "This is Joy Atkins. She's helping with the auction."

"Nice to meet you," Joy said to Pamela.

She smiled and said, "Likewise."

"Rebekah released the paintings today from the station. The sooner they can be restored the better as far as the smoke damage."

That made sense.

On the closest table, lying flat, was a framed portrait of a man. His hair was dark and thick, and he wore sideburns. He sat sideways with his face pointed toward the artist. He wore a white shirt and a black cravat at his neck in a bow tie style. His dark green tailored jacket had fitted sleeves and big buttons. His eyes were dark and bright and his slight smile seemed warm and kind, reminding Joy of Marshall's. "Is that Doc Fleury?" Joy asked.

Abrielle nodded. "I'm not sure what to do with him yet. It all depends on whether Daniella runs another scathing article in the morning or not, since we haven't been able to exonerate him." She sighed. "I'm going to start hanging the paintings for the auction." She turned to Joy. "Would you take over mounting the auction labels on these cards?"

"Of course." The labels and cards were arranged on the back table.

As she worked she peered at the two paintings on the front table. "Pamela, is it all right if I ask you a question?"

"Sure."

"Do you have any thoughts on who might be the thief?"

Pamela shook her head. "I'm not going to touch that with a—" She held up the brush she was using. "A ten-foot pole or brush or whatever. I'm just glad Detective Osborne cleared me."

Joy raised her eyebrows.

Pamela nodded. "She drove all the way to Savannah on Monday to question me. I had an alibi that held—my best friend from Seattle was visiting and we left Savannah Friday morning to spend the weekend in Augusta. The detective wanted to know who in the business might be involved. Sure, I can think of a half dozen people who might be audacious enough to try to pull something like this off, but no one who would be malicious enough to leave these two paintings in a closet and then set it on fire."

Joy nodded in agreement. "It's odd, isn't it? That's the part I don't understand either. I get stealing the Joubert, but why set the fire?"

They continued with their work in silence, and when Joy finished, she stacked the mounted labels and said to Pamela, "It's been nice to meet you."

"Oh, you'll see me before I leave," Pamela said. "I'll probably be working on these right up until the time of the auction tomorrow."

As Joy headed toward the door, shouting at the front of the gallery startled her. "I just want you to be honest," Abrielle yelled. "Why in the world would you show up now, after all these years? I know you always wanted that painting."

Joy hesitated a moment, not sure whether to continue up the hall or not. A long pause convinced her to but when she reached the lobby, Belina, who was in the front gallery with Abrielle, said, "I should have known you would blame me for stealing *Belina in the*

Garden, but do you really think I could set a fire in our church, in a closet with the other two paintings?"

"Yes, I do," Abrielle said. "Absolutely. To hurt Claire and me. You grabbed what you wanted. You don't care about us."

Joy slinked over to the counter by Grey. He made a pained face. "I came home to spend time with Daddy."

"But didn't tell us you were here. We wouldn't know even now if Joy's sister hadn't pulled in front of JD's pickup."

"I was working up the nerve to contact you," Belina said. "I didn't expect *this*." She paused. "But I certainly expected some sort of drama coming from you."

"From me?" Abrielle's voice was incredulous. "The drama is from you. Every. Single. Time. You come home."

"Do you realize how ridiculous you sound?" Belina said. "Do you think I could disarm the security system? Delete the video?"

"No," Abrielle said. "But I think you and JD working together could. Just look at his record."

"Petty larceny," Belina said. "From almost thirty years ago. And he was going to return the wallet." She lowered her voice. "I adore JD. I always have. But he's not bright enough to pull something like this off." Belina stepped toward the french doors, where Joy could see her.

"You could have easily guessed the security code," Abrielle said. "It was your birthday."

Belina crossed her arms. "I never would have guessed it—but someone else might have. The Belina House Gallery. The birthday of the sister named Belina? Who chose the code?"

"Daddy chose this one, a month ago. When the new system was installed," Abrielle answered.

Belina shook her head. "Weird."

"And your alibi—that you were sleeping on JD's couch—can't be corroborated," Abrielle said, "not when you and JD are both suspects."

"My alibi is as good as yours," Belina said. "You live above the crime scene. You knew the code—and the security system."

Abrielle's voice grew even louder. "Who else would have taken it besides you? We're running out of suspects."

"How about Jacque De Villiers? Has he been cleared?"

"Why would he steal something he can buy?"

Belina shrugged. "Maybe you should ask him."

"I'm not going to accuse one of Europe's top art collectors of stealing from us. I can only imagine the reaction to that from the art world. I don't know how I'm going to make this business work as it is. I'd be closed by Monday if I went after Jacque De Villiers."

"And yet—" Belina's voice trembled. "You have no problem accusing me, your own sister." She turned toward the counter and then winced when she saw Grey and Joy. She opened the french doors, stepped into the lobby, and then quickly left the gallery.

Joy squared her shoulders and gave Grey what felt like a sad smile. She did feel sad. About the missing painting. The damaged ones. And the rift between the Fleury sisters. The paintings could be a metaphor for their lives—Belina leaving, Abrielle and Claire staying, but showing damage.

She thought of what Regina said about families being fragile systems. That was certainly true. But she reminded herself that what mattered was that the conflict was repaired. Joy said a prayer for healing for Belina and Abrielle.

Joy hoped Abrielle would come out of the gallery and follow Belina, but she didn't. Finally, Joy stepped into the gallery and said, "I finished the labels."

Abrielle, who had a painting in her hands, said. "Thank you. Put those on the lobby counter. I'll get to them next. Would you ask Grey to come help me? And could you keep an eye on the front door?"

"Sure." Joy did as Abrielle asked and then stood at the counter, thinking through the case. Pamela was off the long-shot list. So was Lloyd.

If Abrielle hadn't let the insurance policy lapse, she'd be a viable suspect. But as it was, she had everything to lose—and nothing to gain.

Belina was the likely suspect. She had the motivation to steal the painting, and it was plausible she or JD could have figured out the security system. She definitely had a lot of resentment toward her sisters, Abrielle in particular.

Joy had a text from Anne that Addie wasn't feeling well so she wouldn't be stopping by the gallery after all. Joy let Abrielle know and then admired the artwork in the first room. There were landscapes, seascapes, and cityscapes, all of or around Charleston.

A few more artists dropped off their paintings, and then Abrielle and Grey decided to take a break. "Come sit in my office for a minute," Abrielle said to Joy. "I want to hear your opinion about something."

Joy followed Abrielle down the hall.

When they sat down, Abrielle asked, "Did you overhear my conversation with Belina?"

"Some of it," Joy said. "I'm not sure how much."

Abrielle put her head in her hands. "I hate this conflict between us, but I'm sure she took the painting. You don't know how many times over the years she's claimed ownership, just because she shares a name with it. That was all chance, right? She shouldn't have any more right to it than Claire or I do."

Joy wasn't sure what to say. "What does your father say?"

"That the three paintings belong to all of us. That we have to work it out."

"I did overhear you say that you believe Belina could have pulled off the theft with JD's help."

Abrielle nodded. "She says she couldn't have figured out the security system, but she's worked in all sorts of places that would have had similar systems."

"I know you've been asked this over and over, but can you think of anyone else who might have known the security code? Watched you key it in? Someone with an interest or motivation?"

Abrielle shook her head.

"You showed the paintings to Jacque after hours," Joy said. "Did you ever give anyone else a private viewing?"

She started to shake her head again but then stopped. "Patrick. He was here about a month ago, just after the new system was installed. Before, he always came during business hours, but this was after he believed that *Belina in the Garden* and the other two might be Jouberts and Pamela had looked at the paintings a couple of times. He flew in that afternoon and had some other appointments that lasted past closing time. He asked to see the paintings, and I obliged. He may have seen me key in the code."

"You didn't change it since then?"

Abrielle shook her head. "Stupid, huh? Especially after it seemed I might have at least one Joubert on the premises. And even more so after I let the insurance money lapse." In a quiet voice she said, "I got so angry at Belina—but really I'm angry at myself. It was my job to protect those paintings, including from Belina, to keep them safe. And I failed. Foolishly."

Joy reached over and patted Abrielle's arm. "Don't be too hard on yourself. It won't help find out who took the painting or where it is."

Abrielle's shoulder's shook. Was she crying?

"This all goes back to when Mama died. And I think I've had an epiphany about all of it," Abrielle said, her voice muffled. "Belina blamed herself and so did I. Belina was brilliant but wild in high school, hanging out with JD and his crazy friends. A week before her graduation, on a weeknight, she was out really late and Mama went looking for her, afraid she was in danger. Belina was down by the river, partying. A semitruck driver drifted into Mama's lane and she swerved but then overcorrected, sending her down an embankment and down into the river. Belina never got over it—and neither did I. She blamed herself, but I blamed her even more. She had reason to resent me all these years, far more than I had to resent her. Belina was seventeen, doing what teenagers do. I see that now, but I've never told her that."

"It's not too late to tell her," Joy said.

Abrielle, her eyes heavy, said, "I doubt she'll listen to me now."

"You can try."

Abrielle nodded, her expression still sad, as Joy's phone dinged. It was a text from Amy at the college. I FOUND A BOX OF DOCU-

MENTS CONNECTED TO ARTHUR FLEURY. CAN YOU COME TAKE A
LOOK?

I'LL BE THERE ASAP, Joy texted back.

She looked up at Abrielle. "Amy from the college library found
another box of documents connected to Doc Fleury. I'm going to go
take a look."

"Great." Abrielle stood and flapped her hand. "Go, go. Let's
hope you find something."

Fifteen minutes later, Joy stood in front of the counter, staring at
a gray archival box.

"I found it on the shelf behind the binders of letters," Amy said.
"For some reason, it doesn't seem like the contents have been invento-
ried." Amy slid a pair of archival gloves toward Joy and then the box.

"Thank you," Joy said. As she headed for the table, she whispered a prayer that she would find something—anything—that
might exonerate Doc Fleury. Or prove him guilty. She simply wanted
the truth.

Joy pulled the documents from the box, one at a time. It was
much like the collection Hope had gone through that morning with
a mismatch of items, business documents mixed in with personal.
Near the bottom of the box were two pieces of attached paper. She
picked them up. The top one was some sort of form.

At the top, the letterhead read, *United States Customs Service.*

It was dated September 26, 1873. The ink was faint but under
Items was written *3 paintings.* On the next line was written *gift.* At
the bottom was the signature of Dr. Arthur Fleury.

The second paper was a French document. She could make out
the word *trois articles* and *les peintures, de Theodore Joubert et BJ*

Joubert and *cadeau*. At the bottom of the document was the signature of Belina Joubert.

Relief flooded through Joy as she took pictures of each document. Now Marshall and the Fleury sisters could unveil Doc Fleury's portrait with pride. The three paintings had been a gift, sent by Belina in 1873.

Joy put the items back in the box and then texted the photographs to Claire and Abrielle, adding PLEASE LET BELINA KNOW. Then she texted Evelyn, Anne, and Hope the pictures, along with GOOD NEWS!

When she returned the box to Amy, she explained what she'd found. "It was exactly what I'd hoped for."

"Great! I've already contacted the historical society," Amy said. "They're going to send someone over to inventory the box on Monday."

As Joy took the stairs down from the library, her phone blew up with return texts.

ALEXANDER AND MICHAEL STARTED THE BELINA HOUSE GALLERY IN 1901, Abrielle texted. WOULDN'T THEY HAVE IDENTIFIED THE ONE PAINTING AS A THEODORE JOUBERT THEN?

No, Joy texted back. IF THE JOUBERT FAMILY FOUND OUT, THEY MIGHT HAVE EXPECTED THE PAINTINGS BACK. BUT THEY REALLY WERE SENT AS GIFTS, STRAIGHT FROM BELINA'S HEART.

Claire sent a smiling emoji and then, IF ONLY THE PRESENT-DAY MYSTERY COULD BE AS EASY TO FIGURE OUT.

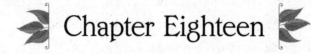

Chapter Eighteen

FRIDAY EVENING, ONCE SHE RETURNED home, Joy checked her laptop to see if the French author had emailed her back. She hadn't.

She then called Abrielle. After they chatted about the customs receipt, Joy told her about the woman who was an expert on French female painters. "If she responds, are you okay if I tell her about the three paintings Belina shipped to Arthur, the postcards, and all of the letters between the two families?"

"Of course," Abrielle said. "I'll ask Claire and Belina for their permission too."

She soon texted Joy to tell her all of them were thankful for her help.

Joy checked her emails several more times during the evening and then before she went to bed, but there was no response.

However, the majority of her evening was spent hanging out with Hope on the patio, talking about the solved mystery from the past, the current mystery, their childhood, and more.

Joy could feel something shifting. She was grateful for her sister in a way she hadn't been before. She took a deep breath and said, "I don't think I ever thanked you for being such a good aunt to Sabrina. For playing with her. Buying her gifts. Taking her on adventures."

"It was my pleasure," Hope said.

"I know—but it had a big impact on Sabrina. And, in being a good aunt to her, you were being a wonderful sister to me. Thank you."

Hope's eyes grew misty.

"I'm glad you're here." Joy reached across the table. "I hope I can be as good a sister to you as you've been to me."

Hope wiped her eyes. "You are being a good sister to me. All week you have been. Thank you." Hope then changed the subject, pointing at Joy's black bamboo. "I'd love a start of that someday."

Joy smiled. "It's yours. I'll have a start transplanted by the time you move into your apartment."

Saturday morning, Joy woke to the smell of coffee brewing and bacon frying again. Having Hope stay with her had turned out to be a blessing in more ways than one.

She opened her email before going down to breakfast and then, excited, clicked on the message from Deborah Bernard.

Hello, Joy Atkins, it read, thankfully in English. *I am grateful you reached out to me. I'm wondering if you residing in Charleston, SC, the same town that has the newly identified painting by Theodore Joubert, is a coincidence or if there is a connection? I'm guessing there is a connection. Please let me know.*

As far as your question, I didn't have enough information to confirm my theory, so I couldn't include anything about what I believe to be true in my book. But, from my research, I'm certain that one of Theodore Joubert's sisters also painted. There are a few paintings that weren't Theodore's that stayed in the Joubert family, and their tradition says that a female relative in the 1800s painted them, but they're not sure which ones. These are not Theodore's offspring—he did not have children. I've long wondered if the painter was one of his sisters, who was influenced by his work, but I haven't been able to verify my suspicions.

Sincerely,

Deborah Bernard

Joy quickly emailed her back, explaining about the three paintings, the letters and postcards, and finally about the customs form.

It appears Belina Joubert was the painter who learned from her brother and studied in Paris. Perhaps the documents now housed in archives in Charleston could help you with your research.

Joy paused for a moment. Belina Fleury would be the perfect contact person for the author. Belina knew art history, French, and how to paint. She added Belina's name and her website.

Joy stared at the screen a moment longer and then added to the email.

Are you familiar with Jacque De Villiers? He has spent some time in Charleston. If you know him, or know of him, I would appreciate any insight you might have as a member of the European art community.

Sincerely,

Joy Atkins

She closed her laptop, returned it to her desk, slipped her robe on, and then went to join Hope for breakfast.

After breakfast, Hope insisted on cleaning up.

"Isn't it painful to be on your foot?" Joy asked.

Hope shook her head. "The boot really helps. I honestly think I'll be fine starting work on Monday."

A half hour later, Joy backed her Mini Cooper out of her driveway and headed to the Fleury estate to pick up Claire. She'd offered to go to the historic City Market with Joy to pick up the flowers for the auction. Then the two would return to the Fleury Estate, clean the stems and fill the vases on Claire's patio, and then take the arrangements to the gallery.

Joy called Claire from the street to tell her she'd arrived.

"Joy," Claire said, a little breathless, "do you mind if we stop by the church on the way to the market? The church's copy machine broke down yesterday so I had to copy the bulletins at Lloyd's office. Now I need to drop them by the church."

"No problem," Joy said.

Claire arrived with a box in her hands.

When they reached the church, Joy parked her car out front.

"Come with me," Claire said. "I won't be long."

Joy turned the engine off and climbed out. She was happy to see the inside of the church again.

Claire took out her phone and sent a text as they walked to the front door. After waiting just a minute, Reverend Martin opened the door for them. "Come in, come in," he said. "I have something for you to give your father, Claire. It's in my office. I forgot to bring it."

Reverend Martin led the way, with Claire and then Joy trailing after him. He walked through the sanctuary and down the right side aisle, then through a door and into a small room with a desk and three chairs. On the desk was a book. "This is an old prayer book I found in my bookcase. It has the name Fleury written in the front. It's for your father to keep."

"Thank you," Claire said, taking the book and holding it close. "Daddy will be so happy to get this."

"The publishing date is 1892. Maybe he'll know who it might have belonged to."

Claire glanced at Joy. "Any idea?"

Joy smiled. "My guess would be Alexander, your great-great-grandfather." Joy turned toward Reverend Martin. "Any more thoughts on who might have unlocked the back door?"

He nodded. "I was so sure someone had a key, but then I remembered an odd visitor we had. Perhaps the door was unlocked from the inside, not the outside. A scruffy-looking fellow who said he was researching the Huguenots stopped by the day before the fire. He had an odd accent—he said he was from southern France."

Scruffy didn't fit the description of Jacque De Villiers, but Joy took out her phone anyway and googled a photo of him. One popped up that was a few years old but looked like the man she met the night before. She showed Reverend Martin.

He shook his head. "The man in the photo is much too clean cut. The man who stopped by here had a scruffy beard and hair. It's hard to tell if it could be him."

Joy pulled up a full body shot.

Reverend Martin stared at it for a long moment and then said, "The body build is the same, actually." He shook his head. "I don't know if this is the same man researching the Huguenots, but I think I may have seen the man in your photos last Sunday, on the steps of the church when I was greeting congregants."

Claire turned toward Joy. "Didn't Jacque say he was already in Richmond by then?"

"That's what I understood," Joy said.

"It's probably not him then," Reverend Martin said. "And the man who stopped by the church—it was last Saturday—his name was Pierre." He paused for a moment and then said, "You know, I had a phone call while he was here. I excused myself for a few minutes." He shook his head. "It might have been long enough for him to unlock the door."

"But wouldn't Raymond check the door to make sure it was locked each day?" Claire asked.

Reverend Martin shook his head. "Raymond had already gone home. I didn't think to check it, because no one had used it, or so I thought." He frowned. "When I finished my phone call, Pierre was back outside my door. Maybe he didn't unlock the door—but I can't be sure."

Joy took her phone from her purse. "This is all information that Detective Osborne needs to have."

The tourists were out in droves on both the sidewalks and the streets, but finally Joy found a parking place by the City Market building.

They entered through the front archway into the brick building. An interior archway had ESTABLISHED 1807, CHARLESTON CITY MARKET painted on it. Booths with ceramics, linens, candles, candies, pastries, Christmas ornaments, woodworking, jewelry, and all sorts of other items lined both sides of the market, including flowers. Halfway through, they reached the Flower Farm booth. Not only was Gwen working the booth but so was Belina.

"Hi," Claire said to her sister.

"Oh." Belina raised her eyebrows. "What are you doing here?"

"I came to help Joy with the flowers."

Joy waved. "Hi." She turned to Gwen and told her hello too.

"The order is in the truck," Belina said. "It's out back."

Joy paid Gwen, got a receipt, and then she and Claire followed Belina through the market and out the back. Belina led them to a panel truck parked in the lot.

"I'll go get my car," Joy said. "And be right back."

"All right," Claire said. "We'll be here."

Joy walked at a brisk pace, breathing in the beautiful September morning, dodging couples and families on the sidewalk.

When she reached her Mini Cooper, she pulled it out onto the street and then into the back parking lot, stopping behind the panel truck. Belina and Claire already had the five buckets of dahlias on the blacktop, waiting for her.

They quickly loaded the flowers into Joy's car. As they readied to go, Claire turned to Belina, "Please come tonight and bring JD."

Belina shook her head. "Abrielle would throw a fit."

"She won't, I promise," Claire said. "Daddy wants you to come. And so do I. I'll tell Abrielle you're coming."

"She'll make a scene."

"She definitely won't make a scene," Claire said. "She'll be focused on the auction."

Joy wished Abrielle would talk to Belina about the epiphany that she had, but it didn't seem like that was going to happen.

"All right," Belina finally said. "I'll think about it." She waved at Joy and headed back to the market.

As Joy turned onto the street, Claire kept her eye on the market. "I don't understand her," she said. "She was the most talented of the three of us. The smartest. And all she's doing is selling flowers in the City Market." Claire shifted her gaze to Joy. "What happened?"

Joy gave Claire a sympathetic smile. "She doesn't seem unhappy. Maybe it's what she wants to be doing."

Claire shrugged. "I can't imagine why."

Joy didn't answer. From what she'd seen, Belina actually seemed to be the most settled of the three sisters.

When Joy and Claire arrived at the gallery with the flower arrangements, the first thing they did was step into the front room to see the portrait of Doc Fleury.

Claire clasped her hands. "Aww, there he is. Innocent as can be." She turned to Joy. "Thank you for the research you did that exonerated him."

"You're welcome." Joy kept her eyes on Doc Fleury's kind face. "I enjoyed every minute of it."

After Claire and Joy put the flower arrangements on the food and cocktail tables, Claire stepped into Abrielle's office to update her sister on the mysterious man at the church while Joy waited in the hall. "Joy already left a voice mail for Detective Osborne."

"I'll call her too," Abrielle said. "She needs to question Jacque ASAP."

All the paintings were hung, and Pamela was still in the workroom repairing *Abrielle Overlooking the Village*. Joy told her goodbye and then she and Claire left.

When Joy arrived home, there was a note on the table from Hope. I'M OVER AT SABRINA'S. CAN WE ALL RIDE TOGETHER TO THE AUCTION? OR DO YOU NEED TO GO EARLY? LET US KNOW. ROB WILL DRIVE.

Joy had expected that Sabrina, Rob, and Hope would meet her at the auction because she needed to be there thirty minutes early. But having them all ride together sounded like fun.

She sent Hope a text asking if they minded going a little early. OF COURSE NOT, Hope texted back. DO YOU HAVE SOMETHING I CAN BORROW TO WEAR?

OF COURSE, Joy replied.

After their exchange ended, she headed upstairs and grabbed her laptop, hoping for another email from Deborah Bernard. Joy plopped down on her bed and opened her app. Her email downloaded, and one from Deborah popped up on the screen.

Dear Mrs. Atkins,

I was delighted to hear about the correspondence and other documentation concerning the Joubert family. If the Fleury family in Charleston would be willing to let me see their family collection, I believe I could arrange a research trip and go through the documents, along with those that have been archived. I believe you are right that it was Belina Joubert who was the female artist in the family. I found a record of a B Joubert studying at the Academy in Paris. I didn't feel

I had enough information before to write about Belina Joubert, but with the help of the Fleury family, perhaps I still can.

Joy's heart warmed at the thought. Good would come out of this. She continued reading.

As far as Jacque De Villiers, this is completely off the record and something I probably shouldn't put in print... But he shouldn't be trusted. Strange things happen when he's around. Paintings are sold for a fraction of what they're worth. He's bought paintings, only to have some completely disappear, never to be seen or shared again. A few years ago in Poland, Jacque was staying at a hotel not far from a museum that caught on fire. No one could prove Jacque started the fire, but a painting he once tried to buy went missing that night.

Joy gasped.

A few people suspected Jacque was involved, but the local police never pursued him as a suspect. Beware.

Joy wasn't sure what to write in response. That there was a fire at the church where two of the paintings were found?

Joy closed her laptop. She'd wait and email Deborah back after the auction. She needed to call Rebekah again, now. The call went straight to voice mail, so Joy left a detailed message and then read directly from Deborah Bernard's email. She ended the call by saying, "Hopefully Jacque De Villiers is still in Charleston. He needs to be stopped."

Chapter Nineteen

HOPE AND JOY STOOD IN front of the full-length mirror in the upstairs hallway. Hope wore a forest-green gown with a wide skirt, which practically hid her boot, and a bolero jacket. She'd pulled her dark hair back on both sides with Joy's gold combs and wore a gold locket around her neck.

Joy wore a long black column dress with a sweetheart neckline, along with drop pearl earrings, a pearl bracelet, and black sandals with more of a heel than she usually wore.

"It's so fun to play dress-up with you." Hope smiled into the mirror, her eyes sparkling.

"I agree." The doorbell rang and Joy said, "I'll get it." And then, "Be careful coming down the stairs."

"I will," Hope said.

Joy opened the door for Sabrina and Rob. He wore a tuxedo and Sabrina wore a wine-colored maxi dress that accented her dark hair, which she wore up.

"You both look beautiful," Sabrina gushed. She pulled her phone from her purse. "I want a picture of the two of you."

Joy put her arm around Hope, and they both hammed it up with big smiles. Then Joy took a photo of Rob and Sabrina.

Ten minutes later, the four arrived at the Belina House Gallery. As soon as Joy stepped inside, Abrielle grabbed her arm and whispered, "I want you to meet someone—give me your honest opinion. But later."

Abrielle pulled Joy into the front gallery as Joy waved at Hope and Sabrina and said, "I'll be right back."

A short, round man with a full head of sandy hair stood in the center of the room with a drink in his hand.

"Patrick," Abrielle said. "I'd like you to meet Joy Atkins. She works at the hospital and has been a great help with the auction. She's really carried me through this entire week."

He beamed as he shook her hand. "Joy, I'm so pleased to meet you. Thank you for being here for Abrielle. I left her adrift all week— that's why I flew down today. I needed to make sure she's all right. I think we all feel as if our favorite child has been kidnapped." He shook his head. "I just can't fathom what happened to that painting."

"None of us can." Abrielle was at least six inches taller than Patrick. "Have you heard from Jacque?" she asked Patrick. "Last night he said he'd be here for the auction."

"Oh dear. I forgot to tell you. I had a text from him when my plane landed. He's on his way back to Europe. His father has a lead on a painting in Italy that he wants him to look at. He's still interested in buying the Joubert, of course, once it turns up. He's sorry he didn't say goodbye—he knew you were busy today."

Abrielle shook her head. "Do you know if Detective Osborne spoke with him?"

Patrick shrugged. "I have no idea."

Joy shot Abrielle a glance but didn't say anything. If Patrick wasn't trustworthy, she didn't want him to know what Deborah Bernard had said about Jacque or that Joy had passed the information on to Detective Osborne.

If Jacque had the painting, would the Fleury family ever get it back?

Claire, Lloyd, and Marshall arrived, followed by Roger. Abrielle soon sent everyone to their places. Joy was stationed at the back door, which was completely off-limits. No one was to enter or exit through it. Roger, who wore a dashing tuxedo, was stationed halfway up the hall, where the two could easily see each other.

Thankfully there was a table of food in the workroom, which drew people down the hallway. Garrison was one of the first guests to arrive. He found Joy and gave her a questioning look. She should have texted him earlier. She gave him a thumbs-up and said, "Doc Fleury is innocent."

Relief washed over his face.

"I'll give you the details later."

It wasn't long until Daniella from the *Dispatch* found Joy. "Did you clear Doc Fleury or is a rumor floating around?"

"Who said something to you?" Joy guessed Garrison.

"Abrielle told me to talk with you—that you'd give me the whole story," Daniella said. "She said you have information that exonerates Dr. Fleury."

Joy sighed. She might as well give the information to Daniella now. She'd do the same for Garrison when she saw him next. "I do." She took her phone from her clutch purse. "There's a customs form from 1873 that shows that Belina Joubert shipped three paintings to Arthur Fleury as a gift." She held the phone so Daniella could see it.

"Interesting." She peered at the screen and then said, "Do you mind texting that to me?"

"Not at all." Joy asked for her number and then sent the text. "There are letters too, which you can access at the hospital, from the Jouberts that seem to corroborate this document."

"Well, it sounds as if another article is in order."

Joy nodded.

"I just wish I could update what's going on with the current case," Daniella said.

"Don't we all." Joy pursed her lips. "So who was your anonymous source?"

Daniella's face reddened.

"Someone who lives in Charleston?"

Daniella shook her head.

"Someone who used to live in Charleston and returned recently?"

Again, Daniella shook her head.

"Someone who lives in Europe?"

"I really can't say," Daniella answered. She pointed toward the workroom. "Is that where the food is?"

Joy nodded again. "Abrielle wanted to draw guests down the hall so the gallery rooms don't get too crowded. Help yourself."

Joy thought of the two paintings back in the safe, *Abrielle Overlooking the Village* and *Claire on the Church Steps*. Hopefully Abrielle had renewed the insurance policy on the family's collection.

When Daniella left, Joy thought of the young woman's discomfort when she asked if the anonymous source lived in Europe. Had Jacque De Villiers planted the idea that had perhaps been passed down in his family, that Doc Fleury stole the paintings? She turned toward the window looking over the alley. A light in the building across the way caught her attention. It quickly flicked off and as it did, Joy wondered if she'd seen a pair of binoculars. She shook her head. Was she seeing things now?

"Joy!"

She turned. Regina, with Shirley following, came toward her.

Joy gave them both a hug. "Mercy, this is quite the event," Shirley said.

Regina wagged her finger. "I told you it was."

"Uh huh." Shirley's eyebrows shot up. "It turns out Mama has been coming to this auction every year for the last three decades. This is where she sees Marshall Fleury every year. They just caught up in the lobby in a half-hour conversation."

"Oh, he's such a lovely man," Joy said. "What a nice person to have as a friend."

Regina nodded in agreement.

"There's a food table in there." Joy pointed to the workroom.

"Are you trying to get rid of us?" Regina asked.

Joy laughed. "Of course not. I just want to make sure you get enough nourishment."

Regina grinned.

As soon as they left, Joy turned back to the building across the way. The light was on again—but it flicked off, once again.

She kept watching, and soon saw a man coming down the outside steps of the building, illuminated by a streetlight and carrying a large bag. He was followed by a woman. Was that Pamela DePass? Joy squinted. The man had a thin build like Jacque. But he was already on his way home, right?

Joy pulled her phone from her clutch again and quickly placed a call to Rebekah, leaving a message. Then, as Shirley and Regina came out of the workroom, she said, "Shirley, would you go get Abrielle? Tell her to come quickly. And Roger too, if you can." There were so many people in the hallway that she couldn't see him.

Then Joy pushed open the back door, which made the alarm start to blare, and stepped outside. Regina started to follow her. "Stay inside," Joy urged her.

"No thank you, ma'am." Regina pulled a flashlight from her purse and flicked it on, lighting the alley.

Joy didn't have time to argue with Regina. She started down the back stairs. "Jacque! Pamela! The auction has started!"

The two kept walking, up the alley.

Joy quickened her steps, yelling loudly over the alarm, "Where are you going?" She lifted her dress and started running after them. "Come back!"

Suddenly, Jacque turned around. He hadn't shaved and his hair fell over his face instead of being styled as it had been the night before. "Do I know you?"

"I'm Joy." She slowed to a walk. Regina caught up, and the beam of her flashlight illuminated the alley. "I met you Thursday evening at the Fleury Estate."

"Ah."

"And I met Pamela this afternoon," Joy said. The woman was still walking, at a rapid pace.

"Well, thank you for the invitation," Jacque said, "but we're on our way to the airport."

Joy still held her dress with one hand and her clutch with the other. "Pamela too?"

The woman stopped walking and turned slowly. "I'll be flying back to Savannah."

"Oh." Joy wasn't sure how to keep stalling. Where was Abrielle? And Roger? "Did you finish the repairs on the two paintings, Pamela?"

"Yes, ma'am," she said, as if through gritted teeth. "I did."

A voice came from the other end of the alley. "Jacque." It was Roger.

Behind Joy, Abrielle yelled, "I thought you already left."

Jacque smiled, by the light of Regina's flashlight beam. "Abrielle, I'm glad you came out. I wanted to tell you goodbye."

"Is that Pamela with you?"

"It is," Jacque said. "I'm giving her a ride to the airport."

"You two know each other?"

"We just met. Today," Jacque said. "I stopped by the gallery but you were indisposed."

Joy turned to see how Abrielle responded, but her face wasn't giving anything away. Standing just behind her was Daniella, tapping something into her phone. Notes? A text? A tweet? Who knew.

Joy shifted her gaze to the back door of the gallery. Belina and Marshall were headed out the back door, with JD behind them.

Claire came rushing by JD and then past Marshall and Belina. "I just checked the safe. The other two paintings are gone. We've been robbed again!"

Everyone froze for a long moment until Jacque nodded toward Pamela and said, "We need to get going or we'll miss our flights."

Roger took a step forward. "You'll need to wait."

"Until?"

"Detective Osborne arrives," Joy said. "This is, once again, an active crime scene. Nobody leaves."

Jacque chuckled. "You have too many of those police shows here in the US. *Everything* is a crime scene to you. Believe me, Pamela and I haven't committed any crimes. And if we don't get to the airport, we'll miss our flight."

Joy chirped, "Flight?"

Jacque smiled. "Flights. I stand corrected." He turned toward Pamela and took her arm. "Let's go."

Where was Rebekah?

JD hurried up the alley and stood with Roger. Rob and Sabrina joined him. Joy turned around. Behind her, Abrielle, Belina, Claire, and Marshall all stood together, blocking that end of the alley, alongside Hope, Shirley, and Regina, who still held her flashlight. Joy guessed Lloyd, Anne, and Evelyn, along with Ralph and James had stayed in the gallery with the guests, the ones who didn't know what was going on.

Shirley activated her phone's flashlight and so did Hope. Joy turned toward the other end of the alley. Roger, JD, Rob, and Sabrina all had their flashlights on too.

Joy pulled her phone from her clutch again and redialed Rebekah. This time she picked up the call. Without saying hello she said, "I'm almost there."

"Hurry." Joy ended the call and held her breath.

Jacque and Pamela stood still, but they were definitely agitated. Finally Jacque said, "What is this? Some sort of vigilante, Wild West justice?"

Patrick stepped down the back stairs of the gallery and called out, "Jacque, what have you done?"

Jacque waved his hand, as if in disgust.

Just then, flashing lights appeared in the alley behind Roger's group. They stepped aside, and Rebekah stopped her car in front of Jacque and Pamela. She turned off the engine and climbed out of the car.

"Detective," Jacque said, "we're simply trying to catch our flights. Would you instruct these unstable people to let us go?"

"Of course," she answered. "But first, I need you to answer some questions."

She motioned to Abrielle and Claire. "Come tell me what's going on."

Abrielle grabbed Belina's arm with one hand and Claire's with the other, and they all hurried up the alley. Joy smiled at the sisters, all three of them together. What a welcome sight.

Claire pointed to the large rectangular hard-sided bag in Jacque's hand and then to Pamela. "The two smaller paintings are missing again. Pamela was working on them."

"Abrielle returned them to the safe," Pamela said.

"Well…" Claire planted her hands on her hips. "They're not there now."

"Mind if I look in the bag?" Rebekah asked.

"Actually, I do," Jacque said.

"All right. I'll get a search warrant then. Come on down to the station with me while we wait." She pointed to Pamela. "You too."

Pamela gave Jacque an icy stare and stomped her foot. "We're busted."

Jacque shook his head.

"It's over. You can't get out of this."

Jacque's voice was as calm as ever. "Of course we can. We are. No one has a right to look in this bag."

"Actually, I do," Rebekah said. "Now, with even more probable cause than a minute ago."

Sunday morning before church, Claire called Joy and invited her to meet with the three sisters and Rebekah at the gallery.

"Isn't it still a crime scene?"

"We're meeting in the lobby," Claire said. "And apparently the crime has been solved—Rebekah wants to give us an update."

"Are you sure you want me there?"

"Absolutely," Claire said.

Joy texted Sabrina, asking if she could pick up Hope for church.

A quick YES! from Sabrina answered her question.

Joy texted back, I'LL MEET YOU THERE. AND THEN LET'S ALL GO OUT FOR SUNDAY DINNER.

PERFECT, Sabrina replied.

Joy drove to the gallery. When she arrived, Abrielle and Belina stood on the front steps. As Joy approached, the two sisters hugged. It appeared repairs to their relationship had finally started to take place.

"Hello," Joy called out as she started up the stairs.

Abrielle turned and smiled at her. "I'm so glad you're here. Rebekah and Claire are already inside."

Five chairs were set in a circle and Rebekah sat in one, a cup of coffee in her hand. The other women sat down.

Rebekah glanced around the circle and said, "Good job, ladies. You found the burglars."

Claire clapped her hands. "Obviously, Jacque and Pamela are guilty, but why would a multimillionaire want to steal the paintings?"

Rebekah shrugged. "That's the big question. But I think I have an answer from what I can piece together from questioning both Jacque and Pamela." She took a sip from her mug and then said, "This goes back to the 1870s. Theodore Joubert was an up-and-coming painter and the De Villierses, because they knew his family, felt entitled to buy as many of his paintings as they could. But one particular painting they wanted—*Belina in the Garden*—was sent to the US instead. The De Villierses never forgot that, so when Jacque found out from Patrick that the painting was in Charleston, he wanted it. But he decided to steal it instead of pay for it, believing it was actually stolen from his family all those years ago."

"But why did he steal the other two paintings?" Joy asked.

"He knew they weren't Jouberts," Rebekah said, "but he hoped to frame Abrielle for the theft—figuring people would think she staged it for the insurance money. But he didn't know it had lapsed. He planned to leave the two paintings in the church all along, as if Abrielle had hidden them there and the fire started accidentally."

Joy thought of Deborah Bernard's assessment of Jacque. It was clear he wasn't a stable man. But, in fact, he was downright malicious to leave the two paintings where he did and then set fire to the closet.

Rebekah continued. "But then Jacque's father, because of a collection of paintings by Huguenot artists, became interested in the other two paintings, once he heard they might be painted by a woman in the Joubert family." Rebekah took another sip of coffee. "Jacque contacted Pamela and arranged for her to let him into the back room as she was cleaning up, promising to make it worth her while. He broke into the safe a second time and took the paintings again."

Abrielle shook her head. "I'm a fool."

Belina laughed. "You definitely need assistance with your security systems."

Abrielle met her sister's eyes. "Will you help?"

Belina nodded.

"What now?" Claire asked Rebekah.

"Both Jacque De Villiers and Pamela DePass are under arrest, although I'm guessing they'll be out on bail soon. At least Jacque will. The DA will take the case before a grand jury, and it will proceed through the court system like any other case."

"What about the three paintings?" Belina asked.

"We'll hold those as evidence for the time being," Rebekah said, "but then they will be returned to you, as before, although maybe not quite so soon."

Claire glanced from Abrielle to Belina. "And then what will we do with them?"

"Keep them," Abrielle said. "Belina's going to help me manage the gallery. No doubt, business will increase. But with Belina's help, I think we can do it right. The Theodore Joubert will spend its time in museums, most likely, which will bring in extra income. But we'll make the perfect place for the other two—as we showcase an early female painter."

That sounded marvelous. Joy stood. "Thank you, ladies, for including me. I appreciate the closure, and I'm so glad things worked out."

"Where are you headed?" Claire asked.

"Church. With my daughter and her family—and also with my sister," Joy answered.

"We should get going too," Belina said. "We don't want to be late. Daddy and Lloyd are going to meet us for the service."

As they all left the gallery, Daniella Hattel hurried toward them, calling out, "Do you have a time for an interview?"

Rebekah glanced at Abrielle. "I'll do it. You go on."

"Thank you," Abrielle said. "Tell her to call me this afternoon if she wants a statement."

"Will do." Rebekah waved at Daniella while the other women scurried away, in the other direction.

As Joy called out a goodbye to the Fleury sisters and then climbed into her Mini Cooper, she thought of the beautiful art they owned. But, more importantly, she thought of the beautiful hearts they possessed.

They'd all learned a lot during the last stressful week, but they all seemed to come away stronger. Including herself.

She looked forward to spending the day with her own sister, knowing the future held more for their relationship too.

Dear Reader,

In *A Change of Art*, Joy becomes enamored with the two Fleury sisters and their seemingly enchanting life—just as her sister Hope arrives in Charleston, stirring up old conflicts in their relationship. She can't help but envy the sisterhood between her two new friends. But soon, Joy discovers the Fleury family has a painful past that includes a secret.

Joy is reminded that all families have their problems. As she hopes for reconciliation in the Fleury family, Joy longs for healing in her relationship with her own sister too.

I've long been captivated with the relationships between sisters, partly based on the fact that I have two (plus a brother who is as close as a sister). I'm finding the older we grow, the more aware I am of their influence on my life—and how much I truly need them. No one else shares the same memories and values in the same way as my siblings. I thank God each and every day for all three of them.

I hope you'll think about your own long-term relationships as you read *A Change of Art* and travel through the streets of Charleston with Joy, her sister Hope, and the Fleury sisters.

Enjoy!

Signed,
Leslie

About the Author

LESLIE GOULD IS THE NUMBER one bestselling and Christy Award-winning author of forty novels. Besides writing, she also teaches part-time at Warner Pacific University in Portland, Oregon. Leslie and her husband, Peter, enjoy hiking, traveling, and hanging out with their four adult children.

The Story Behind the Story

A FEW YEARS AGO, MY husband and I spent a lovely week in
South Carolina, including time in Charleston. The main motivation?
Attending a service at the historic French Huguenot Church was
literally on my bucket list.

A couple of years before, we'd gone to France to research the
Huguenots, the French Protestants who faced persecution from the
1500s until the Edict of Versailles in 1787. Many fled France over
the centuries to find refuge in the New World.

The Huguenot Church in Charleston, which began in the late
1600s, is the only one left in the US. The current church was built in
1844, and I had to see it.

The Gothic-style church and Calvinist service did not disap-
point, nor did the gracious congregants who warmly welcomed us. I
felt as if we'd stepped back in time, a feeling I had the entire time we
were in Charleston, from the horse-drawn carriage ride to the walking tour through the cobblestone streets of the European-designed
city and everything in between.

Charleston quickly became one of our favorite places, putting a
return trip on our current bucket list.

If you visit Charleston, I recommend taking the "Heavenly
Charleston" tour. Sometimes called the "Holy City," Charleston

has the largest concentration of churches in the US with some dating back to the 1600s. The architecture of the church buildings and the wide religious representation are highlights of the city.

Good for What Ails You

ANNE'S PECAN PIE

Crust Ingredients:

1¼ cups all-purpose flour

¼ teaspoon salt

½ cup butter, chilled and diced

¼ cup ice water

Directions:

In a large bowl, combine flour and salt. Cut in butter until mixture resembles coarse crumbs. Stir in water, a tablespoon at a time, until mixture forms a ball. Wrap in plastic and refrigerate for 4 hours or overnight.

Roll dough out to fit a 9-inch pie plate. Place crust in pie plate. Press the dough evenly into the bottom and sides of the pie plate.

Pecan Pie Filling:

3 eggs

⅔ cup sugar

Dash salt

1 cup dark corn syrup

⅓ cup butter, melted

1 cup pecan halves

Directions:

Beat eggs, sugar, salt, corn syrup, and melted butter. Add pecan halves. Poor into pastry shell.

Bake at 350 degrees for 50 minutes or until knife inserted half-way between center and edge comes out clean. Cool.

Read on for a sneak peek of another exciting book
in the Miracles & Mysteries of Mercy Hospital series!

Conscious Decisions
by BETH ADAMS

ANNE MABRY PUSHED THE WHEELCHAIR toward the glass doors, which whooshed open as they neared. The oppressive heat of the South Carolina summer had finally given way to warm October air, and the afternoon sun reflected off the hood of the SUV waiting at the curb.

"It looks like your ride is right on time, Robin," Anne said as the passenger side door opened. Anne recognized the man who hopped out of the driver's seat as the patient's husband, Wallace, who had been faithfully at her side since Robin had been admitted with chest pains the day before.

"Hold on to me," Wallace said, leaning forward so Robin could grab on to him.

"I'll be okay," Robin said as she pushed herself up carefully.

He put his hand on her arm and guided her into the passenger seat of the SUV. Off in the distance, the sound of sirens wailed.

Anne knew that Robin would be all right, at least for the time being. What they had feared had been a heart attack turned out to be nothing more serious than severe indigestion, but Wallace had stayed by his wife's side throughout the battery of tests they'd put her through. He'd finally been persuaded to go home to rest in his own bed the night before. Anne was pleased to see how devoted Wallace was and knew that he would bring his wife back in if anything changed.

"Thank you so much for all your help," Robin said, waving from the front seat. "Everyone here has been so wonderful."

"You take care of yourself," Anne replied. She couldn't take any responsibility for the care Robin had received here at Mercy Hospital, but she was glad to know Robin's experience had been as positive as it could be. "And don't take this the wrong way, but I hope we don't see you here again anytime soon."

Robin laughed and buckled herself in, and Anne waved as the car drove off. What a nice couple, she thought as she turned and began to push the empty wheelchair back inside the hospital lobby. She had just gotten in through the sliding doors when her phone buzzed. Anne waved at Peggy, the volunteer who was covering the front desk today, and moved out of the doorway before she pulled her phone out.

ANY CHANCE YOU'RE FREE TO HELP OUT WITH A PATIENT IN THE ER? It was a text from Shirley Bashore, her dear friend and a nurse currently working in the emergency room.

Anne texted back, ON MY WAY, and after she returned the wheelchair, she walked down the hallway toward the doors that led to the ER. Anne's curiosity was piqued. She was just a volunteer, not a medical professional, so she wasn't sure what kind of help Shirley was hoping for, but Anne knew Shirley would explain as soon as she could.

IN THE TRAUMA CENTER, Shirley texted back. She must be in a rush, Anne saw. Shirley was known for being no-nonsense, but she wasn't usually so short in her texts. Anne walked more quickly and saw that the emergency room was a flurry of activity today. Doctors and nurses were rushing around, and there was more noise than usual in here. Anne found Shirley in a patient room in the trauma area, as promised, tending to a woman on the narrow patient bed. She had an oxygen mask over her mouth and nose, and she appeared to be unconscious.

"Thank you for coming. It's crazy in here today," Shirley said. She was watching the readings on the heart monitor.

"It did seem really busy. Did something big happen?"

"Apparently there was a pileup on the highway," Shirley answered. Her black hair, threaded with gray, was pulled back into a bun and she held a clipboard. "A tanker truck overturned, and that led to a chain reaction. Something like seventeen cars were involved in the end."

"Oh goodness." Anne said a quick prayer in her head for the victims who had just been going about their day before an unexpected wreck changed everything. "Is it bad?"

"There are a few with serious injuries, but many are just being checked out as a precaution." Shirley looked away from the monitor and noted something on her clipboard.

"Is this one of the crash patients?" Anne gestured to the woman. She was probably in her early thirties, Anne guessed, and had long brown hair and fine facial features, at least from what she could see behind the mask. Angry purple bruises rose on her right cheek and her forehead.

"No, this woman was brought in just after that rush began. She was found unconscious in Hampton Park at the bottom of a flight of steps. There's a big gash on the back of her head, and the EMTs found a broken stairway with no railing, so they think she tripped and fell."

That sounded terrible. "Will she be all right?"

"It's too early to say," Shirley said. "We'll have to run some tests to find out what's going on. But it's not happening as quickly as I would like because we're swamped."

"I totally understand," Anne said. "How can I help?"

"We don't know who this woman is," Shirley explained. "She had no ID on her, and the EMTs didn't find a purse or anything that would hold any information about who she is. Police responded to the scene, and I spoke with an Officer Escobar a few minutes ago. He said she fell, but no one at the scene actually saw it happen. He didn't have any idea who she was and said there was nothing to identify her. They did find a cell phone near her, and they brought that in with her." Shirley pointed to the phone in a black silicone case. "But it's locked, and we don't know the passcode."

"Oh dear." Anne's concern for this woman grew. "You need me to try to figure out who she is?"

"It would be a huge help," Shirley said. "Right now she's listed in the system as Jane Doe, but I would love to know what her name really is."

"We'll need to let her family know," Anne said. "They'll want to be here with her."

"Exactly," Shirley said. "And the doctors will need to know about any medical conditions or allergies she has. Would you be able to work on it?"

"Of course. I'm happy to."

"Thank you so much." Shirley looked down as the pager clipped to her waistband buzzed. "I'm sorry, I have to run."

"Go ahead. I'm on it."

Shirley thanked her and bustled out, and Anne was left alone in the small room with the unconscious woman. With Jane Doe—but Anne couldn't bring herself to really call her that. Whoever this woman was, she had a name. She had a family and friends and a life, and Anne was going to do her best to find out who she was and let her family know where she was. Hopefully she would wake up soon, but wouldn't it be wonderful if her family was already by her side when that happened?

Before Anne began, she gently placed her hand on Jane's arm and began to pray. *Lord, please be with this woman. Give the doctors wisdom about what she needs, and heal her quickly. And please help us to find out who she is so we can let her family know where she is. Amen.*

Anne let her hand rest on Jane's arm for a moment, watching her chest rise and fall gently. Anne studied her, searching for any clue that would reveal her identity. Her brown hair had soft honey-colored highlights that brightened it up, but her nails were plain. Much of her face was obscured by the oxygen mask and there were the bruises and some swelling around her right eye, but she was pretty, that was clear. Striking, Anne would venture to say. She wore a maroon blouse, fitted, but no slogans or marks and anything that would offer a clue as to who she was. Black pants, slim-fitting. Someone had taken off her shoes, which were set on the floor next to the bed. They were black ballet flats. Fashionable, the kind she saw young people wearing, but not identifying in any way. She didn't wear a wedding ring—no rings at all, in fact, and no earrings.

Who are you? Anne asked in her head. The only response was the beep of the heart rate monitor next to the bed.

Anne walked around the bed and picked up the cell phone that rested on the small table at her side. Most people had enough information stored in their phone—call logs, contact names, text messages, photos—to identify them quickly enough. It was a standard iPhone, Anne saw. A newer model. The black silicone case revealed nothing about its owner. She swiped up to wake up the screen and saw that the lock screen held a photo of a brown dog. A very cute brown dog—maybe a poodle or a poodle mix.

She felt the strangest feeling of triumph. A clue about Jane Doe—she liked dogs! And maybe had a dog of her own. But Anne quickly realized that got her pretty much nowhere. *Everyone* liked dogs, or most everyone anyway. Without some more information about this dog, it didn't get her any closer to finding out who Jane Doe was.

Anne then pressed the button on the side of the phone, and a message that said FACE ID appeared on the screen. The phone had facial recognition technology, then. It didn't recognize Anne's face, though, so a series of buttons popped up for her to enter a passcode. Anne had no idea what to enter. Could she just guess Jane's passcode? She hesitated. Most people used a number that was important to them, like a birthday or an address, as their passcode. But if Anne knew what those were, Jane Doe wouldn't be unidentified. Even if Jane had somehow picked one of the most common passwords, which seemed unlikely, Anne didn't think she should just guess at the code. There were only a limited number of tries before the phone locked, she knew, and she didn't want to use up tries if someone more knowledgeable could get into the phone.

She walked closer to Jane, pushed the button on the side of the phone to make the screen dark, and then pressed it again to open it. If she had it right, the phone would try to recognize Jane's face and unlock itself. But Anne waited, and it didn't unlock. She reset it and tried again, moving the phone closer to Jane this time, but once again, the screen didn't seem to recognize her face.

Was this actually even her phone? Anne wondered. Was it possible the paramedics had picked up a phone that didn't belong to Jane? Maybe, Anne thought. But it was more likely that the oxygen mask over her nose and mouth obscured her face enough that the phone didn't recognize her. Anne knew better than to remove the oxygen, though she was tempted. Just for a second, she thought— just long enough to get a good look so she could unlock the phone. But she knew she could not do that, not without permission from the emergency room doctors.

Still. If she could get permission to try that, it could make all the difference in identifying Jane Doe. She took out her own cell phone and sent a text to Shirley: IS THERE ANY CHANCE WE COULD REMOVE THE OXYGEN MASK BRIEFLY SO I CAN UNLOCK THE PHONE? IT HAS FACIAL RECOGNITION. Anne looked down at the phone, but there were no dots that indicated Shirley was composing a reply. She was probably wrapped up in whatever had called her away from here. This newer model of phone didn't have the little button at the bottom that could use a fingerprint to unlock it, so using the woman's fingerprints wasn't an option.

There had to be a way to figure out who this woman was. Anne thought for a minute, and then she had another idea. She walked out of the room, turning to take one last look at the woman sleeping peacefully on the narrow hospital bed. Then she walked up the stairs to the volunteer room to report to her supervisor, Aurora Kingston, what she'd been asked to do.

Aurora listened as Anne explained how she'd been asked to find the woman's identity, and Aurora nodded.

"That should definitely be your first priority," Aurora agreed. "The hospital will need to know who she is, so if you can help, that's great."

Anne thanked her, and then she walked back down the stairs and into the lobby of Mercy Hospital. Anne saw that Peggy was still at the front desk. Peggy was a beloved presence, welcoming patients and visitors with her wide smile and upbeat outlook. Anne sometimes covered the front desk when needed, and she always tried to be as welcoming and helpful as Peggy was.

"Hi there, Peggy," Anne said as she approached the desk.

"Hello, my dear. How are things going for you today?" Peggy smiled at her over the top of the desk.

"I'm doing okay. But I just spoke with Shirley, who told me about a patient in the ER who came in unconscious, and she doesn't have any identification on her. I'm trying to figure out who she is."

"It's good they've got you on the case," Peggy said. "You and your friends have solved quite a few mysteries in the past few months. I'm sure you'll get this one figured out right away too."

"You're so sweet." Anne and Shirley, along with their friends Joy Atkins, who worked in the gift shop, and Evelyn Perry, who managed the hospital records, *had* managed to solve some puzzling mysteries recently. "But I suspect this might have a fairly easy solution. Has anyone called the hospital looking for a missing friend or family member?"

Those calls were always the worst ones she had to deal with. Anne had spoken with a number of frantic relatives looking for a missing person, hoping against hope to find them in the care of Mercy's doctors and nurses. Sometimes Anne was able to tell them she knew their relative was here and safe, and other times she had to say that they had no record of the person they were looking for, but in each case, she said a prayer for the distraught family member, asking God to bring peace to them.

"Not since I've been here, no." Peggy shook her head. "And I've been here since eight."

"Would you be able to let me know if you do get a call?" Anne asked.

"Of course."

Anne thanked her and turned and walked down the hallway to the gift shop. The smell of flowers and coffee hit her as she stepped inside. She found her dear friend Joy Atkins ringing up the biggest bunch of pink balloons she had ever seen for an older couple and a young boy. Welcoming a new member of the family, Anne guessed. Once the customers had left, the little boy clutching the strings of the balloons tightly, Anne approached the counter.

"Hi there." Joy gave Anne a warm smile. "How are you doing?"

"I'm all right," Anne said. "Just on a hunt for information."

"About what?" Joy cocked her head.

"There's a patient in the ER who was brought in without any ID. She's unconscious, so I'm trying to figure out who she is."

Joy's eyed widened. "Will she be all right?"

"I'm not really sure," Anne admitted. "I hope so. But that's why I want to figure out who she is quickly. Her family will want to be there with her."

"Of course."

Joy had lost her husband, Wilson, nearly two years ago, and Anne knew she had spent as much time by his side as she could when he had been in the hospital back in Houston.

"I'm about to ask Norm Ashford if he could help me find out whether anyone has called the police department to report someone matching her description missing."

"Ah." Joy nodded, understanding dawning. She stepped around the counter and started across the small shop. "Let's get you a cup of coffee to bring him."

"Thank you." Joy always kept a pot of coffee brewing in the gift shop and was quick to share it with visitors. Anne knew Norm would be willing to help her in any case, but it didn't hurt to bring him a gift.

"Do you know how he takes it?" Joy was already pouring steaming liquid from the pot into a paper cup.

"Light and sweet."

"Coming right up." Joy poured in creamer and three packets of sugar, stirred it up with a wooden stir stick, and snapped a lid on the cup before she handed it to Anne.

"Thank you." Anne smiled at her friend. "I really appreciate it."

"It's no problem. Just please keep me updated. I hope you figure out who she is quickly."

"I will." Anne stepped out of the gift shop and walked down the hallway to the little security office at the rear of the hospital. Anne waved at two pediatric doctors as they passed, chatting about a television show. She smiled at a few people wearing visitor passes, knowing how bewildering and scary a hospital could seem when you were here to visit a loved one. She used her elbow to knock softly on the door of the security room, and a voice called for her to come in.

"Hi there, Anne." Norm Ashford, a retired member of the Charleston Police Department, sat in the small room, monitoring a dozen screens showing security cameras from all over the hospital.

"Hi, Norm. How are you today?"

"Just dandy. And yourself?"

"I'm doing well." She stepped inside the office. "I come bearing gifts." She set the coffee down on the desk.

"You are amazing." Norm popped off the lid and took a sip. "Light and sweet, just like I like it."

"I was pretty sure I remembered that correctly."

"You did. Now, to what do I owe the unexpected gift?"

"I was wondering if you might do me favor," Anne said. "There's a woman unconscious in the ER, and they don't know who she is. I'm hoping to find out if anyone matching her description has been reported missing."

"I can certainly call the station and find out for you," Norm said. "What can you tell me about her?"

"I'm guessing she's in her late twenties or early thirties," Anne said. "She has brown hair with lighter highlights."

"When did she come in?"

"Not too long ago." Anne wasn't exactly sure of the time, but she knew it wouldn't have been very long. "In the past couple of hours. An Officer Escobar was at the scene but didn't find anything to identify her."

"The police won't consider a person missing for at least twenty-four hours." Norm took another sip of the coffee.

"I know," Anne said. "But that doesn't mean someone won't call the station asking, right?"

"That's true. I'll give them a call and ask them to let me know if someone does call the station looking for her."

"That would be wonderful," Anne said. "Now I have another question. The paramedics brought in a cell phone they think belongs to the woman, but it's locked. Is there someone who could unlock it? Does the police department have someone who knows how to do these things?"

"That is an interesting question," Norm said. "The technology exists to allow law enforcement to break into locked phones, but I don't know if the Charleston PD has access to it or whether they would use it in this case."

"Is there a way to find out? Or is there someone who has done this kind of thing before, using the most common passcodes or something like that?"

"I can ask." Norm nodded. "There are privacy issues at play, of course. And there's some gray legal territory here, at least if the police are doing the unlocking, if she's not suspected of a crime."

"But isn't finding her identity the most important thing at this point?"

"I would think so. But a lawyer might not." He took a sip of his coffee. "I'll see what I can find out. I'll text you when I hear something."

"That sounds great. Thank you so much."

"Thanks for the coffee." Norm held up the cup as a thanks as Anne waved and walked back out into the hallway. She tried to think of what to do next and decided she should talk to the paramedics who had brought Jane Doe to the hospital. They would have responded to the 911 call and driven to the park to get the woman and brought her to the emergency room. Maybe they would be able to tell her something about the scene or something they had noticed in the park where she was found.

Anne walked back to the emergency room, which was still bustling with activity, to the ambulance services room near the ambulance bay at the rear of the building. This was where the team of paramedics worked when they were not out on calls or transporting patients. But when Anne poked her head inside, no one was there.

"Need something?"

Anne turned to find Stuart, a paramedic with a bald head, walking past. Like everyone else in this area today, he seemed to be in a hurry. Anne knew that when the ER was busy, members of the paramedics team sometimes helped out with patients if they weren't needed on an ambulance call.

"I was hoping to talk to the team who brought in the woman who was found in Hampton Park," Anne explained. "Do you know who that would be?"

"Stephanie Cain and Tom Whitehead," Stuart said. "They're out on a call now, but I can ask them to give you a call when they get back."

"That would be great," Anne said. She quickly gave Stuart her number, and he promised to have them contact her. Then he rushed off again.

Anne went to check on Jane Doe and found Shirley and another nurse getting ready to wheel the bed out.

"Where is she going?" Anne asked.

"CT scan," Shirley said.

That made sense, given the woman's head injuries. They would want to see if there was bleeding or trauma to the brain. Anne stood out of the way, and once they had wheeled her out, she picked up Jane's phone again and saw there was a text message on the screen. The message was from a sender named Rick, and it was direct and to the point: YOUR CHECK HASN'T ARRIVED. WILL LET THE LAW-YERS KNOW IF IT'S NOT HERE BY THE END OF THIS WEEK.

What did that mean? Anne shook her head. It wasn't her business. All she needed to do was find out who this Jane Doe was. She was running out of ideas, and it broke her heart to see this poor woman here all alone.

"I'll figure out who you are," Anne said quietly. "I won't give up until I do."